What readers are saying

'Totally gripping from start to finish. I couldn't put it down!'

Rose M, Devon

'Wow! You have done it again. Another book you have written, that I have struggled to put down.'

Denise H, Oxfordshire

Dear Kingsley

Enjoy!

Love,

Andree (AJ Ward)

x

AJ Warren worked as Head of an Early Years setting for 18 years. She lives in Oxfordshire with her husband, her two Romanian rescue dogs, grown children, their spouses and her three beautiful grandchildren.

She works hard for her community, from organising regular coffee mornings, to washing dishes at the local community kitchen, and supporting her GP practice. In addition to writing novels, and looking after her grandchildren, AJ works voluntarily for Age UK. She enjoys swimming, singing, reading and writing.

AJ writes from the heart about family, drama, resilience and love. With a little bit of murder and mystery dropped into the mix. Her books, The Lamp-post Shakers, The Ghost Chaser, The Box and The Lost Soul are all available at Root One Garden Centre, Wallingford and on Amazon in both E-reader and book format. The books can be read alone, or as part of the Lighthouse Series. The Invisible Ones is the fifth instalment of this series.

A short word from the author:

'Hello, I'm Andrea, alias AJ Warren and I started writing in 2018, at the end of project managing our house extension. With a concrete floor, but a brand new dining table, my son – home from Uni and a friend fitting the new kitchen, I put my laptop on the new table and announced, 'I'm going to write a novel!'

The Invisible Ones has been a labour of love, and grew as a seed of hope a few years ago. Two sides of one coin. Two people, with similar experiences. Two outcomes. They go under the radar, assuming their daily life. Showing a façade to the world. The invisible ones.

If you have enjoyed reading The Invisible Ones, please let me know. Share on social media or write a review on Amazon. Reviews are the key to making a pushing my books onto the next level.'

You can contact me, via my website:

https://ajwarrenauthor.wordpress.com

or via my Facebook page.

Other books by AJ Warren – in the Lighthouse Series

The Lamp-post Shakers (Book one)

The Ghost Chaser (Book two)

The Box (Book three)

The Lost Soul (Book four)

The Invisible Ones

'The shadows are as important as the light.'

Charlotte Brontë

The Invisible Ones

Part One: Lottie – Eleven years ago

A smile can say so much.

Without words or gestures, the lifting of the corners of the mouth transforms the face until it reaches the eyes, to represent a single moment of happiness. Laughter lines that settle around the eye and mouth areas over years, marking physical memories of a life well lived.

I have many of them. Laughter lines.

Having once googled the meaning of the word 'smile', the verb description read: *'Form one's features into a pleased, kind, or amused expression, typically with the corners of the mouth turned up and the front teeth exposed.'*

Here, at this very moment in time, as I stand in the red walled library of Basildon Park, an eighteenth-century mansion, in Berkshire, I feel as though I am doing all of those actions.

In this grand house, I envisage a pattern of similarity to myself and Lady Iliffe, who purchased the house with her husband in the 1950s. I can well imagine being the lady of the manor, walking through the rooms and making decisions to take the house from its state of disrepair and bringing it back to life with carefully selected fine furnishings and Old Masters.

One can dream, of course.

My shoulder length red hair is a natural mass of ringlet curls and has been styled by my friend, Jenny, into a loose bun with soft curling wisps that frame each side of my face. Set with a tight comb into the top of my scalp, is an ivory bird cage veil.

My make-up is applied professionally, from a friend of Jenny's, and I wear a deep-rose coloured lipstick that never seems to fade, no matter how much I smile.

'What are you thinking about, Mrs Forster?' Simon, my husband of two hours, whispers warmly against my cheek, as we stroll leisurely through the library adorned with white, decorative bookcases filled with all manner of literature.

My husband takes my hand in a loving gesture and steers me to a set of closed doors and our reception area, which is being held in the Octagon Room.

A young blonde-haired man, dressed in a navy suit, and white shirt, wearing a name badge which reads Tristan. He opens the large white doors, gesturing for us to step into the room.

Just inside the door a woman, wearing a white blouse and navy skirt, holds a silver tray filled with several glasses of champagne, she leans forward to offer us a glass. We each take one and smile our thanks.

Standing silently beside us, Tristan steps forward and announces loudly to the throng of guests, 'Ladies and Gentlemen, please raise your glasses to toast the newly married, Mr and Mrs Simon Forster.'

Cheers and shouts of 'Here, here,' fill the room, followed by the sound of people sipping their drinks. I am so thankful to have these people in my life. Mum and dad stand quietly near the huge stone fireplace, they are the only blood relatives here.

Taking a small sip, I allow the bubbles to tickle my throat, before placing my glass onto a nearby table. I can't stop marvelling at the elegance and grandeur of this large room, from intricate gold mirrors hung high onto deep red walls, to oil paintings displayed within thick gold frames.

And I feel extremely lucky to have the wedding of my dreams, here in this stunning house. I smile, capturing the moment. I don't want to miss a thing.

High decorative ceilings, trimmed with gold, are pulled together by a single exquisite, crystal chandelier which hangs beautifully from the centre of the ceiling. Pinching myself quickly, it finally dawns on me that I married Simon, my best friend and soulmate, in a civil wedding ceremony here, earlier today.

My friends, Stuart and Jenny Greyson and Jem from Shore House, stand quietly talking by the table planner, drink glasses in their hands. I met Jem when she came to stay at the refuge home which I manage for the Greyson's charitable company, The Lighthouse Charity. This is part of the international Gloverman Corporation, the company Jenny inherited from her parents on her twenty first birthday.

With messy, short dark hair and a designer stubble beard that shouts unapologetically, 'I don't give one iota if you like it or not,' Simon reminds me of Stuart Greyson, with his laid-back confidence and easy-going manner. When they speak, you want to listen.

It's not that I've had much experience with romantic relationships, but Simon stands out from the others not just because of his good looks, which make me think of a certain male character in Fifty Shades of Grey, but because he exudes an aura of mystery and excitement. Although, unlike the charismatic Christian Grey, Simon isn't fifty shades of messed up and doesn't have a 'red room of pain.' Well, not one that I've discovered yet!

Simon knows what he wants in life, and he knows how to get it. He oozes a calmness and confidence which draws people to him. Me included. How did I get to be this lucky?

One of the things I love about my new husband is that he approaches life with passion and lives each day as though it is his last. This passion shows in his successful security software company, which he started five years ago. The drive and confidence that seems infectious to everything he touched, pulled me to him like a magnet. From our very first meeting, he enthralled me, and began to show me what being loved and being in love really meant. I am so proud of him. How focused and committed he must have been to build something from nothing. An empire and a legacy.

He wears the charcoal morning suit well, the white shirt complimenting his lightly tanned skin. A matching dark grey tie completes the look. The only hint of colour is the pale pink rose buttonhole that sits on his lapel.

Turning slightly into the warmth of his body, I reach for his hand and lace my fingers through his. My heart skips a beat. I close my eyes briefly, making a snapshot memory of this moment in time, needing to keep it safe. We have a lifetime to make memories and to build a life together.

Images of our first meeting swirled through my mind. Stuart had been in touch, asking me to attend a meeting on software security as part of my role as manager of Shore House, the first refuge home purchased by the Lighthouse Charity. We look after women and children in need of a sanctuary from abusive partners and family members. There are funds to offer additional support from counselling to childminding, training and qualifications to setting up new lives. This flagship charity was borne to show how women and children flourish when living in the right environment, where money and resources are no object.

***

I rush through the huge revolving doors of Simon Forster's London office, Forster Cyber Security XL. The building is based at Paddington Basin, close to the station, and is as impressive as I had imagined. Tall, sharp angles made of glass and steel, glide gracefully into the grey sky. It had been a long journey. which involved picking up a busy train at Axminster. This took me to Waterloo, once there, I just needed to use the tube to get me across London to Paddington Station.

Unsurprisingly, at some point the journey began losing time, forcing me to almost sprint the last hundred yards to the building. I check my watch, damn – it's 11.59am I was due at Simon Forster's office at 11.30am.

A short-haired man wearing glasses and a black jumper with a white collar, smiles warmly from behind the sleek steel reception desk, as I bustle in with my long red curly hair flying everywhere. I'm wearing a soft grey woollen jacket which falls haphazardly along my shoulders, followed by my favourite crossover hessian bag, and a long navy skirt freckled with tiny lighthouses.

'Charlotte Peckham,' I introduce myself to the young man. 'I had an appointment at 11.30am to see Simon Forster. I'm so sorry that I'm late. I'm with the Lighthouse Charity.' I tell him breathlessly.

'Let me call through to his office,' the young man smiles, before reaching for the phone and talking quietly. 'I have Charlotte Peckham here for you, Sir. She was due to see you at 11.30am.' The man listens, 'I see. Thank you, Sir.'

Putting the phone down, the man looks my way, smiling. 'Mr Forster will be with you momentarily, he is just finishing some paperwork,' the young man reassures me. He gestures to the brown leather seating area and asks. 'Would you like to take a seat?'

'Thank you,' I smile back, looking at the two comfortable looking sofas, separated by an oak and metal coffee table, and make my way to the nearest. On top of the table sits a vibrant purple Peace Lily in a ceramic white vase. Beside the vase sits several magazines, neatly stacked on top of each other.

The man steps from behind the desk, and moves behind me, asking, 'Can I offer you a tea, coffee or something cold?'

'Thanks,' I smile, dipping my head to allow my bag to slip over, and catching the long handle. 'A glass of water would be good,' I smile with appreciation, dropping my bag onto the sofa.

I feel him before I see him. Shuffling out of my jacket, I fold it onto the sofa with my bag, and turn to face the glass lift. I cannot fathom why, but there feels a need to follow the lift slowly as it descends to the ground floor. The man inside stares out, hands casually pushed into trouser pockets, and then his head lifts and his eyes find mine. My breath hitches, as our eyes meet for the longest time.

Sweaty palms are rubbed down my skirt. Bloody hell. If that's him, I'm done for. My mouth suddenly becomes dry, and I wish the glass of water that I had asked for, would materialise.

The door opens and I forget to breathe. For the most beautiful man, dressed in a navy suit, crisp white shirt and burgundy tie, steps outs and strides towards me. He looks serious, intent.

'Charlotte Peckham?' he offers his hand for me to shake.

I nod, forgetting to take the outstretched hand. My reaction to this man is confusing, embarrassing and very much unwelcome. I don't do flustered. His face is angular and classic and when I look up, I am lost in the clear aquamarine seas of a much-loved Corfu holiday. His eyes drop to my hand, and I quickly raise my right hand and grasp his. Soft and warm to the touch, the contact sends a frisson of electricity up my arm.

'Lottie,' I smile, wondering what he would look like if he smiled. If the smile would reach his eyes, or what his laugh sounded like. 'So sorry, I'm late,' I begin, 'my journey has been long, since I left Lyme Regis this morning, and we lost time getting to Waterloo and,' I stop, as a shadow catches my eye. Walking slowly towards me is a tall woman, dressed in what seems to be the customary white shirt and black trousers, and carrying a water filled crystal glass balanced on a small white tray. 'Your water,' she offers.

Carefully I reach across and take the glass, murmuring my thanks, and the woman smiles 'You're welcome,' as she walks away. I look at Simon, who raises an eyebrow in question, goodness – this is ridiculous! Quickly, I tip the ice-cold liquid into my mouth and gulp it down.

The water catches, causing me to cough and without a sound, Simon steps forward:

'Are you alright?' he asks quietly, concern in his face. I nod, putting my hand to my mouth to cover the last few token spasms. I am shocked by my reaction to this man, and for what is probably the first time in my life, I am rendered speechless.

I simply nod. My world just changed upside down and it has completely thrown me.

It was supposed to be an average day, a day of training and learning about the new software that would keep us and our clients safe. But there was nothing average about meeting Simon Forster, or my reaction to him.

'Send refreshments to my office,' Simon tells the man on reception with authority, as he takes the glass from my fingers and puts it onto the coffee table. Simon Forster appears to be a man who is very at ease with himself, he has an arrogance that borders on annoyance, as he reaches down to the sofa to collect my jacket and bag.

'I think I'm going to enjoy getting to know you, Lottie from Lyme,' his tone is lighter than before, and I shake slightly when he puts his hand gently in the small of my back, to guide me to the lift. As we move together in silence, and enter the lift, I realise that his hand remains in the small of my back.

***

A pressure on my fingers brings me back to the here and now.

My wedding day.

'I am putting this moment in my memory box,' I tell him, turning my head and feeling my auburn curls softly trail across my cheek. Looking into Simon's blue-green eyes, my voice is husky with emotion, and my words are for his ears only. 'I'm going to remember every single thing that happens today.'

In the corner of the room sits a four-piece quartet playing Mozart's Marriage of Figaro.

Simon's eyes hold mine, full of love and promises, and I watch mesmerised as he lifts a hand and gently tucks a stray curl behind my ear. Warm fingers linger on the sensitive skin of my neck, so I close my eyes briefly and sway to the music. Strong arms bring me out of my reverie, as Simon holds me close and begins to caress my back, through the thin lace of my antique ivory wedding gown, slowly as though he has all the time in the world. The featherlike touch of his fingers, linger as he dares to go lower to cup my bottom through my floor-length, wedding dress. I lower my lashes, blushing slightly, savouring the feeling.

It's as though there is only us in the room.

And then, as I drape my hands around his neck, he carefully bends me backwards, like a scene from an old black and white movie with Fred Astaire and Ginger Rogers, and swoops down to take my lips in a long lingering kiss.

'I am going to love you forever,' his voice is hard, as though it's a threat. His eyes darken with intent. 'I will make you smile each day, and I will love you long into each night.'

His words, force my eyes to fill with tears.

'Now, let's get through the wedding breakfast and reception as quickly as we can, because I have plans for you tonight, and nothing is going to stop them.'

Shaking my head, I listen to the promises of my new husband and watch him take two filled champagne flutes from a nearby table. He hands me one.

'I can't wait,' I smile, taking the cold glass. My voice filled with emotion, of love and hope.

But no one knows where the journey of life will take us. Where it will begin or, indeed where it will end, do they? If our future were easy to predict, someone would have written a book and made a fortune from it, by now. Of that, I'm sure.

And, as I reach for Simon's hand and lead him to our places at the far side of the room, I realise that, for this moment in time, I am the happiest I have ever been.

Part Two: Lottie – Now (Eleven years later)

The moon watches on, silently. Waiting for me to lose my mind.

My heart thuds wildly. Thump. Thump. Thump. Deep in my chest.

I feel like I've been running for hours. My legs are heavy, my feet bloody and sore, and my white, sleeveless nightdress is torn at the neck and bodice from negotiating the trees in the dark forest. But I keep running. Even though the pain catches in my chest with each breath, and the burn sears my throat as I frantically draw air into my lungs, I can't stop.

Someone or something is chasing me.

Heavy footsteps echo through the night, following my own, I turn briefly, but see nothing. What the hell is it? If this is a nightmare, I need to wake up soon.

My heart pumps so hard, I fear it will burst from my chest. My foot catches on a low branch as I push through the heavily overgrown trees that line the narrow woodland pathway, near my home. Before I can stop myself, I fall to the ground with a heavy thud. The damp ground is cool, hard and unforgiving. Stones and twigs dig into my knees and hips, taking my breath away.

Pain sears through my body, and I swear several times to cope with the excruciating trauma. Dark shadows surround me, hauntingly sounds of wildlife causing goose pimples to form along my arms.

'Lottie?' a deep, familiar voice, full of anguish repeats, 'Lottie, it's me.'

No, it can't be.

A shroud of light appears above me, and I rub my eyes in wonder. What the hell is happening? Am I losing my mind? I close my eyes and when they reopen, the shroud of light has disappeared. In its place, as though he never died and left me alone, stands the tall familiar shape of my husband.

Simon, with his short dark messy hair, steps closer to me, reminding me of the husband I used to know and the memories of our life together. Worry is etched across Simon's angular face, and his hands reach to take mine, but I brush him away.

Instead, I use my arms to block his loving face from me, because this is all too much. I feel like I'm losing my mind. Sobs form in my throat,

'For Christ Sake, Lottie, it's me!' He says with urgency, 'At least let me help you up.'

Slowly, I uncover my eyes and watch Simon bend to his knees, his face full of concern. Panic consumes me, and settles along my spine, making my whole body feel heavy and rigid.

There is no way it can be him. No way at all. For my husband died four years ago from pancreatic cancer which came on very suddenly, destroying the person he was, as it spread its evil way through his body in a very short space of time. Four weeks. That was all it took for him to leave me, a widow with a young child to raise.

It was as though I was being punished for being happy. Simon paid the price.

We all paid the price.

Thank goodness for my ten-year-old son, Harley, for Jenny, Stuart and Shore House. Thank goodness for friends such as Jem and her husband, Noah, who live nearby. For without them, I would have crumbled and given up. My mind is playing tricks and instinct kicks in, I shuffle my cold, aching body along the muddy path, away from him.

'Lottie?' his voice sounds hurt.

Loud sobs echo in my ears, making me look up and check out my surroundings. Who else is here? Hot wet tears run down my face. Forlornly, I realise that the sobbing is coming from my own throat.

A draining feeling overwhelms me and then the world goes blank.

Opening my eyes, I take in the darkened room, and familiar shapes of my bedroom and, to my dismay, I realise that there is no sign of Simon. He will never be here again.

The nightmares keep coming, filling my nights with restlessness and panic. Why? It's been a week now, and I need to stop them haunting me, draining me.

The only clue as to why I may be having the dreams, is that it's my wedding anniversary tomorrow. Perhaps that's why I'm so unsettled. Four years without Simon, of being both mum and dad to Harley. Thank goodness, I have a good network of friends, and family – or I would be climbing the walls some days.

I reach out to the lamp on my bedside table, press the button and bring the room to a soft white glow.

'Mum?' The soft voice of Harley, my ten-year-old son, breaks the silence. He stands in the shadowed light of the open door, eyes still half-closed with sleep. 'Are you OK? I heard you crying.' His face is full of worry, making me feel ashamed for frightening him. I wipe my wet face with the palms of my hands.

'Hey honey,' I say, holding my arms out to him. Wearing his favourite blue and red coloured, Marvel action hero pyjamas, he shuffles toward to me, reminding me once again, how quickly he is growing up.

'I just had a bad dream,' I reassure him softly, chastising myself in my head, for putting my boy through the aftermath of my nightmares. 'Want to jump in with me?' I offer quietly, shuffling into a half-sitting position. And, for a moment, I wonder if he thinks himself too old to snuggle with mum.

Harley's eyebrows burrow together, as he contemplates what to do. He brushes his hand through short auburn bed-messed hair and gives me the briefest of nods, before my skinny son – who never stops eating, waits for me to pull back the duvet, before climbing into bed beside me.

'It's OK Mum,' he says quietly, laying his head on a pillow. 'I'll protect you from the bad man.'

I try to hide the lump in my throat, the thought of my young son fighting my demons for me, causes my heart to ache. This little man is just like his father, sure of himself and willingly protective of those he cares about. The auburn hair and freckles, he gets from me, but the nose, the eyes and the lips are all his adored father.

'The bad man?' I query, turning off the lamp, before we snuggle down together, his back to my front. The warmth of his body begins to quieten my thoughts and settle the chills that overwhelm me. He must be speaking in a general way, right?

Stroking Harley's head, his voice is sleepy when he finally answers, 'if he comes back, I'll protect you.' His last words hover in the air as I stroke his hair, before turning off the lamp and allowing myself to drift back to sleep.

In the darkened room, lit only by the brightness of the moon as it filters through the thin cotton curtains, I am oblivious to the stranger standing in my garden, staring up at the bedroom window.

Back in that in-between state of consciousness and sleep, I pull the heavy duvet around me as my breathing slows completely and I finally allow myself the privilege of rest.

The moon watches on silently.

Waiting.

Part Three: Cameron - Now

I stand in the garden of the end-terraced house and stare as the upstairs bedroom window becomes shrouded in darkness. I think of her lying there in the bed, soft and pliant in a black lacy nightdress, her red curls splayed across the pillow, like an ethereal Nicole Kidman. And, my groin begins to thicken and twitch, making the urge to touch her, almost overwhelming.

Memories of a night long ago, whirl through my mind making me giddy with pleasure. Hairs stand up on my arms as I think of the flowing beer and spirits, the vodka bowl. High spirited drinking, combined with free drugs, dotted in bowls like a sweet shop pick and mix, became intoxicating and pushed all inhibitions into a secluded part of the brain.

That's when the drinking started. It stopped the monotony and pain of everyday life, it kept the problems locked away, so I could function. Sort of. The problem with remembering, with your mind trying to find memories that link you to the here and now, is that they can trick you. Sending out false memories, ones that we want to have happened, rather than what did happen, also tricking you into believing that everything is all right. When, deep down, you know it's not. And then you realise that reality has become flawed.

My fists tighten, it would be so easy to kill her right here, right now. No one would be any the wiser. She lives alone, apart from that son of hers, which is a pain. That's why I've decided to leave her a little present. To give her something to think about.

The Invisible Ones

An excited shudder runs through me. I hope so. Reaching into my back pocket, I bring out a small, silver hipflask and untwist the lid. I take a deep breath, savouring the smell from within. It's Jack Daniels today, but I'm not too fussy. Anything with a kick will do. I down the entire contents, enjoying the burn as it hits my throat.

Moving closer through the early morning darkness, I lean my face against the cold, hard kitchen window and imagine her tossing and turning.

My hands clench by my sides. One of these days, I'm going to get her back for what she did to me, a pain sears through the top of my right thigh and doesn't stop until it sits behind the back of my knee. Wincing, I momentarily panic, wondering if this is the time, it will completely give in, or if it is just another warning sign. My right leg has been well and truly broken and won't ever be right again.

Another memory, and this time I'm tied to a chair, alongside my friends and this time I don't get to walk away. Whoever gave me this bloody injury has a lot to answer for. I'll be looking for them next.

'But, for now,' I tell myself. 'Don't rush. Bide your time. Stick to the plan.'

Walking slowly along the paved path to the garden exit, I grit my teeth as each step causes a stabbing pain through my injured limb, until I finally reach and quietly open the latch to the gate. I use my phone to lead me safely down the dark, narrow alleyway that leads to the front of her town house.

Everything takes longer with this blasted leg, so when I finally walk through the small gated front garden, it feels like a lifetime has passed. Taking the wooden box from my large black, crossover bag, I reach the blue painted door and lower myself as closely as I can to the ground.

30

Then, I leave the woman's gift on the doorstep.

'Take that, Charlotte,' I whisper, with a note of satisfaction. If only I could see the look on her face, when she opens the box. That would be beyond my wildest dreams.

'Enjoy your gift, it is the first of many. No more than you deserve. And, now I've found you, I'll be making the most of renewing our acquaintance.

The name Charlotte rolls off my lips, again and again, like a mantra until eventually, tired and weary, I call an Uber to take me home.

Part Four: Lottie – Now

'Harley. Are you taking your iPad?' I shout, from the top of the stairs to my son. We were supposed to have left, forty-five minutes ago. 'Hurry, we're going to be late!'

'Yeah, I think it's on my bed,' my son's voice booms through the house, as I quickly turn around to face his bedroom, and push his door open with more force than I intend to. The door handle hits the wall, with a thud.

Harley is mad on anything to do with space, in fact there is a feature wall showing the planets and solar system, in his bedroom. It is a work in progress, because he continually adds something to the wall, either by sticker or hand.

The floor and bed are littered with clothes and trainers. For a young boy, he certainly knows how to ensure that everything he owns is on display, always at hand when he needs them. I spy the iPad with its red cover lying on a space shuttle pillowcase, grab it and the charger that sits in the usual place on Harley's bedside table and force myself not to give the room a quick tidy before we leave for our short break.

Taking the handle of the large yellow suitcase in one hand, I tuck the tablet and charger under an arm and haul the lot down the stairway, one clunk at a time. Izzy, my assistant manager, is covering my duties at Shore House for the week.

I can't believe that we're going away for six days over the summer holidays. My close friends Jenny and Stuart Greyson have hired a manor house, in the village of Sutton Courtenay, near

Didcot Parkway in Oxfordshire for a family get-together. If I'm honest, I'm looking forward to the break. I love working for the Lighthouse charity, and being based at Shore House, which is very important and rewarding work, but caring for women who have suffered systematic domestic violence, can be intense, challenging, and heart-breaking.

The multidisciplinary team and I, work for the Greyson's Lighthouse charity, who house vulnerable women and children in several specialised houses dotted around the country. I'm based at Shore House in Lyme Regis, and we help the women to come to terms with what has happened to them, to understand why it has happened, and finally to help them to move forward with their lives. We have had quite a few success stories.

Jem, Steph and Sasha are wonderful examples of how lives can be turned around.

Harley looks at me with auburn hair, curly like mine and a little on the wild side. He's a good-looking boy and carries himself with confidence and a casual – I don't care stance. He's thrown on jeans and a black hoodie and is holding a whole slice of heavily buttered toast.

'Mum, I can't find my swim trunks,' he says, taking a huge mouthful.

'Have you looked in your bottom drawer in your room?' I ask, opening the front door and about to haul the yellow suitcase down the step to the driveway. Something catches my eye. There's a brown coloured, wooden box on the doorstep, it is the size of a large iPad, and looks nothing like an Amazon parcel.

What on earth is it? I stop, look to my left and right to see if there is anyone about in the road. Not a soul. Leaving the suitcase, I reach down and pick up the box. I'm surprised by how heavy it is. Attached to the lid of the box is a white printed label, with letters in black ink the letters to my name, ***Charlotte***. There's no doubt about it; this gift is meant for me.

I hold up the box and retreat into the house.

'Everything OK, Mum?' Harley asks, in a concerned voice. I can feel his presence, as he moves closely to my side.

'What's that?' He follows me as I walk into our square shaped kitchen, with the dark wooden units, chrome handles, bright white walls and large window that faces the back of the house. The kitchen that Simon and I had chosen together. Harley watches closely as I put the box on the oak dining table.

'I'm not sure,' I say. 'I'm not expecting anything,' my heart begins to race, and I'm unsure what to say. 'Let's open it up and see.'

Suddenly, the skin on my arms becomes cold, and there is a sickening feeling forming in my stomach. Something feels wrong.

Slowly, I open the box, and the first thing that hits me is the pungent smell of death. Immediately, my stomach rolls and sickness rushes to my throat, in a panic I thrust my hand hard against my mouth, force myself to breath and swallow until I feel the rolling motion stop.

What the hell! A terrible sense of foreboding begins to seep up from my feet, a coldness makes its way up my body and doesn't stop until it settles at the base of my neck.

Using both hands I lift the lid completely off the box and set it on the table. I step back in horror. For inside, lying on a small bed of hay, is the body of a dead rat. On top of the rat is a small pale blue rectangular piece of card, with the words ***Charlotte*** handwritten on it.

No one has called me Charlotte for years. Almost everyone I know, apart from my parents call me Lottie. What the hell is going on? Who sent this? I turn the card and find more words. *'Enjoy your gift. The first of many. X'* In full panic mode, my brain searches for memories to shed some light onto what is happening here. Why the hell would someone send me a dead animal?

'Urghhh,' Harley exclaims loudly, stepping away from the table.

I turn to him quickly and point to the fridge at the far side of the kitchen, 'Harley, go and stand over there,' my voice sounds harsh, but I need him to move fast, for his own sake. He's already seen enough. When he's moved away, I turn back to the wooden box and its gruesome contents. I don't think of myself as a squeamish person but seeing the body of the dead rodent encased in the wooden box, in my kitchen is very unsettling.

'Mum,' my son's voice breaks into the silence.

'Stay there,' I warn, studying the dark brown creature. 'Have you got your phone on you?' I take out my own phone, and begin taking photos of the box, the free-standing lid and finally, the rat and card.

'Yes,' he replies, his voice quiet.

'Can you call Jem and ask her to come over? Noah too, if he's there.'

'OK,' he whispers.

As he talks into the phone, I walk to the sink unit, open the cupboard beneath and reach in to take out a box of disposable gloves. Slipping a pair on, I open the 'mess' drawer and search for a pair of tweezers. When I'm satisfied that I have everything I need, I return to the dining table.

'Jem is on her way. She says Noah's at the office,' Harley's voice cuts through my focused thoughts.

'Good, thanks,' I feel better hearing that one of them is on their way. I glance quickly back at Harley, 'stay there, will you.'

Taking a deep breath, I look again at the rat, curled up and force myself to touch it. The body is hard, in full rigor – as though asleep. The fur is dark brown, short and neat, and the tail is curled around the body. There is no evidence of injury, it looks as if it is resting, but I know it's not.

This is beyond weird.

Using the tweezers, I pick up the card.

It is then, that I notice the small lumps of blood around the eyes of the rat. But where the eyes should have been, there is nothing but empty sockets.

I step back, the card and tweezers slipping silently through my fingers, to the floor, and by the look of concern on my son's face, the horror and panic that is rushing through my veins is clear for all to see.

Quickly, I recover myself and put the lid back on the box, before picking up the tweezers and card and laying them both on the dining table. Snapping off my gloves, I rub my hands down my jeans and turn to Harley.

'Come here,' I tell him.

Harley steps forward slowly, he stares at the box on the table, the only sign that he is worried. My brave young boy doesn't stop until he stands before me, his face pale, protecting me. Just like he has always done. I take a deep breath and pull him quickly into my arms. 'It will be alright,' I whisper, 'don't worry about anything, I will sort it out.'

The doorbell rings, breaking our moment of calmness.

'That's probably Jem,' I say, releasing him from my arms, and walking to the door. The outline of my old friend, holding her three-year-old daughter, Edie, trickles through the coloured glass of my front door.

Throwing open the door, I smile my thanks to her, for dropping whatever she was doing to come and support me.

Jem is an artist. A very successful artist, the flair that she wears clothes, mis-matched, and with huge confidence that says, 'It works!' Today she wears a long linen khaki dress with a tulip-shaped hemline, and a long purple cardigan. Short, dark curly hair sits in abundance, framing her heart-shaped face, and casually looped around her slender neck, is a pale green scarf with penguins delicately printed onto it.

Putting her down, Edie dressed in a pair of green and yellow dungarees and a purple long-sleeved top, toddles into the house. 'Aunty Lottie, Aunty Lottie,' she smiles as I scoop her up in my arms. 'How are you angel?'

Jem dumps a large grey bag in the hallway and closes the door, before leaning into me and kissing my cheek. 'We were already heading this way to visit Maureen,' she explains, 'when Harley phoned,' she nods to Harley who stands beside me.

'What's up?' Jem asks as I gently lower Edie to the floor and guide her to the bright yellow living room, which is lucky to catch the sun for most of the day. I lead Edie beside the well-worn leather sofa and to the large, rattan box of children's toys.

'Harley,' I say, 'can you please keep an eye on Edie for a few minutes, while I talk to Jem.'

He nods, he knows it's important, he saw, albeit briefly, what was in the box that was left on the doorstep.

'This way,' I take her through to the kitchen, leaving the door open so that we can hear the children.

Moments later, we both stand over the dining table looking at the box which holds the body of the deceased rodent, with the missing eyes. Jem's smile is gone, and her face is pale. There is no mistaking that this 'gift' is a sign, the start of something, and I'm not good with surprises.

I like to be in control of my life and what happens within it. Apart from losing Simon, there has been one time, a few years ago, when I lost control, and my world came crashing down. Dark days and nights had followed, until eventually I had shaken the misery off and pulled myself back into the light.

From that day, the one when I looked forward and not backward, I made a promise to myself that I would never allow that to happen again.

'Have you called Stuart and Jenny?' she asks quietly.

'No.' I shake my head, 'not yet. I was going to leave it until I got to Oxfordshire.'

Jem steps closer, until she's no more than an inch from me, and puts her hands on my shoulders. The contact is comforting and with a deep sigh, I realise that I've been holding in my worries. Fears that someone is watching me, or even Harley. God, Harley. What if they're watching him too? I hold back a sob, wipe a treacherous stray tear that threatens to fall, I don't want Jem to see how frightened I am. Pulling myself together, I force a smile and face my friend.

'It'll be all right,' she says, leaning against the table, her voice is husky with conviction. 'We'll find out who's doing this, and they will be punished.'

Absently, I tuck a stray curl around her ear and not for the first time, realise how lucky I am to have a friend like her.

'No more kissing, Edie,' Harley's half-joking voice cuts into my thoughts, 'or I'll turn you into a frog!'

We turn at his words and walk into the living room, to find my ten-year-old pinned to the wooden floor by a smiling Edie, who sits astride him, looking as though butter wouldn't melt in her mouth. Until she leans down and plants an open-mouthed kiss on his cheek.

'Urgh...' Harley, winces in disgust, and I suddenly feel the need to smile.

'Edie!' Jem chastises her daughter with mock anger. 'Do not sit on top of Harley and stop kissing him!'

'But I love Harley,' the little girl says sweetly. 'I'm going to marry him one day.'

'Heaven help us all!' I smile, momentarily distracted from the shadow that is now haunting my day. 'No more talk of weddings,' I pat Edie's head gently. 'I'll pop the kettle for a quick cup of tea before I carry on loading the car.'

'I'm mostly packed,' Jem absently pulls a piece of fluff from her linen dress as she leans against the fridge, watching me making the drinks. 'He's finishing work early, so we can set off as soon as he arrives home. I'm looking forward to seeing Steph, Jack and Ben again.'

'Me too,' I hand her, her tea of choice. A peppermint tea, with the bag left in. 'I really need this break. It is way overdue.'

Jem rests her hand on mine, 'It is,' she says, 'you deserve this break.'

I pat her hand warmly, 'we all deserve this break.'

There is a short silence as we sip our hot drinks before Jem asks, 'Is Daniel coming to the house?'

I put my mug of tea on the oak coffee table. Taking my time before answering, I am still unsure about whether I should move on with my life romantically, I don't need a man. I'm an independent person in my own right, I have Harley and a strong effective group of friends.

'I don't know,' I tell her honestly, 'I never asked because I didn't want to worry about what meeting Daniel again would mean.' And if I'm honest I'm not ready to talk about my feelings, not ready to think of the man who used to counsel me many years ago, following the kidnap of my friend, Jenny. We had met for coffee a couple of times and then kind of drifted apart.

A few moments later we're in the living room, where Edie is upending the rattan toy box and searching for small dinosaurs. Harley has returned to his bedroom, to look for his swim trunks, and I take this moment to talk quietly to Jem about my worries.

I look at the photos of family and friends, that sit along the white marble mantlepiece. All different size and style of frames. The memories and smiles warm my heart and remind me of a life well lived, of treasured moments that will stay with me forever.

The photo of Simon and I on our wedding day sits in a plain silver frame in the middle of the group. We look so happy, ready to take on the world and build a life together. Thankfully, at that moment in time, we never knew that our life together would be cut short, our dreams turned to dust and that Harley would grow up without his father. Thank goodness, we never knew.

Taking a sip of my hot, sweet tea and peering over my mug at Jem, 'I've no idea who could have sent this, I've never consciously hurt anyone in my life.'

She looks at me, creases forming on her forehead. 'It's got to be someone from your past, someone who knows you.'

Searching my mind just brings up blanks, offering no input into what's going on.

Shaking my head, I acknowledge what she's saying, 'I know, but I can't think who.' I tell her with some frustration.

And then my phone pings.

It's a text: *'I hope you liked your present, Charlotte. The first of many!'*, and suddenly all I can hear is the loud thud of my heart, beating hard and frantic in my ears.

Bloody Hell! What is going on and how did they get my number?

Part Five: Harley

It feels like I've been the man of the house for a thousand years, and not four, Mum always calls us the A Team, saying that we can do anything that we set our minds to. She is always trying to big us up, telling me that we're invincible.

But more than anything, Mum is my hero.

She was devastated when Dad died, we both were. An image of him lying in the hospice, nothing like the man he used to be. Nothing like my dad. The cancer took over and he didn't stand a chance, becoming more poorly as each day went by. I was so angry, angry with him, as though he had allowed himself to 'catch' cancer. It was totally unreasonable. I was angry with Mum, with her wet face and red, swollen eyes, holding gently onto his frail hands and shaking her head, muttering, 'I thought we had more time.'

Silent tears had rolled down my cheeks when he had beckoned me closer to his side. With pale skin, his blue eyes caught mine, and he whispered, 'Look after your mum, son.'

I wiped panicked tears away with the sleeve of my jumper as his breathing slowed and I knew he was close to the end. 'I will,' I whispered back, before throwing myself over his body and sobbing. 'Don't go,' I had said, loudly as though it would make him hear me, but it was too late.

Opposite me, Mum slumped from her seat to the floor with a thud and started howling like a wounded animal. Jem stepped forward from the doorway, knelt down and hugged Mum as though the

43

whole world was about to end. Lost in my own sea of misery, I stayed rigid on the bed, my body plastered against my dad's, holding him tightly.

For the first time in my life, it felt like I was suffocating, as though oxygen was being sucked out of the room and I began clawing at the neck of my green hoodie, as gasping sounds forced themselves from my panicked throat.

That was the first time I had ever experienced a panic attack.

Strong arms pulled me backwards, reached under my armpits and dragged me from the body of my dead father. 'Come on, Harley,' Stuart's deep voice broke through my daze. He held me from him, facing me, 'Deep breaths, son. That's it, look at me and keep taking deep breaths.' His voice soothed me, forcing me to concentrate and after a few breaths, the world stopped spinning and my lungs began to fill with air.

'Good boy,' he said, before pulling me close and holding me tight. 'I've got you,' he kept whispering, 'I've got you.'

Jenny and Jem looked after Mum, while Stuart stayed with me, as we waited for the doctor to come to confirm the time of death. Nurses hovered in and around the room. I thought about their jobs and what it must be like to be surrounded by death, it wasn't something that I would want to do when I was older. It was too hard, too painful.

***

My friends at school rib me about being a 'Mummy's boy,' but, I know they're just messing about. I never wanted or planned to be a 'Mummy's boy,' it just happened that way.

Justin, my best friend, is a serious nerd. He is tall for ten, and his long, dark floppy hair drapes over his face when he gets lost in a book or looks at the floor during one of his 'thinking' moments. He loves telling me about statistics. Like 'Did you know that according to the statistics for 2019 that there were 2.9 million lone parent families in the UK?'

No, I didn't, and he had better not be having a dig at me. At the same time, I bet he didn't know that there are 238,855 miles between the Earth and the moon, either.

He had asked me during lunch break at school, and my first thought had been to roll my eyes upwards, to the grey ceiling of the dining room, and kick his leg hard under the table.

'What's that for?' He looked at me, surprised by my reaction.

'For being a nerd.' I tell him, pushing pasta around the plate.

'I wasn't getting at you, you know,' Justin pushes his long hair off his face, 'I wouldn't do that.' He pushes a packet of crisps my way, as a peace offering.

Taking a deep breath, finally I tell him, 'I know, sorry. It's just that life sucks sometimes. I wish things were different.'

Without a thought, Justin takes one of the segments of his satsuma and says, 'Open wide, this is what you get for being a dick.' Of course, I wasn't quick enough and completely missed the piece of flying fruit as it shot across the table.

I grabbed the fallen satsuma segment and push it into my mouth.

'Asshole.'

***

Jem and Mum are downstairs talking, with Edie. Things are a bit calmer now and I have left them to sort out the dead rat.

That was pretty gross.

As I lie on my bed and look up at the artexed, grey, white ceiling I think of Mum and worry about what is going on. Who would give her something so disgusting? And why? These two questions worry me the most.

My phone beeps, and I wonder if it's Mum checking up on me as usual. But it's a number I don't recognise. Mum always tells me not to answer unknown numbers.

This time though, even though I know it's wrong, I find myself swiping my finger across the screen to open it.

'Hello?' I ask, waiting for the voice to answer on the other end.

A man's deep voice asks, 'Harley?' A stranger's voice.

'Yeah, who wants to know?' I ask, picking at dust on my bedside cabinet.

'I know your mother.'

'Do you?' I whisper. There is something about his voice that makes me feel uneasy. I'm not sure if I believe him, then he mentions my mum's name, and the world stops. Now, I am listening.

'How?' I say, my voice quiet.

There is a long pause, as if he's thinking about what to say.

'How?' I repeat, I can feel an anger building inside me. Why won't he tell me.

'I'm your mother's cousin, Cameron.'

'She never mentioned you,' I say, wondering why I've never heard of this man before. She never mentioned she had a cousin. Something doesn't feel right here, but it's my job to look after her, so I plan to find out what this man wants.

The man was persistent, 'My fault, we grew apart over the years. It's her birthday in ten days, and I was kind of hoping to take you both out for a meal. To make amends for the loss of contact.'

Oh no, I'd forgotten about her birthday.

'Tell me more,' I say. Wondering if I am doing the right thing, but unable to disconnect the call.

I don't trust this 'cousin' of my mum's. Not one bit.

And I'm going to play along, to see what he's up to.

As we talk, I realise two things.

One, that this man is very good at talking and sharing with others, without actually revealing much about himself. He is very good at bigging himself up, particularly to strangers who he doesn't know.

Two. This man assumes that everyone is an idiot.

Which of course, isn't the case. Just wait until I tell Stuart, he's going to go ape. Stuart and Jack will rip Cameron apart if he so much as looks at mum the wrong way.

Part Six: Cameron

'Do you want your eggs fried or scrambled?' Mum looks away from the smoking induction hob, in the kitchen. Today, she reminds me of a plump bulldog, her face is covered in wrinkles and her abundance of wild grey hair is held together with a colourful scarf, which sits in a messy knot on the top of her head. I swear, she thinks it's trendy, like the ones Jo Brand used to wear. But, in my eyes, she just looks stupid.

Wearing a long, bright orange kaftan printed with leaping black cats, that makes you wonder if the artist was wearing a blindfold. It is garish. The furry black slippers peeping out from the bottom as she moves, reveal the tiny feet that originally had a petite body to match. By all accounts my mother has let herself go, since Dad left mother for his tall, red-headed personal secretary at the office three years ago. At least he left her the house and she is financially independent. I stare across at her and see the red painted lips hold on tightly to a lit cigarette that she lets ash carelessly fall across the black tiled kitchen floor.

My eyes flit to the dirty silver handled knife, resting on the kitchen counter covered with tomato ketchup and butter, where she has just cut up a bacon butty. Mum is the epitome of someone who cares little for hygiene. I really don't care anymore. I mean, I'm thirty-four years old, still living at home, and work part-time in a local book shop. I love books, they are my saving grace. I particularly love horror stories and real-life serial killer books, such as Stephen King and Mo Hayder. The more disturbing, the better.

Back to mother dearest, she could give me a stomach ulcer and I would still smile politely, before thinking about ways to slit her throat and shut her up. Permanently. Sometimes the feelings to hurt someone are so bad, I need a drink to take the edge off. Vodka, wine, whatever I can get my hands on.

'Fried,' I respond flatly, there's no point in being polite to her, she wouldn't notice. I could be sitting here dressed as a geisha and she wouldn't even look at me. I sit down at the table, dragging the heavy, wooden chair across the cold, tiled floor and study the food. It is literally swimming in fat. There is smoke in the room, and there are few windows due to the age of the old two bedroomed cottage.

'Can you clean your room at some point today. There is a horrible stench coming from in there.' Mum's raspy voice, cuts in as I raise my cutlery to slice a piece of sausage.

Looking up from the plate, I force myself to answer, saying harshly. 'I haven't got time.'

We used to live in a fairly large town in Oxfordshire, called Didcot. It was a nice house, with four bedrooms, a tidy back garden and overlooking the Ladygrove Lakes, on the big estate. It was a nice enough place to live, apart from the bloody noise from geese and ducks on the lakes. They never shut up, always squawking, especially when the kids were feeding them.

But two years ago, we moved to this cottage in Charmouth, a village in the west of Dorset. It's a beautiful place, but it's always full of tourists in the summer, which is annoying. I had hoped that mum would find and get a grip on life again, but she didn't. She leaves the cottage twice a week, to buy shopping and her cigarettes, she attends medical appointments, but that's where it stops. Limited contact, limited choices. It's sad to see, but she's given up.

When we moved here, I managed to get a job in a book shop in the town for a couple of days a week. Declan, the owner is laid back and kind, so there is no pressure on me, but to serve customers and browse the books. This is ideal for me, especially when I never know how painful my leg is going to be from one day to another.

Thank goodness it's Saturday and I don't need to work. By all accounts, the weather is going to be nice, and I feel optimistic that today is going to be a good day. My phone rings, and I see my friend, Vincent Camprinelli's name flicks across the screen.

'What?' I ask, what can he want at 9.30am on a Saturday? Nothing good.

Vincent's gruff voice replies, 'I need your help Cam.'

Rolling my eyes with frustration. It bloody never stops, I've been here with Vincent before. He is like one of those funny characters in a gangster movie, who you know will end up dead in the end. He has no brains, and is gullible, to the point of believing that Queen Elizabeth II had a twin and lived in Didcot when she was not residing at Buckingham Palace, a prank from one of our school group, Eric when he was sixteen.

Vincent also has a quick temper and hangs out with the wrong people. Nasty, get rich quick, people who would smile as they shoot him in the back if he said the wrong thing. When he gets into trouble, I am usually the first person he calls.

'I haven't heard from you for three months. What the hell do you want, Vincent?' I can hear the weariness and disinterest in my voice, but I can't help it.

'It's my uncle,' he says quickly, desperation in his voice. 'He thinks I've been selling steroids at the gym.'

The silence is heavy as I process this information. Vincent's uncle is a local gangster called Gino Camprinelli and is well known in the area for being a cross between the Kray twins and Mother bloody Theresa! He's got more personalities than a set of Teletubbies. Bloody hell, this isn't good. I've heard the rumours about Camprinelli. He likes getting his hands dirty, particularly while playing loud classical music.

'Please tell me you haven't been doing that!' I can feel a headache starting just above my right eye and rub my finger absently over the area.

'Cam, it was only a few. I thought it wouldn't hurt. An easy way to make money. But then things got out of hand, and one of the men I sold to started acting really aggressively. Somehow my uncle found out.'

'You are a fucking idiot, Vincent,' I tell him. 'Why can't you just keep your head down?'

'Please Cam,' Vincent's voice whines. 'I just need to talk.'

'Look,' I shake my head, looking at the plate of food in front of me. Feeling my appetite waning. 'I'm just about to have my breakfast. When I'm ready, I'll drive over to meet you at the usual place, but it'll take me a good couple of hours. Make sure no one is following you.'

'Thanks, Cam. You're a good friend,' he says with conviction. 'Sorry, mate.'

'Sure,' I tell him, staring at the plate of food in front of me, suddenly I don't feel hungry anymore. A heavy fog fills my brain, and destructive unwanted thoughts pound through my skull.

I want to hurt something.

Badly.

Charlotte's face replaces the fog and I calm a little. But bloody hell do I really need to get involved with Vincent again?

Fuck it, I pick up the plate and throw it hard at the nearest wall before storming out of the room. Amid the pounding in my ears, my mother's loud, raspy voice shouts. 'Bloody hell, Cameron. Come back here and help clean this up!'

'Fuck off! And don't go in my fucking room!' I shout from the hall, the need for alcohol hits me hard. Storming to my room, I go in search of the alcohol bottles hidden in various crevices, grab a vodka bottle from the bottom drawer of my wardrobe, carelessly toss the lid aside and gulp the liquid down as though I was dying of thirst.

Part Seven: Ferret

I casually hand my boyfriend his coffee. Stepping through the dense undergrowth that sits between the expanse of two large fields, where all we can hear is the noise of nearby traffic and the snapping of branches as we make our way forward. It's much darker under the cover of the thick shrubbery and branches, than in the field, making me feel a little uneasy. My free hand sits in my jacket pocket and touches the cold silver finger chopper and wire cutter, reminding me that I have work to do today.

I force a smile on my face.

'It's a cappuccino, just how you like it.' I smile at him.

'Thanks babe,' Eric says, 'can you hold it for a second, while I sort the dog.' He stoops down to detach the white Shih Tzu from its lead, and we watch, as the dog happily runs off into the expanse of field and shrubs.

I link his arm, happy for the first time in many years. Eric is the man of my dreams and everything that I could have wished for in a partner. He is funny, kind and attentive; and often tells me how much he loves me, even though we've only been dating for three months.

And then a song that used to be a favourite of mine, suddenly pops into my thoughts:

***

'Three, six, nine, the goose drank wine,

The monkey chewed tobacco on the streetcar line,

The Invisible Ones

The line broke, the monkey got choked

And they all went to heaven in a little rowing -boat.'

Everything is dark and I am cold. Freezing cold. A nagging ache churns at my temples and there is a thud to my heart, as it kickstarts into panic mode. Taking a moment, I focus my eyes, searching through dark shadows looking for anything that feels familiar. Nothing. Damn, where the hell am I? Carefully, checking my body with chilled fingers, I am shocked to find that I am wearing only my bra and pants as I lie rigidly on my back. The small bed, possibly the size of a single, is made up with a mattress, sheet and a thick woollen blanket.

What happened? My fourteen-year-old brain asks me. For the life of me I can't remember. Ouch, my left eye is sore, and I gently explore to find that it is swollen shut. Hot tears stream from my eyes and fall down the side of my face. I begin to whimper. Something bad has happened to me, and I don't know what.

Last night had been my fourteenth birthday. I went to the cinema with friends, then out for a meal and to a bar. I look older than my years, well I did last night, when I was made up. We started chatting to some older boys at the bar.

I remember laughing and giggling. Drinking too much.

Before, my world stopped swirling and everything went black.

The beginning of a shiver causes a tingling sensation to creep up my legs and torso. A sudden cramping takes over my body, making me wince in pain and discomfort. Holy mother of God, what is happening to me? I try to call out, but my voice won't work. The shivering continues, working its way up to the top of each arm and then stops. Reaching out for anything to keep me warm, my hands clumsily move about until they reach something loose and thick that feels like a woollen garment. the garment, I find sleeves and open areas for a head to go through. It's a jumper. Possibly mine.

Quickly, I pull the thing over my head and relish the warmth that it brings to my skin.

Movement from outside of the room alerts me, and I inhale sharply. Footsteps moving quickly across a hard floor, a male and female voice chat, and the sound of music lingers in the air. The Clapping Song.

'Three, six, nine, the goose drank wine,

The monkey chewed tobacco on the streetcar line,

The line broke, the monkey got choked

And they all went to heaven in a little rowboat.'

A door suddenly opens, and I blink. Standing in the lit up, open doorway is a bearded man, who reminds me of my grandad. Dressed in baggy, faded denim overalls over a black and white checked shirt.

In a loud gruff voice, he booms: 'Who the hell are you? And what are you doing in my storeroom?

**

When I first saw Eric at the pool, pushing through the water in the fast lane with a graceful front crawl. I didn't know it was him. I thought he was sexy and oozed confidence. And then he stopped to rest, took off his goggles and I knew it was him. I was so taken aback, that my first thought was to leave the pool immediately and never come back. It was as though he had violated my sanctuary.

Turning away, I rested my arms on the edge of the swimming pool and sunk my head. Hot tears formed quickly in the corner of my eyes, and I brushed them away with the sleeve of my swimsuit. No, this cannot be happening, I kept telling myself and then the first burst of anger began to surface.

How the fuck can he turn up in my private space when it was one of the few pleasures that I had?

The anger boiled within me. Fuck him! Fuck his friends! I am not that girl anymore. I am not a victim. And then, an idea came into my head. What if he didn't recognise me? What if I could get close to him? What if I could be as cruel to him as he was to me?

That defining moment, brought clarity to my thoughts. Words whirled through my head. Opportunity. Pain. Justice. Revenge.

The Invisible Ones

The opportunity was surprisingly easy, as I looked across at him, yes Eric Weston. I'm glad I ran into you.

Clearly, he didn't recognise me, even as we both stood in different swim lanes side by side, and I took a deep breath and summoned the courage to speak. 'Hi' I said, to break the ice and was pleased when he began to make casual conversation. I complimented him on his style and strokes, and it wasn't long before we were conversing like old friends.

I thought the Gods had sent him to me for vengeance. Giving me a chance to claw back some of my old self, the self who didn't realise that people and the world could be so cruel.

The self who had hopes and dreams.

Fate, or whatever it was that had led me to the pool that day, left me feeling that something had aligned, without me understanding why or what my destiny was. I usually went to the pool, three times a week in the morning. Sundays, Mondays and Wednesdays. Clad in my long sleeved, navy swim top, which hides the marks on my arms, and matching swim shorts, which automatically make me stand out from the other swimmers, I often feel the need to enter the water as quickly as possible. Mostly to hide my embarrassment. If my arms were too sore, I would simply miss a session.

Strangely, there was some relief with being in the water, it left me feeling cleansed, almost normal. I didn't need to think about what my plans were in life. Or feel bad about not going to college or university. Twenty or thirty lengths later, and I was done, then I usually headed back to the flat in my old dark green Peugeot 2008 that Mum had bought me.

When I left home, soon after passing my test at eighteen, I took a job in an Italian restaurant in Didcot, serving tables. Surprisingly, I made a friend called Lou, she was pretty and confident, and I found myself telling her snippets of my life. She was horrified about what had happened to me. And, very protective. 'Don't let the bastards grind you down, Fee,' she would say, putting a reassuring hand on my shoulder.

Sadly, last month the place went bankrupt, and all of the staff, including me, were made redundant. Now I'm getting some financial help from the government toward my expenses, while also living off my small redundancy package. Life sucks. The good news is, that I can swim any day I want to now.

The bad news is that I need to get another job soon.

***

Meeting Eric and making him fall for me, making myself into everything he would wish for in a girl, has given me a new focus. Taking an interest in his hobbies, such as cheering him on during the local park run was all part of the plan I am putting together. Setting the scene, collecting the actors along the way, allowing the action to play out, scripting in the direction that I want.

The Invisible Ones

I smile at Eric, it's a sad smile. One of resignation. I know how this story ends, for a moment, I wonder if I should keep him. Whether I should move forward and start again. It is such a shame that this happiness inside me won't last. It never does.

Taking a sip of my latte, I allow myself the satisfaction of watching him take a long gulp from his hot drink. The one that I've added my online Rohypnol to. The date rape drug that will incapacitate him, so that I can end his life.

'Mmm…' Eric says, 'this is delicious, it smells like almonds.'

'It's hazelnut syrup, sugar free. Thought you'd like it for a change,' I reply, rubbing my right arm, through the thin black jacket. It's something I do when I'm agitated or nervous.

He takes another sip. 'I'll definitely have this again.'

I don't think so, I smile brightly at him, giving the Rohypnol time to work.

For there is a secret I have. My fingers stroke the wire and cutters sitting in my pocket again. Not long now, I tell myself and a sort of calmness begins to settle over me.

'Glad you like it,' I say, thinking of the small hammer, the rectangular piece of cardboard with the number '1' and a smiley face written on it in thick blue ink and the six-inch screw I'm going to use to hammer it into his groin, all carefully wrapped in an old tea towel in my crossover bag.

There are days when I feel like screaming, when the feeling of uselessness overwhelms me. The darkness drags me down and I spend all day berating and hurting myself at home. I don't know why I feel this way, but I'm pretty sure that the rape didn't help my mental health.

This is a new beginning for me. Eric starts to sway, and his eyes look glazed. 'I don't feel well, I feel dizzy.'

Here we go, I take his arm. 'Here, let me help you,' I tell him soothingly.

I look forward to starting again, for a life where I am safe, and no one can hurt me ever again.

Part Eight: DCI Brian Carter

The first thing I notice are the dirty fingers of the man's right hand, as he lies on the hard ground. The second thing I notice, is that the little finger on his right hand is missing. Red blood has stagnated around the stump, just above the knuckle and the body is surrounded by an avenue of trees and wild shrubbery. What the hell happened here?

His dirty, dishevelled body is dressed in a crumpled black leather jacket, dark green T-shirt, black jeans and a dirty pair of expensive looking black Skechers. Dark leaves are scattered over him, as though an artist had stood above him and sprinkled them from high above for effect.

Mature trees and wild shrubbery divide two large field areas, with an opening at both ends to allow access to both fields. Situated near the village of East Hagbourne in Oxfordshire, it is owned by a farmer who hires the fields out throughout the day, via an online platform to local dog owners, my DS, Laura Sheppington, and number one informs me. She is fondly known by almost everyone at St Aldates as Shep.

A death in the pretty Oxfordshire countryside, surrounded by pretty villages with their bunting and summer fetes, my mind wanders. Who wouldn't want to live here?

Well, obviously this man.

Feeling around in my trouser pocket, I snap on disposable blue gloves before leaning closer to the body.

The undergrowth from the tree-lined, shrubbery has caused wet patches to form on his jeans. It looks like someone has tried to decapitate him with something thin and strong, like a piece of wire or cord. Blood tissue has settled thickly around the large neck wound and his eyes are closed.

Dark facial hair forms into a heavy beard, matching thick hair that is pulled backwards using a band of sorts. A small, heart shaped red birthmark sits on his forehead, above his left eye. For some reason the mark looks familiar, but my memory brings up nothing. So, I store the thought until I can process it properly. My gut though, tells me that I might know this person. I just don't see it yet.

'Do you know him, Boss?' Shep says, briefly looking my way, before stooping down to observe the body. A few rays of sun bounce through stray branches and glisten onto the short, red strands of her hair. It suits her better than the dark purple she had last month. She changes the colour of her hair more often than I change the sheets on my bed.

I shake my head, 'No, I don't think so. But there's something about him.' I study the man's face again but there is just that feeling again. Niggling deep within my brain. Perhaps it's my mind playing tricks on me.

I look at the two beat police officers standing behind me, acknowledging them and asking, 'Any sign of a weapon?' My eyes scour the fields.

'No, Sir, nothing found so far, apart from a couple of beer cans.' The taller of the two replies.

Looking across at Shep, I raise an eyebrow and ask, 'What do you think happened?'

Her attention moves to a thin, rectangular piece of what looks like cardboard which sits over the man's groin area. The colour is light in contrast to the black jeans he wears. It has a silver pin of sorts, pushed through it and I wince when I realise that it has been hammered with some force, into his groin. In thick, blue ink, on the rectangular shape, sits the number '1' and a smiley face.

Fuck, this is looking sinister.

Shep looks around, the wind is picking up, making her long navy skirt billow in the wind. 'Do you think he was walking his dog?'

'Not sure,' I rub my chin, I bloody hate days like this. I'm getting too old for this job.

Glancing at my watch, I see that it's 2pm and hear my stomach rumble.

'Best take a good look around,' I say, watching her strut with purpose across the nearest field. I don't feel hopeful. No howling or barking sounds can be heard in the immediate environment.

'Maybe, he wasn't here to walk his dog?' I tell my long-term friend and colleague Maggie, who is known as Dr Lawson. As the residing forensic pathologist, she is dressed in a full white protective body suit, and full protective gear. We've worked together on several cases before, and she knows I'm not usually a guesser. Maggie celebrated her fortieth birthday last year, and my wife, Julie and I attended her surprise party at her home, an old Rectory on the on the outskirts of Didcot.

I gaze around my immediate environment, searching for anything that might look out of place, that will give me a clue as to what happened here. And, although I don't want to appear the world-weary DCI, who can't help but think of worst-case scenarios, there is no feeling of joy when I realise that I might be right.

A streak of sunlight settles on a nearby cluster of broken twigs, which are bolstered by a cluster of unruly roots. I don't know what it is, but my eyes sense something. Carefully, I take a twig and use it to move the layers. A dirty red oblong shape stares back at me, and then I realise what it is. The feeling of nausea threatens to force itself upwards, so I take a deep breath and close my eyes briefly.

It's the other part of the finger.

'Found the rest of the finger,' I say, feeling inside one of the pockets of my coat for an evidence bag, and carefully place the small digit inside.

Maggie raises her face to look up at me, in response. 'Well done.'

We turn at the sound of footsteps behind us, to find Maggie's colleague, the forensic scientist, Sid Braden, dressed in a full pale blue body suit, with a camera around his neck and carrying a large square box. Sid and I nod in unison, before he drops to one knee, next to Maggie. He carefully puts the case on the dirty ground.

'Just in time,' I say, 'I got you a present.' I say, handing him the evidence bag.

'You're all heart, Brian,' he replies dryly, 'All heart.' Sid takes out a pen and begins to write on the bag before popping it into his case.

Maggie is petite and kneels beside the body with ease, studying him visually first, before beginning to touch him with respect and dignity to make assessment samples. She peers over the rim of her glasses as she pulls one of the eyelids upwards to expose the pupil and then, surprisingly, turns to face me. She repeats the motion with the opposite eyelid.

I raise an eyebrow in question, 'What is it?'

There is a quick movement as the pathologist swiftly checks the back of the victim's neck again.

She looks at myself and Sid, her face almost the same colour as her white coverall and says steadily. 'Call an ambulance, I've found a pulse, call one now! And pass me something to keep him warm.'

Shit!

Moving my shoulders, I ease out of my grey raincoat and hand it to Maggie. We're both deep in thought, hoping that it isn't too late for this man. Because, if there's one thing I do know, it's that no one should die like this, alone and in pain. Quickly, I take my phone from my trouser pocket and call the emergency services.

Disconnecting the call, I push the phone into my pocket and stare at Maggie as she kneels next to the victim, watching as she gently puts him in the recovery position, before laying the garment carefully across the victim's body. 'They should be here within five to ten minutes,' I tell her.

'Bloody hell,' Maggie repeats, all the time rubbing 'How the hell did I miss that, Brian?'

'Don't worry,' I reassure her, because I know she'll beat herself up about this. I would do the same. 'You've caught it now, that's all that matters.'

A high-pitched dog whine filters through the air, and I look up to see a white scraggy bundle of a dog with grey furry ears, heading my way. If I'm not mistaken, it's a Shih Tzu and appears very friendly as it jumps over fallen trees and undergrowth and bounds with gusto towards me.

I stoop down instantly, 'Whoa,' I pat the dog's fur on its forehead and scratch behind its ears, and before I can stop the little scamp, it jumps onto my bended knees and rests muddy paws on me.

'Now, who are you and where have you been hiding?' I stare into dark brown eyes and give it another scratch while checking out the genitalia. It's a girl.

She's wearing a red leather collar, from which hangs a silver circular tag. The tag is blank apart from printed postcode and information to say that she's been microchipped and neutered. Someone has taken the time to care for this dog, with her wet nose, bright eyes, and friendly nature.

Maggie reaches into the man's trouser pocket and pulls out a brown leather wallet. 'Here,' she hands it to me, 'let's find out who he is,' she says in her no-nonsense way. Ever to the point, she continues searching for clues, whilst I hold on to the dog collar and flip open the wallet.

With blue-gloved hands, I pull out the driver's licence and read the black print next to the name.

'Eric Weston,' it reads. My blood runs cold, as the name links the heart shaped birthmark and suddenly, the parts of the puzzle begin to click together.

Bugger! I know this man.

I need to speak to Julie. Now.

'Just need to make a quick phone call,' I say, putting the driver's licence back in the wallet. I skim through his credit and loyalty cards, and find the usual credit, debit and loyalty cards. There's also a membership card for the pool in Didcot, which take me by surprise. I wouldn't have taken him for a swimmer. Absently I drop the wallet into an evidence bag, pocket my gloves and stoop to stroke the dog's head. It's tail wags with appreciation, and a reaction that I never expected, takes over. My heart jumps.

'You found him then?' Shep smiles, a bungee-style black dog lead swinging from her hand.

'Yeah,' I hand the dog to her, and take my phone from my pocket, 'and, he's a she. Can you take her to the local vet to confirm through the microchip that the dog belongs to Eric Weston? Find out her name and ask the vet to check her over. Oh, and Shep, give her something to eat and drink, will you? She's probably famished.'

'Sure,' she smiles, 'suits you… with a dog, I mean.' Her eyes are bright as she watches me.

'Haven't got time for a dog, not with the hours Julie and I work,' I mutter. But then, a vision comes into my head of us walking along a woodland trail, lead in hand and a cute dog walking obediently beside us. It's not an unhappy feeling.

'Everything all right?' Maggie's voice breaks into my frantic thoughts, as I absently watch Shep place the dog onto the muddy ground, hold the dog firmly and attach the lead to her collar. I don't answer Maggie until they are out of earshot.

'I'm not sure, but I think I know this man,' I finally reply, turning to look at the woman. In the distance, the sirens from the ambulances become louder as they head our way.

Bloody hell, I can't believe this. Julie and I were planning to keep our heads down, with our aim to finish work on time, at around 6pm tonight. We're taking a break with our friends, the Greyson's and their family for six days, over the summer holidays.

I wasn't too bothered about going to the Sutton Courtenay Manor house when they first suggested that we join them, but Julie has been looking really tired the last month or so and I thought it would do her good. She's a perfectionist and being away from home will, hopefully, allow her time to chill out and give her a chance to recharge her batteries. This is not looking good.

Reaching for the phone in my pocket, I find my recent contacts and call my wife. This is going to make her day.

Part Nine: Julie

'Brian?' I can hear the breathlessness in my voice, as I hold the phone to my ear.

Not great timing, but I know it must be serious if he's calling me during work hours. Picking up speed, I race over grass, down historic steps and along pathways through the beautifully maintained Abbey Meadows ruins in the historic market town of Abingdon-on-Thames. Records show that a Benedictine Abbey was founded on these grounds around 675AD, and I wish I had the time to imagine how glorious it must have looked. Gasping for air, I say quickly, 'This isn't a good time, I'm kind of busy here.'

The young, long-haired man is about ten metres ahead of me, and dressed from head to toe in scraggy denims. Over one shoulder, he carries a black rucksack with ease. He's hardly out of breath, clearly much fitter than I am! Note to self, to work on my stamina and physical fitness. As a DS in the Thames Valley Police, based in Abingdon-on-Thames, I admit, I've probably let myself go a bit over the last ten years. Don't get me wrong, I'm not overweight, I'm just older.

The perpetrator, or perp as we call them, stops suddenly and turns to face me. He has an arrogance about him, summed up by the way he shakes his head and smiles my way, before lifting his middle finger to give me the bird. 'Fuck you! Pig!' he shouts, full of the bravado of someone who thinks he's a cut above the rest.

'That's not very nice language to use,' I call out, wincing at sore heels and not for the first time, wishing that I'd put on my old faithful, flat ankle boots, instead of wearing these new brown ones with a three-inch heel.

'What language?' Brian's voice asks in my ear.

'Not you, Bri. The perp I'm chasing,' I mutter back.

'Ah, OK,' Brian, understands the job, he knows what it's like when you're in the middle of a chase.

'I'll be with you in a minute,' I tell my husband, calmly, before disconnecting the call. staring as the man pushes long, greasy hair from his bearded face.

'Hey,' I call out, trying to distract him. Trying to keep him facing my way. Out of the corner of my eye I see my colleague, DC Chessa Gillwoody, walk slowly into the meadow through the open gates. 'Why don't you just give yourself up, Billy.' I finish, using his name for the first time.

'No fucking way!' He shouts back, 'You think I'm going to let a little shite like you take me in?' He scoffs. He faces a charge of theft, and resisting arrest, since stealing three pairs of expensive trainers from a sports shop in town and wanted for several other suspected thefts.

Chessa, with her mid length dark hair clipped into place at the base of her neck and dressed completely in black, and low-heeled boots, is now almost directly behind Billy.

'In your dreams,' I shake my head, gently. 'In your dreams.'

'Why don't you go fuck yourself, bitch,' he shouts, saliva dribbling from his open mouth as I draw closer, he suddenly turns to flee through the meadow opening, towards the children's play area and the river.

He swears when comes face to face with Chessa. She is standing no more than a couple of feet away and is holding her lanyard to show her police badge.

'Police, stop right there!' Chessa commands. The man turns to face me and swears. We've been watching him for a few days now, Billy Machin, low-life criminal. We've been following his daily routines, and I'm going to make it my mission today to make sure that this man is going nowhere.

'Fuck!' Billy says loudly. Shaking his head, he kicks at the grass in frustration.

Billy attempts to make his escape. He rushes, forward and throws himself at Chessa, trying to knock her to the ground, but this woman is determined to stand her ground and not only takes the brunt of his weight, but grabs his arms in turn, and forces one of the limbs up and into his shoulder. Loosening the rucksack with the stolen goods, she brings his arm down and loops the bag over his hand, before throwing it onto the hard, grassy ground.

With the grace of someone who has done this before, she takes metal handcuffs from her pockets and pulls both arms so that his hands meet behind him, before clicking the cuffs into place. Billy pulls against the restraints and tries to kick my DC. She moves out of the way, missing contact, 'Do that again, Billy and I'll be adding assault to your charges,' Chessa promises, holding his arm to keep him secure.

Moving forward, I reach them and with a sense of pride tell my DC, 'Good job. Now, read him his rights.'

My DC nods and begins citing the words we use during the arrest procedure, to her perp. Raising my hand, I motion for them to follow me through the gate and to the right where we can wait in the Abbey Close Car Park.

When we're where we need to be, I call for a car to pick up Billy. We'll meet him back at the station, because I've got a number of places to visit. There are two businesses who have lost upwards of a ten thousand pounds, through break-ins, and stolen goods. There is a gut feeling that Billy is involved.

Billy is quiet, it's not the reaction I am expecting. It's not often that things surprise me. When you've been doing the job as long as I have, you learn to anticipate behaviours.

'I'll be back in a minute,' I tell Chessa, pointing to the gate we have recently walked through. 'Just need to make a phone call.'

Chessa nods, 'That's fine, Boss.' I disconnect myself from the scene to return to the gate, lean casually against a post and take my phone from my coat pocket. I call my husband.

'Is everything OK?' Brian's voice is full of worry, and I can't help but smile. He knows I'm good at my job, but it doesn't stop him worrying.

'Yep, all under control,' I answer, kicking a stone absently with my foot. 'What's up?'

'I'm in East Hagbourne, with someone who has been savagely assaulted. You'll never guess who it is?' My husband says, and there is something in his voice that sends alarm bells ringing in the deep recess of my brain.

'Who?' I ask, quietly – unsure if I've heard him properly. There is a long silence, before he finally speaks.

'Eric Weston,' Brian reveals sourly.

The name is familiar and straight away it brings back unpleasant memories. There is something in my past. Something that ties me, my husband, Stuart and Jenny Greyson together forever. An unspeakable act that binds us to Lottie Peckham-Forster, like a blood oath, after we made a decision to avenge an evil deed, and to protect that person so that she could get on with her life. Serving justice and making those pay for their crimes outside of the law, takes its toll though, even if the end justifies the means.

My temple begins to throb, and I rub several fingers over my forehead, trying to massage the threatening headache away.

'Eric Weston,' I mutter, 'It's been a while since I've heard that name. Wonder what he's doing over these parts. Didn't he go over to Ireland with one of his mates?' I ask, trying to pull memories, I had in many ways tried to keep buried.

'Yes,' my husband's voice is deep and there's a hint of worry behind his words. 'Eric and his friend, Vincent, went to Dublin to start up a nightclub. Didn't last long though, they both came back, then I lost track of them.'

A police car pulls up in the car park, near to Chessa and soon after, two officers exit the car and make their way to Chessa. 'Bloody hell, Bri. Look, I need to phone you back,' I say, disconnecting the call, quickly and making my way to the police car and my DC. My mind is full of bad memories. I really don't want to be dealing with this today.

I nod an acknowledge to the police officers for coming out. 'Thanks,' I look at the man and woman, who look very similar with short cropped blond hair, in their thirties and both wide shouldered with narrow waists. They dip their heads, and say, 'no problem.'

My voice sounds weary, even to my own ears as I speak to my colleague. Shooting pains sear across the right side of my forehead, causing me to wince. 'Can you sort this out, Chessa? I need a couple of minutes.'

My DC puts a hand over her eyes to shade them from the sun, her eyes catch mine, 'sure, shall I meet you back at the car?'

Our car is parked in the public car park by the council building. 'Please,' I smile gratefully, 'Hopefully I won't be too long.'

Rubbing my temple, I turn and walk away. Spying a wooden bench facing the stream, not too far away, I wait until my bottom touches the bench, before reaching into my small crossover bag and taking out emergency pain relief. Luckily, I am one of those people who can swallow tablets without water, a blessing and a curse. As, I am never sure if they would begin to work quicker if they were swallowed with water.

A sudden feeling of nausea overwhelms me, and I take a deep breath to force it back. Cursing softly, I remember that I skipped lunch and, apart from my breakfast which consisted of an out-of-date slice of toast, I have been running on empty. My stomach grumbles in agreement.

It's been a while since I've heard the name Eric Weston. Vincent, his friend, is the nephew of Gino Camprinelli, a small-time crook who Brian and I have had dealings with over the past ten years or so. There was one more, the cousin. Cameron Frost. Yes, I remember him, he disappeared off grid for a while but resurfaced when his family moved to Charmouth, on the Dorset coast.

They were known locally as the Three Amigos.

Nothing but trouble, especially when they were partying. They developed a liking for young girls and drugs. Moreover, drugging and raping their prey. Which left every single female vulnerable.

Pressing the button on my phone, I wait for Brian to answer.

'Hey,' I say, sitting forward so that I can rest my forearms on my knees. I spit on my finger and rub it against a mark on my black jeans.

'Hey you,' he says, 'everything sorted?'

'Yeah, pretty much,' my voice softens. 'So, tell me about Eric.'

There's a shuffling sound, that sounds like feet moving, and I can almost hear my husband's brain ticking away. He's the best person I know. He sees the world as it is and tries to make a difference. He's patient, methodical and gives people a second chance.

I was a rookie police constable of twenty-five, working at Cowley Police Station, when I first met him, some fourteen years ago. We had worked on a kidnapping with Jenny and Stuart Greyson and Jenny's uncle, Felix Gloverman - who had been the culprit. He had led us a merry dance, drugging and sexually assaulting Jenny and he went on to kidnap and murder Jenny's housekeeper and surrogate mum, Rose.

At the time, Brian had been this big DCI, still is, who I absolutely respected and worshipped. I wanted him to see the potential in me, because workwise, we were both very similar. Never off the clock, never giving up. Once we had hooked up, I decided to transfer from Cowley to Newbury Police, where we could each pursue our own professional journey.

Stuart Greyson once described Brian as tall and brooding, good-looking in a rugged sort of way. But to me, he will always be the good-looking man who stole my heart and gave me the confidence and encouragement to be the best me, I can be. He pushed me to go for promotion to DS and encouraged my move from Newbury to Abingdon station.

'There's not a lot to say,' my husband's voice brings me back to reality. 'We found a dog nearby, so it may be his and he may have been walking it. Weston has a neck wound, a strange hand injury that looks like it's been put through a blender and, here's the weird part, he's got a piece of cardboard, with a number '1' and a smiley face written on it, nailed to his groin.'

'Urgh...torture, revenge,' I picture these injuries. 'Or something related to what we did to the boys all of those years ago?'

The woods might be symbolic and the impaled number. Is this the start of something bigger? A vision of Jesus on the cross causes a sudden shiver to cross my shoulders blades. My brain is going into overdrive, trying to make sense of the information. Torture, symbolism, possible religious connotations, this attack is beginning to worry me, the more I think about it.

This is not your average stabbing or shooting. The assault sounds more specialised, personal even, Particularly, with the genitalia connection. Deliberately pinning an object to a person's dick is symbolic.

There's a deep sigh, before Brian eventually answers, 'I know Jue. I can feel it in my bones. Something is off, very off. And this is just the beginning.'

'Bloody hell!' a shiver of apprehension creeps up my spine.

'Look, I've got to go,' Brian says with a resigned note. I can hear the tiredness in his voice. He needs this break with the Greyson's, as much as I do. As much as I love my job, it needs to stop coming first. It needs to stop being my main priority. Apart from Brian.

'See you tonight,' I tell him. 'And try not to worry.'

'You too,' he says, before disconnecting us.

I stare at the families walking through the meadow garden towards the outdoor pool, splash and play park, some are laughing, some are sullen. A couple of tattooed drunks, with red Mohican-styled haircuts, sit on a bench strewn with empty cans at the far end of the park, talking loudly to people as they walk past them.

Suddenly, my blouse feels too tight, and my skin feels like it's burning, I drop my phone on the bench to release a few of the top buttons of my blouse. I feel like I can't breathe, and my airways are beginning to spasm. Instantly, I recognise the signs of a panic attack.

I am cross with myself. I haven't had one of these attacks for years. Closing my eyes, I focus on the familiar technique that I used to use in my teens. Starting with the letter 'Z' I slowly repeat the alphabet backwards, calming my breathing as I focus. 'Z, Y, X, W.' By the time I get to 'P', I feel notably calmer. Opening my eyes, I allow the cool afternoon air to soothe me. What the hell is going on with me?

A need so strong suddenly forces my hand to my mouth and I rush from the bench and empty the out-of-date slice of toast and two lattes from this morning, into a nearby bush. The recoil and spasms that follow, leave me feeling completely drained.

I take out tissues from my black crossover bag and wipe myself the best I can. There's nothing I can do with the acrid taste in my mouth, that will need a toothbrush, toothpaste and a glass of water. Or something stronger.

My mind wanders back to that night when we rounded up the three young men who had hurt Lottie. They had been in their early twenties, brash and full of attitude.

***

It is cold and dark in the provisions department of the local recently vacated Cash and Carry. Luckily, the electrics are still working, so the three spotlights glare relentlessly at the three frightened men tied to wooden chairs.

I look across at Brian through my black hood, and watch him move around the room slowly, studying the three men. He is such a good man. A man who sees things that others don't. Stuart stands in front of them, as though weighing up his prey. I shudder with the thought of what is about to happen. I zip my own black jacket all the way to my neck, hiding the truncheon that sits hard against my chest.

There is no going back. These men will pay for what they did.

Brian and I have been engaged for three months, just before Rose Dean's funeral. That was one of the lowest points in my career. Losing Rose at the hands of Felix Gloverman. The only consolation was that Felix Gloverman is now dead, which means that he can't hurt anyone ever again.

'Who the hell do you think you are?' Cameron, the ringleader thrashes against the thick rope.

'Do you know who my uncle is?' Vincent shouts, saliva flicking from his mouth. Trying to sound intimidating isn't easy when you're sitting tied to a chair with your two best mates.

I hold my breath as Brian steps forward so that he is standing in front of Vincent, and speaks for the first time, 'I know who your uncle is, and I don't give a rat's arse what you think he will or will not do.'

Stuart remains quiet, simply moves to the back of the room. To me, his lack of words make him appear more dangerous.

'So,' Brian steps back and looks at the three casually dressed men in jeans and hoodies in turn. 'Which one of you made the decision to drug a fifteen-year-old girl at Cameron's party?'

Trying to keep my emotions under control behind the hot mask, the anger simmering just beneath the surface, 'Was it you, Cameron?' I walk forward, unzipping my jacket and taking out my truncheon. It feels familiar, a protective baton to keep us safe on the beat. I know it's not meant to be used as a weapon, but in this case, the end justifies the means.

'What is it?' Brian asks, 'Can't any of you get it up, unless the person is unconscious?' His words are crude and bring home the reality of just how despicable their behaviour has been.

Stuart walks to me. 'May I?' he asks quietly, holding out his hand for my weapon. I don't believe that Stuart or Brian will kill these young men, but I know that they will cause them harm, leave lifelong marks on their bodies to show that they have been seen, served and found lacking.

Silently, I hand him the cold, hard truncheon, my breath catching as I watch him walk to Cameron. Here we go. There is no going back now. In the back of my mind, I hear a trickling sound, and my eyes wander to the chairs and then to the floor, I see that beneath Eric's chair is a puddle of urine. Bloody hell, I can't allow myself to feel sorry for these animals.

'Cameron, did you drug your cousin and then decide that you and your friends would rape her?' Stuart finally asks.

'No way man, I wouldn't.' Cameron starts. The thwack of the truncheon as it is lands with speed on his knees, smashing bone, startles everyone, and I put my hand over my masked face to my mouth. Holy cow, this is really happening.

Cameron howls in pain. 'Yeah, well I don't believe you,' Stuart says flatly, as he makes his way to Vincent. 'Or, was it you?' Stuart raises the weapon and repeats the motion on Vincent.

'No please,' Eric is crying, begging to be saved from the pain of the knee assault.

Brian intervenes, putting his hand up to stop Stuart for the moment. Eric cries, 'Don't hurt me, I'll tell you what happened.'

'Shut the fuck up,' Cameron hisses. 'Don't say another word!' he warns his friend, shaking his head.

Vincent looks up. 'It was Cameron,' he says in a flat tone. 'It was his decision to spike Lottie's drink, his decision to fuck her.'

'Fuck you!' Cameron hisses, rocking his chair forward.

'And did Cameron force you to join in too? Maybe held a knife to your throat?' Brian asks, as he stares at the other two pitiful excuses for human beings. He puts out his hand to Stuart for the truncheon, and I inhale sharply. He briefly glances at me, his eyes hard and unapologetic. Part of me wants to scream for him to stop but it's too late now. There is no going back.

'I thought not,' Stuart leans against a nearby wall, shaking his head. The tension in the room is palpable, an invisible string of intense emotion that coats everything in sight.

Again, Cameron tries for bravado, 'Fuck you and fuck that stupid cousin of mine for opening her big mouth.'

'No' Brian says, walking up to Cameron. 'Fuck you!' He grabs the young man's face hard and leans in close, until their noses are almost touching.

'Bastards,' I whisper, as Brian pulls back his arm and punches Cameron hard in the mouth. I watch in slow motion as the force of Brian's fisted hand, forces him backwards with a sickening thud, and I panic for a moment – worrying that Brian had killed him. Seconds later, Cameron starts a low moaning howl, like the sound of a wounded animal.

Stuart shakes his head, 'Unapologetic, unrepentant, undeserving… you thought you'd got away with it. But we know what you did to that girl, and probably to countless others. But it stops here.' He looms over Cameron, stares at him resolutely. 'I hear you're good at sport?' he says, studying the young man's right leg. I realise what he is about to do, too late. Despite my horror, I can't look away, as Stuart hauls Cameron and the chair upright again, grabs the man's right leg and kicks it hard in a backwards motion, the knee bends and distorts, until it finally snaps.

There is an ear-splitting screeching sound, as Cameron's face screws up in pain. He is howling, his eyes scrunched closed and large, fat tears falling down his cheeks.

The brittle sound echoes throughout the empty room and turns my stomach. This is madness, but the anger within each of us is set, like a concrete pillar, unyielding.

'Not any longer, you're not,' Stuart mutters. 'Not any longer,' he says, handing me back my truncheon.

'Not one of you have asked if she is OK after what you did to her,' I say in a flat tone. 'If we ever find out that any of you are continuing to drug and molest girls, I'll come back with a pair of secateurs and cut off your balls.'

I walk out of the room, leaving the men to finish dishing out justice for Lottie.

Not all justice can be served by the law. It's a hard lesson.

***

Whatever we did to those young men that night, we did it to protect the future Lotties of this world. Or that's what we told ourselves at the time. But the nagging doubt that it is connected to what happened to Eric Weston, won't go away.

I'd better do some digging of my own.

Part Ten: Cameron

They used to call us The Three Amigos when we were at high school. That's me, Vincent Camprinelli and Eric Weston. We first met in reception class at Ladygrove Park Primary School which was situated on the far side of Didcot. And as we followed each other through to Didcot's single sex high school, and moved onto the shared sex sixth form, our main focus and interests were sport, drink and girls. We attracted girls like magnets, which only boosted our already inflated egos.

Football was my life, and I don't mind admitting that I was good at it. I even managed to become the long-term Captain of St Birinus Boys School, and then at the mixed-sex college, which made me extremely popular with the girls in the Sixth Form. My sports coach, Mr Adams, knew a few people in the local football leagues, I trialled and was offered a place at Didcot Youth Football Club.

We thought we were invincible. And we were. Most of the time. Until that fateful Saturday night when my parents allowed me to celebrate my eighteenth birthday at the house. They had booked to see a show at the theatre and stayed over in a hotel in Oxford. The last thing my dad had said to me was to 'not go too wild.'

Too bad I didn't listen to his advice. The drugs had piled up and things had got wild and out of hand. I didn't remember too much about that night due to the drugs and alcohol, but I know that me, Eric and Vincent, did something bad, really bad.

I rub my right knee absently. There is some irony in the fact that I am paying the price for what we did, with the damage to my leg and everything that came after. My overwhelming need to drink alcohol, to dull the pain and my senses, is a problem and I know I need to deal with it but there's never a good time to stop. There's always an excuse. On top of that, it's costing me a small fortune.

Some days are good for driving, other days I might as well have gone back to bed and slept off the pain. Thankfully, today is a good one and the pain is manageable. It's taken me two and a half hours to reach my destination, but I did it. When my leg feels too bad, I call an Uber.

It is bloody freezing. Where the hell is he? I am standing like a lemon in the old disused pub, boarded up at the front, waiting for that idiot, Vincent. The pub stands next to some boarded up properties, ear-marked for renovation, down a side street in the village of Steventon. I had to pull a few boards loose from the back door to gain access.

He is forty minutes late, and my anger is sizzling just beneath the surface. This is the thanks I get for being a good friend.

The distant road traffic is the only sound that interrupts the silence, until the song 'Supermassive Black Hole' by Muse, blares with purpose from my phone. If this is him, I'm going to fucking kill him.

There's no caller ID, but I accept the call anyway.

'Hello?'

The line is open, but I hear no voice.

'Stop pissing around and answer the phone, will you?' I mutter, not bothering to disguise the anger in my voice.

I spent this morning watching Charlotte's front door, from a distance, waiting for her to open it and find my gift. Eventually, she did come to the door, dragging a suitcase, before stopping when she saw the box on the doorstep, and it was pure joy to see the bewilderment on her face as she read the note on the top and picked it up. About twenty minutes later, her friend Jem arrived with her young child in tow, and everyone disappeared into the house.

Charlotte is going away, the look of that suitcase. I wonder if I can get another gift in before she leaves the house. It may be a bit ambitious, even for me. I zip my padded jacket up to the neck and curse Vincent Camprinelli for making me wait in this God-awful place.

My right leg is playing up now, it's usually worse when it's cold, and the temperature is dropping faster than a sack of potatoes being thrown from a plane.

'Stop playing silly buggers,' whoever it is, he or she is trying to wind me up. They're also, bloody succeeding.

'Call Vincent, call him now,' a distorted voice says and disconnects the line. Shit. Who the hell was that? And what the fuck was he talking about?

I call Vincent, and almost immediately the familiar tone of Johnny Cash's 'Ring of Fire,' echoes through the room. Following the sound, I eventually find the damn phone, sitting in an empty larder fridge in the old kitchen corner of the pub. My eyes are drawn to the bloody finger marks on the cover. Shit. I lift the phone, to see if there are any videos or messages on it, but as soon as the phone is moved, I recoil in horror, for sitting under it, is a discoloured, severed part of a little finger.

Fuck. Fuck. Fuck. Hairs stand up on my arms in alarm. What the hell? Regaining my composure briefly, I quickly study the finger before taking out my phone to take a quick photo.

Wincing, I pick the severed digit up and stuff it and the phone in my jacket pocket.

I have no idea what is going on, but there is no way I'm staying in this place.

Rushing to my car, I can almost feel the severed finger as it moves from side to side in my pocket.

Camprinelli wouldn't do this to his own flesh and blood, would he? Well, there's only one way to find out

Part Eleven: Ferret

By definition, a nickname is noted as meaning: 'usually descriptive name given instead of or in addition to the one belonging to a person, place, or thing.' I never really understood that. I mean why can't the use of someone's name be sufficient? Is it to be mean or affectionate? To endear or belittle?

When I was younger, I didn't used to look like this. I was very different. From the age of six, my body was thin, rather like a runner bean. There wasn't an ounce of fat on me. Mum used to say that I was lucky, that I had her genes, and could probably eat anything I wanted to without any weight gain throughout my life. As opposed to my father, who was naturally prone to putting on weight.

Long, limp wavy hair hung down to my lower back. It was completely devoid of style or cut, my mother didn't have the money to pay for extras such as haircuts since my dad became ill with early onset dementia. Very quickly he deteriorated until he was unable to recognise us and became unmanageable. From the age of twelve, my dad was offered a bed in a care home on the other side of the county. This left Mum as the main carer, responsible for keeping a roof over our rented heads and food in our empty bellies.

The eyepatch over my right eye to correct a stigmatism didn't help. By the time I was eight, I was known by almost everyone as Ferret.

'Ow...' a grumpy voice breaks into my thoughts. I look behind me, across the drab flat on Great Western Park, on the outskirts of Didcot, that has been my home for the past two years. It's on the ground floor with a separate entrance, kitchen, bathroom, bedroom and lounge diner. I even have a small garden, which would be useful if I were a gardener, but I'm not. The place needs a lick of paint to brighten it up and some new furniture, but I keep putting it off. The main attraction is its close vicinity to the centre of town, the railway station and the A34.

I sit at my square dining table at the back of the brown carpeted lounge, with my laptop, and a feeling of hopelessness. Everything in my life seems dull and pointless, including my home. Looking around the room, and taking in the small flat screen TV, and pieces of oak furniture that furnish it, I can feel my shoulders drooping with the heavy darkness that lies within me and I start rubbing my right arm. Even the dining table needs a good clean.

The only light in my darkened life, is the taser gun, which sits on the dining table staring back at me, waiting for its next outing. It hadn't been easy transporting it into the UK, but it is surprising what people will do for money. Reaching out to an old friend, Lou – who I used to work with and trust, proved to be a godsend, as she had a couple of Welsh friends who had been backpacking around Europe, and with a cash incentive offered to buy the taser and bring it into the country via the channel tunnel.

An adult wheelchair sits next to the second-hand black sofa. I picked it up from a charity shop a week ago for ten pounds. It seemed like a good idea and proved to be invaluable in moving a drugged man from my Peugeot into the flat.

'What did you do to me?' Vincent asks, holding both hands, bound with red rope, over his body and tied to his ankles. One hand is bandaged and bloody, the one with the missing finger. It took me a few days of watching You Tube videos, to perfect how to tie someone to give them minimal movement. To incapacitate them.

Closing my screen down, I swivel my chair to face him. I'm tired of this man already. Why I didn't kill him, I don't know. But now I'm stuck with him in my home, and that is a huge problem.

Absently, I push up the sleeve of my navy-coloured sweatshirt and rub at the scars on my left arm. There are ten of them, lines across the inside of my arm. Some are thicker than others, if they've been opened several times. Angry and raised. But the feeling of release I get when cutting myself, is better than any drug over the counter.

I take the small, black-handled penknife from my table, hold it carefully with my right hand and begin to stroke it against my left arm. The build-up sensation has me holding my breath with anticipation, until that point of contact which sends a big rush of adrenaline through my body. Yes, of course it hurts, but this huge feeling of excitement kicks in, as the first droplets of blood begin to seep across my pale skin.

The release, when it comes, at the first sight of blood, clears my mind and allows me to close my eyes and just relax.

To simply be

When my arm becomes too sore to the touch, I pull the grey sweatshirt sleeve down and rub my temple to try and calm my thoughts. Then I push my reading glasses up, onto my nose and study this pathetic excuse for a man, from his mussed black hair to his European features and sharp Italian nose. Some people say he's good-looking, but I know what's underneath.

Weakness and destruction. Cruelty and arrogance.

By the look of the dressing I had wrapped around his finger, he's lost a bit of blood, his face is pale. 'I just gave you a taste of your own medicine, Vincent.'

It was weird being in that place again. The derelict pub with the storerooms at the back of the building, most of which were derelict with little footfall. Where I woke up after my assault. It must have been their special place. There is a sudden urge to empty the contents my stomach, but I take deep breaths to overcome it. It was Eric who gave the game away, explaining where Cameron and Vincent and he used to hang out sometimes in one of the pub storerooms in Steventon.

And, all the time, he didn't realise that this was the place they brought me to, to rape me. Maybe they were too stoned or drunk themselves to remember.

I knew straightaway that I wouldn't be able to drug Vincent, as I hadn't had time to befriend him and build his trust. That was where the taser came in useful. It's first outing was a complete success.

Vincent had been sitting on top of three pallets, when I arrived. It took a bit of homework to find his address, so that I could stalk him. First, I checked out every Camprinelli in the phone book, and found that there were only ten of them. Ringing each one in turn, I pretended to sell life insurance, and I was relieved to find that Vincent was number six. Bingo. I had him. Armed with his address, all I had to do was to follow him from a distance.

Thankfully, I don't look anything like the girl he used to know, so I'm not overly worried that he will recognise me. But there is still a nagging voice in my head, telling me to be careful. I have already crossed too many lines by bringing him here.

Pushing myself to a standing position, I walk to the kitchen and take a bottle of water from the fridge, open it and take a long gulp.

'Who are you and what the fuck did you do to me?' He shouts. 'My hand is killing me!'

Taking some codeine from the pocket of my jeans and push out two tablets. Walking into the lounge, I stop in front of Vincent. 'Open wide.' I tell him, putting the codeine into his mouth.

Vincent closes his mouth and peers at me under long dark lashes. I hold the bottle of water close to his mouth. 'Open,' I order. Slowly he opens his mouth and I tip the liquid from the water bottle down his throat, before pulling the bottle away and flipping the lid on.

For a moment, there is silence as I look down at him. I want to feel shame and guilt for my actions, but there is nothing. Just a coldness.

'There's something familiar about you. Have we met before?' Brown eyes fix on me, waiting. My heart starts to thud hard in my chest, and I recognise the signs that I am about to have a panic attack. Shit.

Still standing over him, I close my eyes and begin to count backwards in twos from one hundred. Ninety-eight, ninety-six... Come on Fer, get a grip. Ninety-four, ninety-two, ninety and the spasm that has taken over me, starts to settle. The tremors stop completely. Thank God.

'Hey, what's wrong with you?' He suddenly asks, concern showing on his face.

From my jeans pocket I take out a Snickers bar, and throw it on the sofa, 'eat, you'll feel better soon.' I walk back to my desk and flop into my chair. The need to form a plan is foremost in my mind. What do I do next?

'Now, tell me where to find Cameron Frost?' I look his way.'

'Cameron Frost?' he looks bewildered, as he chews the chocolate bar.

'Wait a minute, you're… you're that girl... from the bar.'

'Yes,' I sigh, moving to his side once more. 'I am. Now tell me where I can find that bastard, Cameron Frost.'

Something tells me that this is going to be a long night.

Part Twelve: Lottie

The traffic on the A303 to Andover is insane. I'm going at a steady thirty-eight miles per hour, with Deacon Blue playing quietly in the background. Google maps on my phone, says it will take just over two and a half hours to get to Sutton Courtenay, but I suspect it will be more like four hours by the time we realistically get there. Harley is next to me, with his neck pillow and earphones, engrossed in his music with his eyes shut.

My thoughts drift to the 'gift' that was left on my doorstep this morning. Who on earth would do such a thing? And, why now? The thought of a deranged person out there, watching me, makes the hairs on my arms stand up and the uneasy feeling in my tummy won't go. Is it someone I know? My mind skips through various memories, searching for possible suspects who may want to hurt me. Could it be a partner of one of the women I have helped over the years? There have been some angry and volatile people left behind, as their beaten spouses grew strong and moved on with their lives.

And the rat? What a gruesome thing to send boxed as a gift. Macabre, sadistic.

The one thought that keeps running through my mind is that this is personal. Very personal.

A weariness comes over me, and I rub my forehead to ease the tension. Bloody hell. With Summer only six days away, I wanted to have some down time with those closest to me. Is that too much to ask?

A shiver travels down my spine. I feel like the world is closing in on me. That I'm about to fall down a huge crater and not be able to get out. I haven't felt this way since Simon died, and I had to find a way to keep looking forward. Harley was my saviour. Harley kept me sane.

The car phone begins to ring, and I check my rear-view mirror, before reaching over to answer the call. 'Hello?' I say, changing down into fourth and then third gear, as we slow to another build-up of traffic.

'Lottie?' The deep Scottish voice is familiar, and one I haven't heard for a long time.

'Daniel? Is that you?' I smile, it's good to hear his voice.

'It is, the one and only.' I can hear the lightness in his voice. 'How are you?'

'I'm fine,' I say, glancing across at Harley. 'I'm heading your way, to Oxfordshire I mean, with Harley. We're staying with Jenny and Stuart for a few days.'

'That's one of the reasons why I'm calling,' he says a few seconds later. 'I just wanted to let you know that I've been invited too.'

'You have?' My breath catches and a frisson of excitement I've not felt in a long time reawakens inside me. I shake it off.

'Yes, which is good,' his warm voice filters through the speaker phone, 'because I was going to give you a call anyway.'

'You were?' I query. 'Why, is something wrong?'

'No,' he reassures me quickly, 'nothing's wrong. Do you remember that support group that you and Jenny set up years ago?'

I check my wing mirrors and indicate to move to the slow lane. I think about Daniel's question.

How can I forget? It was the start of my recuperation, of me facing my demons and moving forward. If I hadn't told Jenny about being drugged and raped by my cousin and his friends when I was fifteen, I would have never been able to completely process what had happened.

You tell yourself you're not a victim, that you won't let it define you, but deep down you can only lie to yourself for so long, because when you look in the mirror you're not the person you used to be. You're different. Damaged. I told no one about my experience, until I was twenty-one when thankfully, I met Jenny at Bournemouth university. We clicked instantly, becoming great friends. Stuart joined us and surprisingly, we all still hung out together. They saved me.

'Yes,' I answer, my throat filling up with emotion. 'Of course, I do.' When I took over the managing of Shore House, the first part of Jenny and Stuart's new Lighthouse project, I moved from Oxfordshire to Lyme Regis. With the setting up of the new house and charity comes vast amounts of paperwork. Many external agencies needed contact to be put in place so that we could support the women coming through our doors.

It was a busy time for me, with my energy and focus being channelled on getting everything for the house ready and waiting for the first guests to arrive. I lost track of the support group and most of my Oxfordshire contacts, as I became more engaged in my new life. I even became distant with my parents. As if the whole rape thing was their fault.

'Well, they are still going strong,' Daniel's voice breaks into my thoughts, 'and Jenny and Stuart are still Trustees of the group, as you know. Not sure if you are aware, but the group is about to celebrate its fourteenth anniversary and are planning a celebration event to show how far they've come. The Counsellor and Leader in charge of the group, Karis, would like you to attend. And I know that Jenny and Stuart would also love to have you there.'

'Me?' I query, 'what a kind gesture. When is it?' I ask, before checking my mirrors to indicate and move into the slower lane.

'Tomorrow evening?' he says.

I suddenly think of the dead rat that was delivered to me this morning. This doesn't feel like the right time to be enjoying myself, until I've got to the bottom of why someone would do such a thing.

'Lottie, you still there?' Daniel prompts.

'Yeah, sorry.' I'm just about to say 'no' when my treacherous mouth, utters the words 'I'd love to attend.' The half-hearted anger I had a moment ago, disappears and I smile.

'That's wonderful,' his voice softens as though he is happy with my decision.

His pleasure sends a warm tingle to my tummy. Oh heck, what am I getting myself in to?

'Is Jenny going?' I can ask her tonight, but I don't want to disconnect the call yet.

'Yes, she and Stuart are going.' He responds quickly.

'One more thing, Lottie,' he says as I'm about to say goodbye.

'Yes, Daniel,' I glance across at Harley, who is still engrossed with his music. 'I wonder if you would let me be your plus one for the evening?'

'You don't have to do that, Daniel.' I butt in. During our previous counselling sessions, many moons ago, he had shown himself to be thoughtful and caring, professional and perceptive. I am not looking for romance, despite my reaction to Daniel over the phone. At thirty-six, I feel that there is much more in life that I can do, particularly in helping abused women.

'I know that, but I want to,' his voice takes on a serious note.

Something inside me breaks during the silence and I know he's waiting for an answer. 'All right, Daniel. You can be my plus one, which means you can drive, and I get to have a glass of wine!' I joke.

'It's a deal! See you in a few hours.' Daniel's deep Scottish voice fills the car, before he disconnects the call, leaving me with an unappealing silence. That voice could slay a thousand demons and leave you feeling cleansed of all the darkness within your soul.

His words 'It's a deal!' echo in my head. I thought for a moment there he was going to say, 'It's a date.' And for some reason, that doesn't frighten me as much as I thought it would. 'You've still got it girl,' I begin to smile, and my heart skips a beat.

There is movement to my left, and Harley's voice forces me to the here and now. 'Everything OK, Mum? Thought I heard you talking to someone.'

'Yes, an old friend of mine and Jenny's, just called. His name is Daniel and he'll be staying at Jenny and Stuart's place with us.

Harley must have realised that I wasn't going to say anything else, because he takes his phone from the charge point and sits meddling with it.

Inwardly, I want to scream, shout, and dance a jig all at the same time.

I've got a sort of date. For the first time in a long time. A real date. My heart beats fast in my chest. What on earth will I wear? And why didn't Jenny mention that Daniel was staying for the break away?

Part Thirteen: Daniel

There are three things that you should know about me.

One. I have a strong sense of morality. Which means that if I think something is wrong, then I have to say something. It also means that I feel extremely protective about the people I know and love.

Two, is that I am a very patient man. My mum always says that it was one of my best assets. My ability to listen, observe and to bide my time before rushing to say something. As a consultant psychiatrist at the John Radcliffe University Hospital in Oxford, this is one of the key skills needed for my job.

Three. I have been in love with Charlotte Peckham since the day I first met her. In fact, from the moment I first looked into her wounded, soulful soft brown eyes I felt a connection. With a head of dark red curls and long, swaying skirts she almost took my breath away. Of course, she was my patient and I convinced myself to wait until the time was right to ask her on a date.

Then life got in the way. My elderly parents needed support and I took some time to return home to Edinburgh to look after them and put things in place to make life simpler and easier for them. To ease the situation, I pay for a helper to go into their home, the one which they've lived in for sixty years, each day to help with chores, bathing and cooking.

I feel quietly optimistic that this could be the solution I am looking for. Jon, their brilliant helper, reassures me that the situation is working well. Being an only child, has its responsibilities and considerations. It won't be easy, but I want to do right by them. For everything that they have done for me over the years, it's the least that I can do.

Well, going back to my story. Things settled down once I had made sure that my parents were cared for, which enabled me to return to work at the hospital in Oxford, my thoughts were focused on keeping my head down and getting back into a routine. This was made harder, when I learned that Charlotte was moving away to live in Lyme Regis, West Dorset.

What a blow! I thought I had forever. But forever never lasts. Lottie met Simon and then they married. I didn't go to the wedding, couldn't face seeing their happiness, looking at the life that could have been mine, if I had only seized the moment.

Carpe Diem.

I don't usually swear, but from the moment that Lottie and Simon married, the first words that came from my mouth each morning when I woke up were, 'Another fucking day.'

Being mad at yourself doesn't help, because you just take it out on others, so eventually, I had to pull myself together and focus on what was important to me. My work, family and friends replaced the anger and self-loathing, and forced me to find my equilibrium again. Even though some days, I still feel like I am only partially living.

After Simon died the concern came back. I didn't want to see her hurting. Couldn't bear the thought of what she was going through and that her son was now without a father. To lose a partner was bad enough, but to lose the father of your child, that must be devasting. I kept telling myself that she would reach out if she needed me.

But she didn't.

And I almost gave up.

The Invisible Ones

Until Jenny called me one day and asked if I would like to spend a few days of the holiday in Oxfordshire with some of their friends. We had discussed the upcoming anniversary of the Lighthouse Support Group that Jenny, Stuart and Lottie had begun many years ago, for those people who had suffered at the hands of others.

Of course, this gave me a reason to call Lottie, to invite her to the support group celebration and to explain that I was staying with Jenny in the Oxfordshire House too.

What I had really hoped for, was that Lottie would show some interest in me, and I wasn't disappointed, she didn't hesitate to agree to my proposition. I could almost hear the smile in her voice during our conversation, lifting me and sending a warmth through my body which I hadn't felt in a while.

Her son, Harley worries me though. I need to tread carefully. He is young and protective of his mum, understandably. I will do everything in my power to make sure that he begins to understand how much I want this to work, and that I'm not trying to take the place of his dad. This is not going to be easy to navigate, feelings can become messy, especially to a ten-year-old, who has spent the past four years living without his dad and therefore being the man of the house.

Children's hearts are fragile, but they are also very resilient, and I am hoping that when Harley sees how happy his mum will become that he will begin to accept me into their lives.

The alarm bells in my head, tell me to take this one step at a time.

My mind flits back to my former girlfriend, Anna, we broke up last September. She was everything I could have wished for, beautiful with long dark hair, kind and smart, she was working on her first psychiatry rotation at the JR. She was everything I should have wanted in life, but something was missing. The connection I had been looking for, the final piece of the puzzle simply wasn't there.

The funny thing was, I knew exactly where that piece of the puzzle was.

Hidden in a pair of pale grey eyes.

This time, I'm determined to get the girl.

This time, Lottie had better be ready, because she's no longer my patient and there are no constraints.

Carpe bloody Diem. I'm seizing the day.

Part Fourteen: DCI Brian Carter

I am absolutely useless with flat pack furniture, fitting things together and following written instructions. I haven't got the patience. Staring at the children's safety gate, as if using telepathy could move the gate and it would fit itself. Of course not. I decide to try again, pulling the extension and trying to fix it to the plaster walls in my hallway. An excited 'yelp,' reminds me why I'm doing this. As I look across the open plan living room of the detached home that Julie and I purchased four years ago.

'That's enough Lola,' I tell my newly acquired, temporary foster dog. 'Julie is going to be mad enough with me as it is. Let's at least stop you from going upstairs.' I know I need to call Jenny to see if she minds if we bring her.

Lola brushes herself softly against my bending leg, not unlike a cat. I stroke her reassuringly.

The house is a converted barn, near Wallingford, Oxfordshire. The land had once belonged to a farmer, and sadly like many farms over the years, the land had been sold to sustain the farm. In this case, the barn was bought and renovated by a young couple six years ago, who sympathetically converted it into a modern living space, with four bedrooms.

Unfortunately, a year after completion, Mr Mack had explained, the couple split up and put the property up for sale. Julie and I couldn't believe our luck when the place came on the market for a quick sale, and before we knew it our offer had been accepted, which left us the proud owners of this beautiful barn. It is all open plan, apart from the staircase. It still retains some of its older features, such as wooden ceiling beams, and a lot of exposed brickwork.

Finally, I add the extender pole to the oak wooden rails and secure the white metal gate to keep our new family member from venturing away from the lower floor.

'Thank God for that!' I mutter, forcing my aching legs to a standing position. Walking to the deep Chesterfield green leather chair, by the wood burner, I flop down and feel surprisingly comforted when Lola jumps onto my knee, licks my face and curls up against my chest.

Where the hell is my wife? I check my watch, 6pm. She should have been home thirty minutes ago. We're meeting our friends, the Greyson's for dinner at their rented holiday house tonight. It's a big family affair.

Absently I stroke Lola. 'Mummy is going to love you,' I smile. 'Particularly after you've had a quick bath.'

I'm about to drag my tired body from the chair, to take Lola to the bathroom for a good clean when the phone rings, I answer without looking. 'Julie?'

'No,' a familiar voice replies, 'It's Gino Camprinelli.'

Leaning back against the chair, I pull Lola's warm body close, so that she snuggles against my chest. Fuck. What the hell does Gino Camprinelli want?

Although we've met several times briefly in the ten plus years since the Felix Gloverman business at Wittenham Clumps, we have no social interaction. Despite this, Gino Camprinelli and I have a common bond, an unspeakable bond, which neither of us will ever discuss with another living soul, because we each have too much to lose. The stakes are too high.

Felix Gloverman, Jenny Greyson's uncle, the monster who drugged and raped his own niece, before leaving her to die in a long, oblong box. The man who killed Jenny's housekeeper and close family friend, Rose Dean. Gino, it appeared was amongst a bunch of people who, for one reason or another, knew Felix and wanted him dead.

The unspeakable bond will never go away, it's as though we've made a blood vow.

So, you can see why the thought of him makes me apprehensive. When the ghosts hiding in your closet come calling, you need to be wary.

Taking a deep breath, I finally speak, 'Gino, what can I do for you?'

He seems wary, unsure for a moment, 'I wasn't sure whether to call or not.'

'Just say what you've got to say,' I order him, I haven't got time for his procrastinating.

'It's my nephew, Vincent. He's gone missing,' he tells me.

That last sentence piqued my interest and made me focus. 'Missing? Since when?'

'Since today, but it's not that. Fuck,' he sounds frustrated. 'Remember he used to hang around with a couple of other kids, Cameron Frost and Eric Weston?'

Shit, immediately I put Lola on the floor and begin to pace the floor. A shiver moves across my shoulder blades, and I run a hand through my already messy brown hair. The Three Amigos. Fuck, visions of the last time I saw them flash through my mind. Tied to chairs. Scared shitless. Fuck. I keep moving, can't keep still...

'I'm listening,' I say quietly, looking out of the window at the overgrown lawn.

Gino's voice is flat, devoid of emotion, as though we were talking about going to the pub next week. 'Vincent was supposed to meet Cameron, but he didn't turn up.'

'Could he have just disappeared?' I ask.

I wonder how much to tell him, I think I can trust him, but the police officer in me questions what is happening.

'Brian,' his use of my first name cements my thoughts on the matter. We have been partners in crime before and it worked out well.

'Yup,' I answer.

'Cameron found Vincent's phone at the place where they were due to meet. And…' he holds his breath.

'And what?' I ask, hoping that this isn't something that will come back to haunt me. 'Spit it out, Gino. And?'

'Cameron found a finger. A little finger.' I stare at Lola, bloody hell. Her eyes are so trusting, even though she hardly knows me. Something tears at me. Don't trust me too much, Lola. I'm not a good person. Not really.

Of all the times for something new to blow up in our faces, it had to be now. Why? How do I tell Julie what I did, all those years ago with Gino Camprinelli? Will she understand, or will she walk away from the marriage?

'Fuck! I will need to get them both analysed for DNA, weapon etc. Can you get them to DS Sheppington at St Aldates? I'll give her a call to tell her you're on your way.'

'Thanks Brian,' Gino's voice is husky with relief, 'I was hoping you would say that.'

'One more thing,' I say, wondering if I was doing the right thing. 'Eric Weston was assaulted this afternoon and left for dead. His little finger is missing.'

There's a brief silence before Gino speaks, 'Jesus! Eric Weston? That means…'

I don't let him finish his sentence. 'I know. But let's keep an open mind, for now. It may not be about the Three Amigos.' I tell him raking my hand through my hair. So much for a break. 'In the meantime,' I say, 'I'll get someone to visit his mother's house in Charmouth.'

'Think so. Yeah, we'll do that for now,' I can almost hear his brain ticking away, 'but if it turns out that someone is after my nephew and his friends, then I'll be making my own enquiries.'

Bloody hell, this man drives me mad. He's mercurial by nature, one moment he's almost begging for my help, the next he's well on his way to threatening me.

'You called me for help, damn it. So let me do my bloody job.' I say harshly, my voice becoming louder.

Disconnecting the call, I walk to the dining area and take a bottle of whiskey from the cupboard, dropping my phone on the hard wood surface, before locating a nearby glass. Pouring myself a quick measure, I tip the glass to my lips and down the drink in one gulp, closing my eyes as the liquid burns my throat.

After I put the empty glass next to my phone, I let the conversation with Gino play around in my thoughts. He's not a work colleague, or a friend, he's that someone in between. The almost friend, the almost confidante who can make a difference.

Of course, the attacks are connected, clearly related, but I need to keep my cards close to my chest. I've told him enough to keep him going, for now. Lola follows at my feet, her paws tapping along the wooden floor, waiting patiently for some attention. Considering that she is someone else's dog, she's very friendly and calm. The sort of dog that will easily fit in with your lifestyle and family.

My phone springs to life and I grab it, hoping it's Julie to say she's on her way.

'Boss,' Shep's familiar voice sounds worried. I begin to take the stairs to the first floor, because if I don't run this bath and get Lola cleaned, we are never leaving tonight.

'Yes,' I rub my tired eyes, making them squeak briefly. This has been a very long day. 'What is it?'

'Eric Weston just died. He had a massive heart attack, the consultant said he didn't stand a chance.'

Oh fuck, now life just got a lot more complicated.

'OK, thanks for letting me know. Gino Camprinelli should be contacting you. His nephew, Vincent, has gone missing. He was supposed to meet a friend but never turned up at a derelict pub in Steventon, the friend found a finger and Vincent's phone. I've asked Gino to bring both of them into the station to you. Can you get them sent off for analysis while I'm away. I want to hear the results as soon as they come in.'

'No problem, Boss,' she says. 'I'll get details about the pub, so I can send SOCO down there.'

'One more thing,' I pause, before finishing the sentence, 'Vincent Camprinelli knew Eric Weston.'

'Jesus!' Shep says. 'Now, we're getting somewhere.'

'In addition.' I continue, rubbing the bridge of my nose, 'they were part of a trio, with Cameron Frost, known as the Three Amigos. See if you can find Cameron, keep an eye on him.'

'Got it.' She replies absently, I can hear scribbling as she makes notes. There is a silence over the phone before she begins to talk again, 'Is Gino Camprinelli going to behave himself?'

'Hopefully, but who knows?' I reply, 'We don't want a retaliation thing starting, or bodies will begin piling up.'

We disconnect the call as I step onto the first-floor landing. There is a feeling of foreboding, now that Eric Weston is dead. I can't help but believe deep in my gut, that whoever attacked him and left him for dead, and has now taken Vincent Camprinelli is seeking revenge. We all know that revenge comes in all shapes and sizes. But knowing why is going to be the key to unlocking these attacks.

When I reach the bathroom, I turn on the light, run the taps and add a few bubbles, while Lola's eyes stare at me suspiciously as though she knows I'm up to something. I test the water.

'Right, young lady,' I say, leaning down to stroke Lola's soft fur, 'It's time for a quick bath.'

Scooping the animal up against my chest, I hold her carefully. 'Yes, then we can have food.'

I hear the front door open as I lower the dog carefully into the soapy water and wonder what will become of her now that her master is dead. Julie is home. I know that sound anywhere, as the clipping of her shoes walk toward the kitchen on the ground floor, and I hear the fridge door open.

'Brian, you upstairs?' my wife calls.

'Hi honey. Yes,' I say, hoping that I'm not going to be in the doghouse tonight. 'I'm upstairs, and I've got a surprise for you. We have a visitor.'

Fingers crossed she's had a good day.

Part Fifteen: Jenny

The large dining table looks fit for a King, with double pedestal legs supporting a polished mahogany top. In the centre sits a wide rectangular silver vase, which is overflowing with beautiful pale roses, spray roses and campanulas.

The floral scent is both intoxicating and calming.

White linen napkins are folded and held in place with silver napkin rings, on top of white plates with gold rims, marking each of the twelve place settings. Silver cutlery is set either side of each dinner plate in various sizes and shapes.

Hanging high above the table, is an over-sized modern silver candelabra, sending ethereal shadows of light from the windows across the table. Deep blue upholstered chairs are tucked under the table, noting each place setting, The elegance within the room is without question, until you take a closer look around the room and spot the wooden highchair placed next to the table, and the large wicker box of toys

To be honest, looking around the dining room, taking in the two stunning ten-foot-high palm trees that are sprinkled with thousands of tiny bulbs, sparkling in front of the Victorian sashed bay windows, this room and this house are simply perfect for our family get together.

Walking to the windows, I look out into the manicured gardens and feel at peace. I was so pleased when I came across this listed ten bedroomed manor house, with its separate games barn, pool and spa area. The house sits in the beautiful Oxfordshire village of

The Invisible Ones

Sutton Courtenay, a picturesque chocolate box village that would do well in an Agatha Christie novel. Quintessentially English, with manicured pockets of greenery and grey stone walls.

We've rented the house for four weeks, as we are having work done on our Chippenham home, I thought it would be a great idea to catch up with family and friends over the summer holidays. The housekeeper, who is included with the house, Mrs Agnes Monk, is a similar height to me, around five seven, with short silver-grey curly hair and a very pretty face.

Mrs Monk lives in the staff bungalow, which is situated on the estate, rather than at the manor house. It appears, that the Chef, however lives in the village.

When I first met the housekeeper, six days ago, my heart skipped a beat because she reminded me so much of my previous housekeeper, dear Rose who had been like a mother to me.

Rose and her husband, Henry, brought me up because my parents were workaholics, and when their plane crashed over the English Chanel on their way back home from a business trip, it was Rose and Henry who took me in as their own.

Carefully helping, supporting, guiding me. I didn't know then that my Uncle Felix would do those horrible things to me, and to Rose. He killed her, and even though he is dead too, I can never forgive him for what he did to her.

Oh, how I wish Rose was still alive. I miss her so very much. I must call Henry and go to visit him soon too. Reflecting on life reminds me of my blessings, to think of all the things I have in my life, rather than all the things I haven't. Sadly, I was unable to conceive but Stuart and I both came to terms with this over the years. It was hard, but we moved on. Found our own family.

We have each other and that is more than enough. I stroke my wedding and engagement rings, feeling their cold smooth surfaces and set a smile on my face.

This week is going to be wonderful. I can't wait to see our friends.

The calmness is broken by a loud crash and a hard thud that seems to come from the kitchen area. This is followed by a flurry of movement behind me, before someone with a French accent, shouts 'Mon Dieu, vous êtes un imbécile!'

I turn to see what the commotion is about, to see a young woman running across the hallway behind me, clearly distraught and sobbing inconsolably. The joy of inheriting a temperamental French chef, who also comes with the house. He doesn't care one iota about the manner in which he talks to people. Which, in a nutshell, is bordering on rude.

Straightening the paisley patterned velvet table runner, with hints of red that match the dining chairs, I inhale slowly before making my way to the kitchen to find out what has happened this time.

'Monsieur Durand?' I say, cautiously stepping into the large domain that the chef rules with an iron rod. How ridiculous that one should feel that they are in the presence of a head teacher when they are near him.

The tall, slim chef is facing away from me, hunched over the counter, concentrating. I can hear the speedy chopping of someone intent on completing his task at quickly as possible. Chef looks young, probably in his early thirties, with long black hair, tied at the back with a band and a tidy beard.

He holds himself with poise, confidence with accents of arrogance, and wears a navy-blue apron over a dark long-sleeved top, paired with black jeans. From studying him over the last few days, I now know that this is his preparation uniform, and he will change into his brilliant whites during the service of each meal.

With a silent chuckle to myself, I wonder how someone who loves to work with food, can remain so slender. Maybe, he eats very small portions!

Chef ignores me, so I look around the room to see if anything is amiss, apart from the obvious disappearance of his assistant. At first glance, I cannot find the source of the argument or the broken crockery, until I walk around the large white marble kitchen island and find that several white plates are smashed on the black stone floor.

Monsieur Durand suddenly turns to me, a large knife in his hand and begins to wave it from side to side. His face is rather handsome, despite the arrogance that screams, I'm French, I'm the chef and I know what I'm doing.

'She was no good. Too clumsy in my kitchen.' His accent is strong, and I concentrate hard to understand him.

'Monsieur Durand,' I say calmly. 'Please put the knife down.' I point to the knife and then to the counter, where he has been slicing carrots, onions and other vegetables. Looking around the kitchen, I realise that it must be every cook's dream to work in such a clean, modern environment.

The kitchen has been sympathetically restored, with a little exterior brick here and there, and a brick inserted arch for the large eight ring gas cooker. 'The knife...' What is it with chefs and their mercurial mood swings? Is it something in their blood? Or is it part of the job description to have a lack of empathy, and kindness?

Monsieur Durand, slowly lays the knife down on the counter, before shrugging his shoulders, 'I only asked her to wash her hands, and she muttered something and knocked the plates onto the floor.'

'I will give Brigitte a call tomorrow to see if we can persuade her to return,' I tell him. Mediating between the chef and his assistant seems to have become my new norm. 'Please try to be nice to the guests when they arrive. They are very old friends of mine.'

He made no move to clear the mess from the floor, so I begin to open cupboards in search of a dustpan and brush. Do you remember that old saying, 'If you want a job doing, do it yourself?'

Mrs Monk bustles into the kitchen, 'Oh François have you upset Brigitte again? You really must try not to frighten the staff,' she admonishes the chef. Agnes is the only person who is allowed to call Monsieur Durand by his first name.

'Madame Monk,' the chef turns to look at her, his face serious. 'I cannot work with these people when I am trying to prepare my famous beef bourguignon.' Agnes moves around the kitchen and stops when she comes across the broken plates. 'Oh dear, I will clean that up, Mrs Greyson.'

'Don't worry, Mrs Monk,' I gesture for her to leave the mess alone, 'I have it in hand.'

I reach the utility room and finally find a dustpan and brush in the cupboard under sink and within a matter of minutes I have scooped the debris from the kitchen floor and deposited it in the kitchen bin.

'What will we do without Brigitte this evening?' Mrs Monk asks in a panicked voice.

'Don't worry, we will muddle through,' I reassure her with a smile, 'everything will be fine.' I rub my hands down my grey trousers to calm myself. My soft pink blouse hangs to my trouser pockets, in gentle flowing peaks, and I am very conscious not to mark it before dinner, which we plan to serve at 7pm.

My phone rings and the name Judy lights up. It's one of our former guests from Shore House. Judy Jackson was a resident at Shore House when her twin daughters, Amy and Anna, were four. They stayed for a year, before moving into their own place in Lyme Regis. Now, she manages a florist shop in the town. The Lighthouse Charity covers childcare costs, so Judy has a part time nanny, Sarah, to help with busy times.

Answering the call, I worry that something is wrong.

'Judy?' I can hear the worry in my own voice.

Judy's voice is soft and deep. 'Sorry to bother you, but I've just had some bad news and I need to talk to you.'

'Bad news?' I repeat. 'What is it?' I walk through the house and until I reach the dining room, find a chair and slump into it.

'Tell me, Judy.' I urge.

'I've just had the results of my tests back from the hospital,' her voice is devoid of emotion, as though she's still not sure of what she is going through.

'And…' I ask, my voice clipped with anticipation.

'It's not good. I've got stage four breast cancer.'

'Oh my God, Judy. I am so sorry. What can I do?' My eyes stare at the table, which is quickly blurring with the tears that have formed at this terrible news.

'There's nothing they can do. Just palliative care now.' Her words are so flat.

'Oh Judy. That's terrible. What can I do to help?' I feel so helpless, so useless. She is only thirty-five years old.

'That's why I'm calling.' Judy's voice is croaky. She is such a strong woman, and I can only imagine the strength it is taking her to talk about this, with such honesty and finality.

I stay quiet. Waiting for her to compose herself. 'I want you and Stuart to take on the legal guardianship of the girls. Bring them up as your own.'

My mind shuts down, as her words freeze in my head. *Take on the girls. Bring them up as our own.*

'But Judy, isn't there anyone else? Any members of your family?' What about everyone in between, my mind races.

'My family and ex partner's family disowned me, when I left him. They blamed me for his downfall. All I know is that if he was still alive, I would be buried six feet under by now.' There is a harshness to her voice.

'The girls will come to us, Judy. We will love them like our own and keep your memory alive. I will speak to Stuart in a few minutes and when our houseguests have gone next Thursday, we will come to Lyme and talk some more. Just concentrate on looking after yourself.'

Finally, Judy breaks down. Sobbing with relief or despair, I'm not sure. But I do know one thing, and that is it's not in my nature to do nothing. I am a doer. And, if looking after Anna and Amy is what Stuart and I are meant to do with the rest of our lives, it won't be a hardship.

I had all but given up on ever being a mother. After my uncle drugged, kidnapped and raped me when I was twenty years old, it's no surprise I was never able to conceive. I kept telling myself, one day it will happen. But one day never arrived. Out of this desolation came our baby, The Lighthouse Charity.

121

'Judy, we love you and the girls.' I say, as tears fall down my cheeks.

'Thank you, Jenny. We love you too. And thank you for everything that you have done for me and the girls. We are forever grateful to have had these years together.'

My heart is breaking for this woman, who will not get to see her children growing up. For those memories that cannot be made.

I think of Stuart, and how hard this conversation will be, as I make my way back to the kitchen. Of course, it's a no brainer. The girls will come to us. The paperwork will be put into place, to give everyone involved stability. Our world will change.

My husband is currently on his way back from Oxford where he is collecting more drink and food supplies. Our friend, Brian called earlier, to say that they were on their way, and could he possibly bring a dog with them, assuring me that the dog was house trained and well behaved. Goodness knows what that was about.

The shrill of the doorbell breaks the brief silence, startling me from my thoughts of Judy and the girls. Checking my watch, I realise that it is 5.30pm, much later than I had realised. This could be the guests arriving.

Mrs Monk motions to the doorway, with a nod and immediately turns to exit the kitchen. 'I'll see to that,' she says abruptly, walking with purpose through the kitchen, into the entrance hall which leads to the front door.

I follow her, my hands becoming clammy with nerves. Was this a good idea? Getting everyone together for nearly a week during the August holidays? We'll soon find out. I hover next to Mrs Monk and force a smile.

'Aunty Jenny!' Harley gives me the biggest smile, and I know that everything will be all right. He rushes forward and gives me the warmest hug. Mrs Monk smiles my way, 'I'll leave you to it if that's all right. Call me if you need me.' I briefly nod to her and mouth 'Thank you.'

My old university friend, Lottie steps forward with a huge grin. 'This is rather grand, Bestie,' she says, throwing her arms around me.

'Thought it would be nice to make an effort,' I reply, reaching out to hold her tightly. We have been through so much together in the early days and now we are tied together with my charity, the Lighthouse. The bond we have will remain with us forever. 'So good to see you,' I whisper, holding her tightly. 'It's been too long, much too long.'

'You too honey,' she replies.

'Let's get your luggage and I'll take you to your rooms. Then I'll show you around.' I tell her with a smile.

We are about to close the door when two cars pull to a stop in the driveway at the front of the house. Immediately, I recognise Stuart's blue Volvo and pull the door open fully to see who the driver of the black BMW is. My husband steps out of his car, faces me and gives me the warmest smile.

I never tire of the way that my husband acknowledges me, and how he makes time to keep our emotional connection, despite the seventeen years that we've been together. I smile back, forever thankful that he walked into the university refectory that lunchtime and came to sit with Lottie and myself.

The tall, confident frame turns to face us, and immediately I recognise the short blond hair, the good looks, the smile. Dr Daniel Scott, with the Liam Neeson looks, hasn't changed at all. He's wearing a navy checked long sleeved shirt, with his sleeves casually rolled up at the wrist, with a zip up green jumper and navy jeans. Stuart turns to Daniel and pats him on the back warmly, as they exchange a few words.

Both men go to the boots of their cars and lean in. Stuart takes out a large cardboard box, and Daniel holds a small black suitcase. Behind me, Lottie inhales sharply as though she's seen a ghost and I turn to catch the flush in her face and lift an eyebrow. Is she fond of Daniel?

'Are you all right, Mum?' Harley asks, his face serious with worry.

Lottie turns to her son, and lays her hand reassuringly on his shoulder. 'I'm fine honey,' she reassures him softly, 'a bit of a dry throat, I'll get a glass of water in a moment.'

Footsteps come closer and I feel the presence of my husband before I see him. A warm breath caresses my cheek, and Stuart's deep, familiar voice whispers, as he leans into me, 'Hey.' I reach out to briefly touch his skin, feel the soft whiskers on his jaw.

'Hey,' I say quickly. 'Lottie and Harley have just arrived.'

I step to the side so that my husband can pass, the box rattling as he moves. 'Hey Lot, good to see you,' he says, without stopping. 'Sorry, can't stop, this box is heavy.' As he walks along the hallway, and zig zags through the house to the kitchen, his deep voice calls outs, 'Harley I can't believe how tall you've grown!'

Daniel moves forward with confidence, setting his suitcase on the floor beside my feet.

'So glad you could make it,' I lean forward, taking his tall frame in a hearty embrace. I genuinely like Daniel; he has been a friend since I first met him in the hospital. The memory is bittersweet, nearly fifteen years ago when I was studying at university, I was drugged and kidnapped - taken from the bedroom in my Gateshead family home, near Stadhampton in Oxfordshire, by my masochistic uncle. Thankfully, Stuart found me hidden in a long wooden box in the Summer House of the Gateshead estate. In the hospital I found to my horror, that my uncle had also raped me.

The memory, as I say is bittersweet. Daniel saw me at my worst over the days that followed. I was angry, frustrated, helpless.

'How are you?' he asks quietly as we hold each other close. He is very much like a brother to me. Checking in with me, to make sure I'm OK. Maybe in another life, we may have become more, but in this life, I have my soul mate, in Stuart. Meanwhile, Daniel is still travelling that road to find the person he's meant to be with.

'I'm good,' I smile into his shoulder. 'You?' He shrugs and looks over my shoulder. Instantly, I feel his body stiffen.

'Lottie, you're here,' he says, slowly withdrawing, and I step away so that he can talk to my friend.

They hover, and for the first time since the death of her husband, Simon, I see Lottie blush over a man.

I watch as they stand, waiting for the other to speak. 'Hi,' they both say in unison, and I put my hand over my mouth to stifle a giggle.

Daniel makes the first move, leaning in to give Lottie a peck on the cheek, she in turn, moves forward and accidentally headbutts his nose. There is a short gasp and an 'Ow' of pain, before they both laugh, and he pulls her forward quickly and holds her close.

'And you must be Harley?' he leans down slightly and studies the young boy. 'I'm Daniel, by the way,' he offers his hand, in a formal introduction. It's a touching moment, Harley is growing fast, like my godson, Ben – who is the son of my friend, Steph and stepson to her husband, Jack. Harley and Ben will be young men soon.

Harley takes his right hand from his jeans and grasps the older man's outstretched hand, 'Hey,' Harley lifts an eyebrow and his mouth lifts at the corners.

I smirk grabbing the handle of the forgotten suitcase bringing it over the threshold of the door. This is going to be an interesting couple of days.

'Let's go inside,' I tell them, 'I'll show you both to your rooms and get Mrs Monk to arrange refreshments. Daniel, can you please give Lottie and Harley some help with their luggage.'

Part Sixteen: Ferret (10 years ago)

The bar in Oxford is noisy, and I can hardly hear myself speak. Looking every inch the girl about town, with my three-inch platforms, low-cut burgundy sleeveless top and short skirt, I feel rather proud of the fact that our fake ID cards were accepted by the bouncers. Although the bright pink jumper lying on the padded seat next to my black bag, might look as though I'm quite a sensible sort, tonight I wanted to let my hair down.

As I sit in a booth near to the front of the bar, I lean closer to the good-looking young man they call Cameron and say loudly, 'It's a bit noisy in here, shall we go somewhere quieter, maybe grab a coffee.' Smoothing my hands down my black leather effect mini skirt. 'There's a coffee and ice cream parlour nearby, which I use a lot on Fridays with my girlfriends, it stays open until 11pm.' Looking across the room to my friends, Marina and Anna, I see that they are talking to Cameron's friends, giggling and pointing to their empty glasses.

Cameron is tall, blonde haired and slim, he looks in his twenties. Or older, maybe it's the confidence that he seems to have, who knows? He's limping a bit, but there's no disguising that he looks chilled and confident in his white T-shirt.

His two friends, Vincent and Eric leave their seats and are leaning on the bar, waiting to be served. They are loud and slur their words, as they attempt to attract the attention of the pretty, young bartender with the tight purple top and tied back hair. She is busy refilling a shelf with clean glasses. Vincent suddenly turns our way and catches Cameron's eye.

Cameron nods. What was that about? Did I imagine that they made eye contact?

'Hey sweetheart?' Vincent calls loudly to the woman and slamming a hand on the top of the bar. 'We need more drinks!'

The young woman stays quiet. There is a resigned sigh as she makes her way to Vincent and places her hands on the bar. 'What can I get you?' She asks, without making eye contact.

'Four Red Witches,' Eric chimes, 'that's blackcurrant, cider and Pernod and we'll have two margaritas too.'

'What about a private show, afterwards?' Vincent won't leave the woman alone. He's lucky he doesn't get a slap across the face. 'I'm sure you won't disappoint.'

Watching the woman's face, I hear the biggest sigh, as she shakes her head. She turns away and concentrates on Eric's drink order.

'Behave yourself lads,' Cameron shouts, 'or you'll get us thrown out.' He brushes his hands through his hair, before turning to me. 'One for the road and then we'll make our way to your ice-cream place.'

He puts a hand on my thigh, making me panic, and wish not for the first time, that I had put a longer skirt on this evening. His hand begins to roam upwards to the edge of my skirt.

Immediately, I put my hand over his and draw it back to its lower, safer position. 'Slow down, Cameron,' I tell him. 'There's no rush, is there?'

A flicker of annoyance shows in his eyes, and his brows draw together before he decides to smile again.

'Here you go, you two,' Vincent says, putting the two margaritas down on the table, 'get these down you, compliments of Eric over there.' I look to where Vincent is pointing and see his friend, Eric, sitting next to the girls again. He raises a glass when he sees me in salute. I smile back, 'thanks.'

Three minutes later, and I am loving my margarita. In fact, the glass is half empty already, and my head is beginning to feel light.

'So, what is a sweet young thing like you doing hanging out in a bar like this?' Cameron asks.

'Who says I'm sweet?' I counter, feeling rather brave. Something doesn't feel right. I shake my head to clear it a little. Sounds are echoing in my brain and when people talk, their words are all distorted.

'I think I drank that too quickly,' I confess, pointing to my glass on the table. My arm feels heavy, and my words sound strange.

Cameron smiles, finishes his drink and looks at me. 'You need some fresh air, let's get you outside.' He takes my hand and pulls me to my feet. God, I feel groggy. 'My bag and jumper,' I mumble. He reaches down and grabs my things. 'Come on. Fresh air and maybe coffee. If you're good, I might even treat you to ice cream.'

He pulls me with urgency through the doors into the coolness of the night breeze.

In my naivety, I believed that everyone was good. And, that if I was in some way compromised someone would help me. I believed in the goodness of people to care, in the dashing knight on the white horse, who rescues the damsel in distress.

But life isn't like that, is it?

There wasn't anyone to save me from my drugged stupor. Just evil people disguised in human form.

Part Seventeen: Cameron

The music is deafening. Shuffling to ease the ache in my back as I lean against the hard wooden chair. I clamp my hands together until my knuckles whiten to stop them from shaking.

Gino Camprinelli sits behind his sleek mahogany desk, his eyes are closed as he listens to a loud, haunting tune, with words that sing about someone called Lacrimosa. It has a hypnotic draw to the soul, and for a moment I forget where I am, until a sharp, searing pain travels from my kneecap down to the ankle of my right leg, and back to my knee again. Instinctively, I rub the top of my knee hard, to compensate for the relentless pain.

I really need to stand up. Stretch my damn leg. But I don't.

The music finishes and Gino opens his eyes. He's wearing a black suit, as though he's going to a funeral, complete with a white shirt and black tie. His hair is grey and hangs to his neck. I've only met him once and it was much shorter then. A time six years ago, at a local bistro in Didcot town centre, having lunch with Vincent. And that was enough.

***

I still remember the moment when everything stopped as Gino and his black suited cronies strutted into the place. It was like one of those moments you see in the movies. The energy level dropped to zero and a heavy threat of something sinister hung in the air. Gino had scanned the room, before eventually looking our way. The silence was deadly.

Gino walked to the table next to us and nodded to the cronies. I watched in horror as they lifted a young man from the next table to us, his two female friends who had been sitting beside him were cowering in shock and fear. I will never forget the screams of the pimple-faced, greasy haired young man, as he was dragged from the bistro to the car park.

'Who the hell is that?' I whispered to Vincent.

'My uncle,' Vincent had sighed in a low voice, just as Gino turned to look at him.

'What are you doing here? You're supposed to be at the gym.' The older man asked in a stern voice.

'I'm on my lunch break, uncle,' Vincent said defiantly, and I could feel the hackles rising on his arms. Mine were too.

'Don't be late,' he muttered before turning to follow the cronies.

'Holy fuck!' I breathed as the door had swung closed.

Holy fuck indeed.

***

'Just exactly, what was my nephew up to Cameron?' Gino says, suddenly focusing on my face. He looks at me as though I am nothing but a nuisance that has been added to his already busy schedule.

'Do you have any idea who might have taken him?' I ask.

'No, but I plan find out,' Gino says, pushing his wheeled office chair backwards, and standing up. 'And, when I do find them, they will pay.'

Gino Camprinelli is an impressive sight when angry! The skin on his face becomes red, seeping down his neck like a silken scarf.

His dark eyes stare at you fixedly, trying to read your thoughts, to persuade you. Take away your free will.

'Was he seeing anyone?' Gino suddenly asks.

'Not sure,' I think of Vincent, trying to remember our last conversations. There had been someone, but I don't know who he or she was, for Vincent liked men and women. Shit. When did I start referring to him in the past tense?

'He mentioned someone a few times, but didn't give any details,' I say, flatly. I'm not taking the blame for this. Vincent was not a child. He didn't need a babysitter and he certainly didn't need to tell me who he was dating.

Gino moves forward, opens the button of his jacket to further expose his crisp, white shirt and leans his rear against the desk.

'He was taking drugs from the gym, drugs that weren't his.'

This isn't a surprise.

'Do you know where he was selling the drugs he stole?' He asks. Now, I know we are on treacherous ground. Drugs always complicated things and made people go crazy.

Shaking my head. 'No,' I answer, shuffling my legs and rubbing my hands together, 'I told him I wanted nothing to do with it.'

'He likes the good things in life. Is he using?' Gino asks.

I look at his sombre, but not bad-looking face, and for the first time notice the genuine concern in his eyes for his unpredictable missing nephew. Dark rings are noticeable under his eyes, as he leans down to bring his face close to mine. Poor sod.

'He does like the finer things in life,' I admit, 'but as to taking drugs, he used to do a bit of coke when out with the boys. That's about it.'

Gino stands upright, pushes his hands in his trouser pockets and begins to pace the room.

'I'll bloody kill him when I find him!' he says, stopping beside a slim console table perched against a white wall, housing a smart speaker and a silver and grey table lamp.

'Echo,' Gino's voice is abrupt, I can tell he's annoyed, but there is nothing more I can say to him that will lead him to his nephew, 'play Frank Sinatra.'

And as Frank Sinatra begins to sing about life, the universe and everything in between, I close my eyes and allow my mind to think of new ways to terrorise Charlotte.

Part Eighteen: Ferret

'Cameron Frost? I don't know anyone called Cameron Frost,' Vincent shakes his head, a little too eagerly.

He must think I'm stupid. A small tick starts at the top of his cheek, a tell-tale sign that he's lying. When he was asleep, I rolled him onto my sofa, tied his ankles together with red rope, bent his knees for tension and pulled his wrists in front of him, so that I could bind them securely with the soft rope. I stare at him as he attempts to move into a sitting position, but the rope restricts his movements.

I cannot believe he is talking such rubbish. He has no shame.

'Cut the bullshit, Vincent,' I say, stepping closer to him. 'I know who you are,' I spit the words that I've been holding back, before pushing a finger, hard into his right shoulder blade.

'Or, should I say, I know what you are,' The anger in my voice rises, as years of tortured thoughts and feelings rush to the surface. 'What you all are, the bloody lowest of the low. Pieces of shit that I need to wipe off the bottoms of my shoes.'

I reach for a nearby dining chair, haul it off the floor as though it weighed nothing, and place it in front of him. Slowly I study his pale face. Brown eyes, hard as flint stare back at me as I drop into the cushioned seat and lean forward, resting my forearms on my knees.

'I don't know what you're talking about, you deluded bitch.' His cheeks grow red with anger and his eyes don't meet mine. They rest on my jean-clad thighs, as though he can't face me directly.

He shows no sign of remorse. There is no inkling that he feels sorry for what he did. He wasn't the one who couldn't sleep at night, because of the flashbacks of these three animals grunting as they took their turns with my body.

Suddenly I feel fractious, and before I can control my feelings, I push out of the chair and begin to pace the room, muttering 'Fuck, fuck, fuck,' under my breath. I can feel the start of a headache, as my body tenses and tries to compensate for my manic state. Closing my eyes, I begin to count slowly to ten under my breath, until I reach the dining table, where I stop and lean lightly against it.

When I feel calmer, I resume our conversation. 'No matter,' I tell him, in a flat toneless voice, 'I will find him one way or another. He will pay for what he did to me, just like Eric.'

'You can't keep me here forever,' Vincent tries for bravado, but I can see the look of panic in his eyes.

'I can do whatever the hell I want with you, Vincent,' I laugh bitterly, turning to this arrogant, cruel man taking up residence on my sofa. The rope grows taut each time he moves. 'In fact, I might keep you here indefinitely. Perhaps you can be my pet.'

'You are crazy.' He mutters, wriggling his body. 'Fuck, I need to pee.'

Bloody hell, I pull away from the table and walk to him. Reaching down, I pick up the grey bucket that I had placed earlier beside the sofa, in case he was sick or something. I hold it out and tell him. 'Sit up.'

'No way am I going to piss into a fucking bucket,' he sneers. Even with his anger, I can see by the shake of his head, that he's resigning himself to his fate. With a bit of luck he'll shut up soon, or I'll put something in his drink to silence him. My ultimate aim is to take away his power, his dignity, like he took mine away. One way or another, he will pay.

Reluctantly, he lowers his eyes as I hold out the bucket.

'Do you need a hand?' I ask.

'No!' He shouts, 'Just give me some privacy, will you.'

I watch as he makes several attempts to pull the zip of his jeans down, he opens the top button with ease. But to release the zip, he needs two hands, and he should be standing.

'Oh, for fuck's sake,' I snap, reaching out to take the cold metal of the zip and yanking it down.

'Give me some privacy!' Vincent glares at me, trying to manoeuvre his hands to find the opening of his purple-coloured boxer shorts. Seconds later he finds it, reaches through the opening and brings out his half erect dick. I watch with interest as he tries to position the piece of flesh, into the bucket that I am holding.

'What, like the privacy you gave me, you little shit.' I mutter. There is no way I am giving him the satisfaction of dictating his wants to me, so when I hear the trickle of liquid hitting the bucket I stand and watch.

***

Some days are very dark. On those days nothing can help me, only the release of pain that I can get with the nearest sharp object.

They say, time heals all wounds.

But they are wrong.

Time can't heal me.

The flashbacks started a year ago. Triggered by the sighting of Eric Weston, when I recognised Eric at the pool in Didcot, I was shocked. I don't think he recognised me, so I used the opportunity to instigate a conversation. By the end of which, Eric had asked me out.

There was a curiosity within me that couldn't be sated, what would he think of me now? Could I make him fall for me? Could I turn the tables and treat him with such contempt?

Strangely enough, Eric didn't turn out to be quite the monster I thought he was. Perhaps, in another life, things could have been different, perhaps we could have been happy. I could have been happy. But the assault changed everything.

More importantly, it changed me.

As we got to know each other Eric told me a little about his home life and college days. He enjoyed talking about a group of friends that he used to hang around with. He said they used to be called the Three Amigos.

In turn, I fabricated a happy childhood and education, growing up on a farm in West IIsley, near the Ridgeway in South Oxfordshire, with my parents. Some good old-fashioned patience and the nerve to keep focused, was all that was needed to do the job. To succeed in this macabre game of hide and seek, is everything to me. There are no options left, but to rid the world of these people, who leave lives in tatters and destroy people's souls.

What Eric didn't realise was that I was making notes of every little thing, to piece together bits of information that would help me find Vincent and Cameron.

One day, over a KFC, we had been talking about places where we used to hang out when we were teenagers. I told him that I used to like going into Oxford with my friends, drinking. And, Eric, unwittingly told me about the disused pub in Steventon. The one with storerooms at the back. The one that he used to visit with his 'Amigos'.

I made a fake profile on Facebook, found Vincent Camprinelli and friended him. My plan was coming together, I just needed to bide my time and be careful not to ask too many questions about his friends. The opportunity to find out more about Cameron and Vincent came quite by chance, when Eric received a phone call from Cameron.

We had been in his car on our way to see the film Oppenheimer, at our local cinema, when the call had come through. To my surprise, he had put the call through the car phone speaker while driving, and motioned for me to be silent, putting a finger to his lip.

'What's up, Cam?' Eric had asked, as he parked in the Oxford Westgate Shopping Centre car park.

'Just wondering. Have you heard from Vincent?' A familiar, hated voice answered.

I froze, when Cameron's voice came over the speaker. That voice. The one that is embedded in my stupid brain. I close my eyes and with fisted hands, begin hitting my forehead.

Eric's worried face stares at me. 'Are you OK?' he asked quietly.

'Yeah, sorry. Just a headache,' I told him, touching his leg. 'It will go in a minute.'

'Is someone there with you?' Cameron's voice resonates through the car speaker phone.

'Yeah, just an old friend' Eric answered, and I raised an eyebrow. 'Look, I haven't seen him in a while. Maybe reach out to him if you're worried. 'We could meet at the old pub.'

The old pub…

My head really starts to pound. Bugger. In the midst of that, a plan began to form, and I waited until I was alone to take out my phone and stalk Vincent Camprinelli on Facebook and in the phone book.

That was five days ago, I now have Vincent's address and found it easy to keep tabs on him. Today, I followed his Toyota at a distance, and it was with a heavy heart that I found myself back here, in the place of my nightmares, the place where I'd been attacked. The old, disused pub in Steventon. Still standing empty, down an empty side street, but now has the addition of a large 'Land for Sale' sign.

I had sat parked in my Peugeot, tucked behind a Waitrose lorry and watched as he walked to the door of the pub, jiggled it slightly and pushed it open He was scruffy with a mop of unruly dark hair, and wearing black jeans, a grey V-neck jumper and brown blazer as he disappeared into the dark, boarded up building.

Reaching over, I had grabbed my black jacket from the passenger seat of the car and slipped my arms through, before hauling it onto my back. Carefully placing a hand into the pocket, I made sure that the taser and cigar cutter were still in there. Then, I went in pursuit of Vincent Camprinelli.

I had found Vincent sitting on some wooden pallets in the large storeroom behind the bar, rubbing his hands together and staring at the empty shelves. He seemed to be waiting for someone. With a rush of adrenaline, I quickly checked the room to make sure that we were alone and took the taser from my jacket pocket. I checked to make sure that it was set to maximum volts.

'Vincent?' I had said, stepping out of the shadows. He turned to look my way and I lunged forward and fired the taser. It was interesting to watch the shock in his eyes as his whole body began to convulse, causing the pallets to shake with him, as his body responded to the massive voltage plummeting through his system. He collapsed in a heap on the floor.

I didn't have long, mere seconds to get him completely incapacitated before he recovered and came at me. Bugger, I hadn't thought this through properly. I quickly checked the room in panic, looking for something to subdue him and protect myself.

I knew I couldn't keep tasering the bastard. In the corner of the room, I found a metal wheelbarrow full of old cooking equipment, ceramic bowls, a toaster, sandwich maker, coffee machine and a kettle.

'Poor Vincent,' I whispered, as I put the taser away and took out the silver cigar cutter.

'It's not nice being out of control, is it?' I tutted, shaking my head. I watched his eyes plead with me. Too late, Vincent, you started this years ago.

In less than a minute his body began to settle back to normal, he started to flail, as the cigar cutter flew from my fingers onto the hard floor. Kicking out with as much force as he could muster, he shouted, 'Get off me!' I shuffled backward, momentarily stunned. Shit. I was fast losing control of the situation.

I hadn't counted on his strength coming back so soon, as he grabbed my hand and pulled me forward over him, causing me to trip over one of his feet. Fuck. This is not what I had planned.

Throwing my hands out to protect my fall, I heard movement behind me. Turning quickly, I came face to face with an angry, unsteady Vincent Camprinelli.

'I'm going to kill you!' He shouted, as spittle came out of his mouth.

Stepping backwards, I tried to keep him distracted. 'You wish, you pathetic little shit.' I spat at him, 'Do you know who I am?'

My knees hit the back of the wheelbarrow, and he lunged for me. 'I don't give a fuck who you are!' he shouted, lunging at me. I reached out behind me and grabbed the first thing from the barrow that came to hand.

'Well, that's a shame,' I said, with the heavy metal kettle in my hand, just as his hand reached my face within a hairs whisper, I bring the kettle smashing down on his head.

He looks momentarily stunned, before he crashed to the floor.

Then, it was time to finish what I came here to do. I found the silver cigar cutter on the floor, picked up Vincent's right hand and placed the cutter in position over his little finger – near his knuckle and slice the digit off. Leaving it on the floor.

I reached into his jeans pocket and found his phone. Throwing it in the direction of the finger.

For some reason, I didn't finish the job, didn't use the wire to slice into his neck. For some reason, I emptied the wheelbarrow and haul Vincent Camprinelli inside it, grabbed the bloody silver cigar cutter and returned it to my pocket, before taking him back to the car.

It is always best when they don't see you coming.

Part Nineteen: Lottie

'I bet you five pounds, that she'll quit before the weekend is out?' Jack says with a smile before taking a large sip of red wine. He hasn't changed in all the time I've known him, apart from the way he worships Steph and Ben, his wife and her son.

Harley and Ben sit next to each other, roll their eyes and smirk. The boys have met several times at family gatherings and get on well together.

Jack notices and picks Ben up on it, 'What? I'm just saying.'

The boys openly laugh, and it warms my heart to hear Harley enjoying himself. He was always trying to look after me, as the man of the house. I guess because it has been just the two of us since Simon died, he's had to grow up fast. It is good to see him being a child again.

'Oh, I don't know,' Jenny says, looking up to check that Mrs Monk has left the room. She had managed to persuade Mrs Monk to help with serving the meal tonight. Jenny aims to serve the starters which is pea and mint soup with a fresh, crusty roll and butter, or homemade chicken liver pate, chutney and toast. Mrs Monk will then serve the main of beef bourguignon, dauphinoise potatoes and fresh greens. Followed by a selection of mini sponges and tarts.

Jenny looks her usual elegant self in her soft pink top, grey trousers and flat shoes. Silver flamingos dangle from her ears, jiggling as she ladles soup into a bowl from a large serving pot. She places it carefully next to the large bowl of bread rolls and individual butter dishes, by Steph. She looks at Jack before slowly letting her gaze move around the table.

'Monsieur Durand seems to have a soft spot for our Mrs Monk,' Jenny says in a low voice.

I look across at Daniel and our eyes meet. He raises an eyebrow and for some reason unknown to anyone at the table, I suddenly burst out laughing.

'Jen,' Stuart's deep voice admonishes her softly, 'You are not to attempt any matchmaking during this holiday.'

'So, she'll either leave or fall into the arms of our temperamental chef?' Noah stretches his hand across the table, mindful of the wine glasses and Jem places her hand over his and smiles.

'My money is on her falling…We all know what that's like!' Noah laughs, and everyone at the table erupts into laughter.

The small white Shih Tzu joins in with a few short barks, and Brian sets his soup spoon in his bowl before leaning down to pet the dog's head. The sound of Edie's soft snoring filters through on the portable baby monitor that is set on the sideboard facing Jem. Upon hearing the noise, she immediately looks at the screen to see if her young daughter settles again. She does. The happy table of people before me, is a stark reminder to make more of my life, rather than simply working.

The evening continues with lively conversation as my friends converse about every topic under the sun, until I look at the clock and realise that it's 10pm and time for Harley to head to bed. I kiss my son briefly on the top of his head, and like many young boys of his age, he shrugs, and his cheeks begin to redden, as he utters the word 'Mum!'

Ben follows Harley up the stairs to his own room, while Noah heads to their room to check on Edie. Jenny and I chat about the

Lighthouse Support Group celebration tomorrow night, and I explain that Daniel has asked to be my plus one. Collecting the last pile of dessert plates from the dining table, I make my way behind Jenny, into the kitchen. As we fill the dishwasher with our used crockery, the only sound is the clinking of plates as they settle into their slotted places and the distant babble of conversation.

Jenny looks at me and raises her eyebrow in query, she asks, 'So, are you and Daniel finally going to get it together?'

'I don't know Jen,' I shake my head, as I roll my neck to ease an ache. 'It's just one night.'

'Oh please…' Jenny smiles, adding a tablet to the dishwasher and setting it on a wash cycle.

I smile at the woman who has been my best friend for so many years. She knows me better than I know myself. Our worlds have collided and been in tune for more years than I can remember.

A cough alerts us that we are no longer alone. Stuart lingers in the doorway, tall and slim in black chinos and a white shirt, open at the neck. He rakes a hand through his hair, a gesture he sometimes uses when he has something on his mind.

'Are you two ready for a brandy? We're in the sitting room,' he states, moving forward and taking Jenny's hand. He pulls her forward and as I move next to him his arm drapes loosely around my shoulder, like he used to do occasionally many moons ago. 'Leave what's here and we'll do it in the morning, when Mrs Monk arrives.'

The group in the sitting room are chatting casually until we enter the room. That is the first indication that something is wrong, and a shiver runs down my spine. Steph and Jack sit on a small dark green sofa, looking extremely comfortable together and still in the

145

throes of early marital life. In contrast, Brian, Jem and Julie, are seated, facing Daniel on the formal velvet green sofas that you only see in Jane Austen films.

Stuart gestures for us both to sit. Jenny moves across the room and joins Daniel on the sofa. I feel a little uneasy, something feels wrong.

'What's going on?' I ask, worry making my voice slightly croaky. Alarm bells begin to pound softly in my ears and my legs feel heavy as I make my way to the sofa and sit in the remaining space next to Daniel. I am acutely aware of the significant change in atmosphere, gone is the fun and laughter and in its place sits a heavy silence.

'We need to talk,' Stuart begins, dropping to half-sit on the arm of our sofa. He rubs his hands together before continuing. 'There's no easy way of saying this, so I'm just going to say it.'

Stuart looks directly at me, and I can feel people watching me as I wait patiently for him to speak.

Have you noticed that in heightened situations, that time seems to stop? That as you wait with bated breath, a minute feels like an hour.

'Remember the night that you came to the hotel and told Jenny about what had happened to you when you were fifteen?' Stuart asks.

And there it is. The past has finally caught up with me. My free hand goes to my mouth and a grey mist begins to seep its way through my brain. A dark memory, that's been locked away for a long time.

'Yes,' I whisper, remembering the last time I saw my cousin. His uncaring face staring at the kitchen floor, because he couldn't look at me. Couldn't face what he and his friends had done. I remember the hate that coursed through my veins, holding me upright, keeping me from crumbling in front of him. I wouldn't give him the satisfaction.

'Yes,' Stuart turns to look at Julie, before turning his attention to Brian and then finally to Jenny. He continues. 'Well, following that conversation, I contacted Julie and asked for her help.'

I stare at our friend. I can't believe that she knows about what went on that night. About the assault, even now I struggle to say the word 'rape.' It wasn't something I wanted to be associated with. Because if it was, that makes me a victim. I certainly didn't want others to know of my humiliating experience at the hands of my cousin and his friends.

Julie's voice breaks into my erratic thoughts, as she continues the story. 'I did some digging and found them. Cameron Frost, Vincent Camprinelli and Eric Weston were put under unofficial surveillance.'

There is a loud buzzing in my head and I want the world to stop and let me lie down in a quiet, darkened room.

A frisson of panic shoots along my shoulders, and I turn to Daniel. His eyes are questioning, I think he's hearing this for the first time too. He reaches down and puts a warm hand on my jean clad thigh. I stare at it, fixated at our connection.

'Unofficial surveillance. What does that mean exactly?' I ask Julie. Why do I get the feeling that there is going to be a big 'but' tagged onto the end of this statement somewhere?

'We did something,' Stuart's deep voice echoes through the silent room. 'It was time to make a bold statement. Time to make the bastards pay for what they did to you.'

'Jenny?' I stare at my closest friend, suddenly feeling old and very weary. All these years I have been focusing on moving forward and making new memories. Only to find that the past won't leave me alone. It is always there. Waiting.

'Tell me what you did,' I say to Julie quietly, dreading the words I am about to hear.

Julie looks to Brian, waits for him to nod. Jesus, what the hell happened? What did they do?

'We kidnapped them,' she says simply.

'Of course, they didn't know who we were because we were wearing masks.' Julie's face is devoid of colour as she tells me about that fateful night in the disused cash and carry.

'Kidnapped them! And, who's 'we'?' My voice rises. 'Why the hell would you do that?'

'Myself, Brian and Julie.' Stuart says, in a harsh tone. 'Because we needed them to understand that what they did was wrong!' Stuart raises his voice. 'They fucking drugged you, Lottie.'

Jenny puts a hand on Stuart's arm to calm him. He gently puts a hand on top of hers.

'Not to mention the other thing,' Julie cuts in, looking everywhere but not at me.

'You can say it, you know,' I say quietly to everyone. 'I won't fall apart.'

But even as I say the words, I lower my head. I cannot look at them. They are my closest friends, closer than family even. They know my deepest, darkest secrets and I am ashamed. If I had pretended it had never happened, it might have been easier, but up until this very moment, I had believed that only Jenny, Daniel and Stuart knew my secret.

'Did you go too?' I ask Jenny. Why do I suddenly feel so cold? My shoulders start to shiver, and I feel Daniel's hand lift from my thigh as he brings a firm, strong arm across my shoulder, cupping it with a warm hand.

'No,' she says softly, shaking her blonde hair.

Rubbing my hands together to warm them and get the circulation going, I realise that hearing that Jenny didn't go makes me feel less betrayed. Although she was the catalyst, she didn't know that they would take matters into their own hands.

'We just roughed them up, Lottie,' Brian cuts in, leaning forward and resting his forearms on his knees, 'It's no more than they deserved. They should have gone to prison for what they did.'

Stuart pushes to his feet and walks solemnly across the room, shoulders slumped as though he is carrying a heavy weight., He stops a few feet away from me. 'We didn't know if they would hurt other women.' His eyes focus on mine. 'We wanted to send them a warning, to make them think twice.'

Mirroring Stuart's movements, I gently disengage Daniel's arm from my shoulder and push myself into a standing position, where I take the two steps to meet Stuart. My anger subsides slightly as I look at his dear, concerned face. I know that he would do anything to protect his family, and that I have the honour of being included within that group.

He is taller than me, and I strain to meet his eyes.

'I'm sorry,' he says, gently putting his hands on my shoulders. 'Really sorry, for raking this up for you.'

'Stu,' how can I be angry with him? He was trying to put right a wrong, trying to protect me. Apart from Simon, Stuart and Jenny are the only people who would step up for me. We were not blood related, but we might just as well have been. Because they are like a brother and sister to me, and whatever challenges we have faced, we have done it together.

'You did what you thought was right, you wanted to protect me. And, for that, I will always be grateful.' I wrap my arms around his torso and hold him tight. 'So grateful,' my voice is husky with emotion as I kiss the warm skin of his cheek.

I remember that night in the hotel so vividly, as though it were yesterday. It was supposed to be about Jenny. Supporting her through her terrible ordeal, making sure she had someone to lean on, but Jenny is stronger than all of us. She turned it around, she knew something was wrong, and before I knew it, a five-year-old deep, dark secret, which I had sworn never to reveal to anyone, began unravelling from my reluctant lips.

And, like all things that have been kept firmly hidden, ignored and unwanted, it began to weigh me down. I didn't realise until I'd told Jenny every last detail from the night of the party just how much weight that secret was carrying. Until my shoulders lifted and I began to relax.

Jenny's quiet sobbing in the background, makes me look up and in two long strides we are in each other's arms. 'I'm sorry Lottie,' she whispers softly in my ear. 'We never intended you to find out, but...'

She stops talking and Brian unfolds his tall frame from the sofa, walks over to the dog and pets it on its ears.

'Yes, there is a but, I'm afraid,' he turns to the group, and I'm suddenly reminded of the JB Priestley novel, An Inspector Calls, with its web of lies and intrigue.

Jenny and I disperse, leaning against the nearby marble mantlepiece.

'Did you know that the three young men, who drugged you, including your cousin, were known locally as the Three Amigos?' Brian asks, pushing his hands deep into brown chino pockets.

Shaking my head, I whisper, 'No.'

Brian glances at Julie, his eyebrows draw together. 'Their reputation was one of heavy drinking, fast driving, charismatic guys. The women loved them.'

'Jesus!' I say, this is unbelievable, so far-fetched.

'Anyway, two days ago one of the Three Amigos was attacked and subsequently died, in a dog walking field, near the village of East Hagbourne.'

Holding my breath, I wonder if it was my cousin. 'Who was it?' I ask quietly.

'Eric Weston,' Brian replies flatly.

'Oh...' I'm not sure how this news makes me feel. They were all guilty, but my cousin, Cameron, was by far the worst in my eyes. He passed the line. He let me down. Badly.

Brian looks to his wife, once more for reassurance. Waits for her encouraging nod, before breaking the silence. 'And today I received a call from Gino Camprinelli to say that his nephew, Vincent, has gone missing. That's number two.'

'Holy Fuck!' Daniel's soft Scottish brogue becomes harsh. 'Is someone taking out the three lads?'

'Well, it's not me, if that's what you're thinking,' I say, with false bravado, trying to lighten the situation. What the hell is going on? Daniel's gaze catches mine and he looks annoyed, with drawn brows and a scowl that is so unlike the man I know. I've spent many hours talking through my attack with him, the bits that I remember, and he always kept a level head, his eyes never wavered. Until now.

'The fuckers,' Daniel's voice is harsh as he leans forward, resting his arms on his knees and grasping his hands together so hard that his knuckles pale. 'They can all rot in hell for what they did to you.'

'Daniel!' I whisper. I have never met this protective side of Daniel before, only the professional one, and although I'm taken aback by his emotion, his language, my heart flutters in response to his words and protectiveness.

'Of course, it's not you,' Brian says, his voice hard, 'but you are a crucial part of the puzzle that links this together.'

Jem has been quiet throughout the whole conversation, as always, she prefers to listen and process everything that is being said. She pushes wayward curls from her eyes, clasps her hands together and speaks, 'You had better tell them about the rat.'

For a moment, I had completely forgotten about the gift this morning. It feels like a lifetime ago when I found the box on my doorstep. The note with my name on it. There is someone out there sending me gruesome gifts and messages. So much for a short break to recharge my batteries and chill out. Something tells me that these few days away, are not going to go the way I had hoped.

A sudden movement in the open doorway, forces the group to look in that direction. Noah stands there, tall and handsome with his mop of unruly hair, and wearing a burgundy zip neck jumper which sits over navy jeans. He oozes confidence and genuine curiosity. 'Rat?' He asks in a deep voice. 'What rat?'

Yes, it's going to be a long night.

Part Twenty: Jenny

I study my beloved husband. He has always been the strong one. Like me, he empathises and cares about the people in our lives and communities, he wants to do good in the world. Wants to make a difference. That's why we started the Lighthouse Charity. To make the Gloverman Corporation give back to communities, to those who are vulnerable and in need of care and safety.

We have come through so much together.

I wanted to find somewhere neutral to talk to him about Judy and our conversation. Somewhere away from the hustle and bustle of the Manor House. A friend of mine had mentioned about a lovely garden centre in Blewbury, they had a nice café called Style Acre, which enables young people with learning disabilities to work and be independent. What a wonderful idea. I can feel a seed of an idea forming already in my busy brain.

Stuart sips his cappuccino and I smile, when the froth and chocolate stick to his upper lip. I gently reach out to wipe it away with my thumb, and just as I'm about to withdraw my hand, he takes it carefully and brings it to his lips.

'God, you're beautiful!' he says in a low, husky voice. He looks dashing in a navy and white checked shirt and jeans.

I smile. I will never tire of his compliments, of the way he's never afraid to show he cares. Of how effortless he makes loving me seem. We are sitting in an enclosed gazebo next to the café, and quite alone.

'Stu,' I whisper, stroking his lightly whiskered cheek with my fingers.

'Yes, love,' he asks, his smile fades and his brows draw together. 'Is something wrong?'

'Yes, and no.' I say cryptically. This is harder than I thought it. 'Remember Judy, she stayed at Shore House for a year? She has six-year-old twin girls, Amy and Anna. Her partner was a drug addict, sold a lot of their stuff to feed his habit. Then became violent toward her and the girls.'

He clenches his fist, as I talk. I know he remembers.

'Yes, I do. Bloody idiot, getting himself stuck on the hard stuff.' He answers, with a grim smile, shaking his head.

I wrap my hands around the warm latte mug. 'Judy has stage four breast cancer. She hasn't got very long to live. It's heart-breaking.'

He reaches out and covers my warm hands with his. 'I'm so sorry. Poor woman. Poor girls, after everything they've been through, and now they're going to lose their mum.'

'That's the thing, Stu,' I look from our connected hands to his handsome, angular face. Hazel eyes hold mine, making my heart flutter. We say nothing for a moment. Savouring the peace, before I say the words. Taking a deep breath, I break the silence. 'She wants us to have the girls.'

My husband closes his eyes and pulls his hands away from mine. I can almost hear his mind ticking away, trying to take in my words.

Not quite the reaction I was hoping for. I try not to get disheartened. He needs time to process this.

'Both maternal and paternal families have disowned her and the girls. They've had no contact since she moved away. Judy is adamant that she wants us to be her children's new parents. It is her dying wish.' My words rush out, and although I've had time to take in the magnitude of what is being asked of us, it still seems surreal.

Stuart's eyes open, and he reaches out to wipe away an unchecked stray tear that rests on my cheek. 'It's a big ask from Judy, but I get why she's asked us.' His voice is husky. 'I have always wanted children, we both have. But I also knew that if children never happened, that we would be enough. That you are enough to give my life meaning.'

Tears fall heavily down my face, and I blink several times to unblur my vision, as I listen to his declaration. In one quick movement he is out of his chair and by my side. Taking me by the hand, my husband pulls me gently to my feet. 'It was always you, Jenny,' he says resting his forehead against mine. 'From the moment I walked into that cafeteria at Bournemouth university, I knew it was you.'

Closing my eyes, I inhale deeply. The sandalwood and pine aftershave soothes my senses. Stuart is my world, I would not have survived the kidnap and rape, without him and Lottie to bring me back to life.

'What do you want, Jen? Do you want to take the girls and bring them up as our own, in Judy's memory?' These heartfelt questions are raw, bringing out the maternal instinct in me to protect Amy and Anna as much as I can. To want to give them a home, to love them, watch them grow and help to shape their lives. To experience firsthand what parenting is really like. The ups and the downs. Until being faced with this dilemma, I hadn't realised how much I would love the chance to have children join our family unit. It would complete us.

'Yes, Stu. Yes. I want us to have them. I want to love them as our own. To experience what it is like to be a family with children.' I rest my hand on his heart and smile. 'What about you?' I ask, 'this isn't something we can just take on and change our minds about when the going gets rough.'

He pulls me close, and wraps his arms around my tall, slender frame.

'I want that too,' he whispers against my ear. His voice gets louder, 'through the good times and bad times, through the pain and the sorrow.'

These are the words I've been waiting for. I'm so full of love for this man that I snake my arms around his neck and pull his face down to me. Bringing his warm lips home to mine.

After the kiss, we pull apart and Stuart caresses my cheek softly with his fingers, before sitting down again. I mirror my husband's actions, retaking my seat and putting both hands around my mug, to take welcome sips of my warm, sweet latte.

'I told Judy that we'll go down next week,' I tell him in between sips, 'and talk some more. Start the paperwork etc. It's going to be so hard watching her fight this awful disease. Especially hard for the girls. We're going to need to spend more time with them. Help them through this. All of them.'

Stuart nods.

We each take mouthfuls of our lukewarm drinks, and Stu's upper lip settles into a cappuccino froth moustache. I smile, he's my man and he won't change.

'Fuck, Jen!' he says, giving me a wink. 'We are going to become parents!'

Part Twenty-One: Ferret

Clothes are strewn everywhere across my bedroom. It's a real mess. One day, I'll tidy up. But for now, I need to get to the pool. Quickly I shimmy into my long-sleeved swim top and boy shorts, in the background, the deep husky sound of Bruce Springsteen, singing Tougher than the rest, sounds from the Echo dot.

Pulling black jeans over my swim stuff, I throw a long, loose black top over my head and step into flip flops. I'm about to grab my swim bag, when a heavy thud comes from the lounge, stopping me in my tracks. It sounds like a sack of potatoes has been dropped from a height on to the floor, followed by the sound of an animal howling in pain.

I rush into the living room. 'For God's sake', I shout, louder than I intend to as I negotiate clothes and mugs on the carpeted floor. 'What is it now, Vincent?'

The sight before me is almost comical. The 'pet' had somehow fallen headfirst onto the floor, his back faces me, rigid and his bottom is in the air. By the shape of him, he is still trussed with rope, like an oven ready chicken.

'What do you think you're doing?' I lean down and haul his heavy shoulders up onto the sofa and push him back into place. It's not easy. He's a dead weight.

'Ow!' he says loudly, like an angry teenager. He looks weak today. My eyes move to his injured finger, it's still bandaged, but amid the dark blood patches, there is fresh red blood there. Bugger, it should have stopped by now.

I should have killed him when I had the chance, slit his throat and be done with it. He doesn't deserve my pity.

'Ferret, why are you doing this?' His eyes search mine, 'I know I did wrong, but I've apologised.'

Focusing on his lips, my words reflect the dark bitterness within my soul. 'You think an apology is enough? For what you did to me? For ruining my life?' I pull the arms of my jumper up, dragging up the sleeve of my swim top too, 'you think these marks made themselves? I am the person I am today, because of what you and your bastard friends did to me.'

His face drops, faces the floor. He is finally beginning to understand what he and his friends did.

'I'm sorry.' He says, with feeling. Remorse in its rawest forms. We make a striking combination, a man with nothing left to lose, and a woman with nothing left to live for.

My heart begins to thud rapidly, and my head starts to pound. This was something I never expected, never thought possible. An apology. Is it genuine? Or just because he thinks I'm going to kill him?

'I hardly remember the night,' he continues, staring at the floor. His good hand clasps his injured hand, 'I never wanted to do it. Cameron bought the drugs. Eric and me, we should have stopped him, but we were too wasted, and did what Cam told us. We always did what Cam bloody told us.'

There is anger in his voice. I don't move. Allow him to talk. He needs to work through this.

'What are you going to do with me?' he asks quietly.

'I'm not sure,' I push my hands deep into the pockets of my jeans and pace the short distance from the sofa to the window. 'It depends,' I shouldn't have said that, when it's so obviously a lie. Of course, I'm going to kill him, I just haven't decided when, yet. Nothing too bloody, I don't want the hassle of cleaning the carpet. A thought comes into my head, I have always wanted to see what happens when you shove a screwdriver into a person's eye. Is that enough to kill them? Do they die instantly? I'll have to experiment.

'It stinks in here. You stink.' I look at him, before walking across the room to open a window.

'My uncle Gino will have people looking for me,' Vincent closes his eyes and leans his head back against the black sofa, 'he's a powerful and violent man.'

'Is he now?' Sarcasm drips from my tongue, 'Shame he didn't teach you some manners.'

'It's no joke,' he looks at me, eyebrows drawn together. 'He will kill you in your sleep and still go and enjoy a three-course meal afterwards.'

'Oh, shut the fuck up, will you. You're giving me a headache!' I snap, I can't hear myself think.

Moving to the kitchen, I run cold water into a glass and grab a box of paracetamol.

I'm about to walk back to the 'pet', when my phone begins to belt out, Meatloaf's 'I would do anything for love.' I know it's my mum calling. I can almost hear her sobbing hysterically on the other side of the line. I walk to the lounge and hand Vincent the glass of water and paracetamol. As soon as he takes them from me, I return to the kitchen area for some privacy. Then taking a deep breath, I answer.

'Hey Mum, what's up?' I ask, forcing my voice to be calm. I don't want to get into an argument with her, not today. Staring into the sink, I answer cautiously.

'Hi sweetie, how are you? Haven't heard from you for a few days.'

Taking a deep breath, I can't help but roll my eyes. She's always fussing. 'I've been busy that's all.'

'Busy? Doing what?' she asks, persistently.

'Oh, nothing really, this and that,' I say, knowing that my lack of information will make her frustrated, angry even. I just can't help it though, what I do is none of her business. Whatever time I have left on this godforsaken earth is going to be done on my terms from now on.

'This and that?' Mum repeats, her voice wavering with worry, 'what does that mean?'

I open the kitchen drawer, the one with the cutlery and odd gadgets that don't fit elsewhere. The brown handled Phillips screwdriver stares back at me next to the cheap silver knives. I take it out, place it on the grey countertop and stroke the cold hard metal. 'It means, I've been busy. Now, I need to get to the pool, so I'll call you soon.' I disconnect the call, grab my keys from the nearby table and without giving my unwanted guest a second glance, I open the front door and make my way to the car.

I really need a swim.

Part Twenty-Two: Lottie

Looking into the gold framed, free standing mirror in my bedroom, I'm stunned at the woman's reflection. She doesn't look like me. Not like the woman who usually stares back at me when I quickly glance in the hall mirror on my way out of the door. The one who is happy to be invisible.

This dress hasn't been worn since my honeymoon with Simon. It is midnight blue silk with matching lace at the neck and short sleeves. It tapers in gently at the waist, which is good because I've added a few inches in that direction since I got married. The dress drops in an A-line shape almost to my ankles, just allowing me to walk in flats without tripping myself up as I move.

To give myself some extra cover, I slip on a longline lace cardigan the type you wear at the beach and move to the bed to find lipstick and mascara from my handbag.

'You look nice,' Harley stands at the open doorway to my room. In jeans and a zip hoodie, with his trademark, short, auburn brown hair he reminds me of the little boy who used to toddle around my legs when I was in the garden pegging out the washing. Giggling and holding onto my legs with joy, his laughter filling the garden with bubbling happiness. It brings back such lovely memories.

'Thanks honey,' I smile, without moving. 'You going to be all right here with Noah, Jem and the others?'

'Yeah, don't worry. We're going to go for a dip in the pool. Julie says she won't bother though, she will just read her kindle.' He moves to sit on the bed.

***

I think of earlier today, when Julie, Jenny and I had been into the Orchard Centre in Didcot, to catch up over a coffee and cake and check out the shops. Julie had stopped several times to use the bathroom, not to mention the sudden need to drink decaffeinated coffee.

On arriving back at the house in Sutton Courtenay Julie had suddenly felt tired and announced that she was going to her room for a rest.

Jenny and I had taken our friend to her bedroom and asked the question that had been on our minds since she had arrived. All three of us had sat on the bed, and I waited for Jenny to speak:

'Julie,' Jenny had begun, putting her hands on our friend's shoulders, 'do you think that there is any chance that you could be pregnant?'

The look of shock on Julie's face had clearly meant that she hadn't.

'Pregnant? Jesus, no... of course not,' Julie's face had lost all colour.

'When did you last have your period?' I asked.

Julie had looked at us both, 'But I can't be. I've never been regular... bloody hell it must have been two months.' She had put her hand over her mouth in complete shock.

I sat down beside her and put a comforting arm around her shaking shoulders. 'First thing, though. We need to get you a pregnancy test!'

***

Harley walks to my side, and surprises me by putting a hand on my shoulder. 'Love you Mum, enjoy tonight.'

My heart swells and I hug my son close. 'Ah, thanks Har. I love you too,' I reply, as I turn to kiss his forehead.

'One thing, though. Make sure Daniel behaves himself!' My son is a force to be reckoned with since his father died. 'Don't worry,' I laugh, 'I will make sure he does.'

Leaving those words echoing through the room, my son saunters away to let me finish getting ready for the celebration. Jesus, what was that about?

An hour later, and I am standing at the white four pillared entrance of the Milton Hill House, a country house hotel near Abingdon. Daniel is by my side. I am excited but nervous. Maybe I shouldn't have worn a dress that I wore on my honeymoon to another man. A vision of my beloved Simon fills my senses, and my eyes blur. Perhaps this is a mistake? Maybe it is too soon.

'Are you OK?' Daniel asks quietly, his soft Scottish accent sending warmth across my shoulders.

I give him a quick glance. He looks handsome in his smart navy blazer, white open-necked shirt and navy chinos. Offering a smile, 'I'm fine.' I say quietly.

A warm hand gently touches the small of my back, making me gasp. 'Let's do this,' Daniel's words are decisive as though he knows that tonight and being here with him is a big deal for me,

We follow the directions to the Lighthouse Refuge Support Celebration event, and meet Jenny and Stuart, who came earlier, in a separate taxi. 'Boy, are we glad to see you,' I say, kissing them both lightly on the cheek. I look around the room, there must be about sixty people here, or more. Tables are laid out in groups of six and there is a stage. Along the far wall is a buffet laden with all manner of finger food. Silver balloons with the number fifteen in gold are strewn about the room.

Jenny is wearing a burgundy velvet ankle-length dress with a V drop at the front, complimenting Stuart's white shirt, black trousers and burgundy jacket. Jenny reaches to take my hand, 'Come,' she says, drawing me forward, 'they've set up a table for us.'

As I walk, I absently reach out behind me and someone takes my hand, linking warm fingers through mine, and instinctively I know it is Daniel. Glancing back, I offer a quick smile. This evening is promising to be a very good one indeed.

Once we're seated, Daniel and Stuart leave Jen and I to chat, while they go in search of drinks.

'Well?' Jen nudges me gently.

'Well? What?' I shrug, smiling.

'How's it going?' Jen asks smiling.

'We've only just got here, Jen,' I wince, taking my bag and reapplying my lipstick.

'You look very comfortable together, though,' she says.

'We are,' I smile, 'very, it's just still very new and we need to see where it goes, if anywhere.'

She laughs out loud, before pulling me into a long hug. This is going to be interesting. It's hard enough starting a new relationship without being closely observed by your nearest and dearest. Still, I feel invigorated and ready to start a new chapter. Harley has been supportive of me moving forward, from his dad's passing for the past four years, so there is every reason for me to start living my life properly again.

The men return and the lights dim, with someone moving onto the stage. A woman I don't know. She is stunning, very tall and slender, with a sleek ink black, shoulder length bob. Her purple jewelled top and long black skirt accentuates her long limbs. We watch as people slowly make their way to their seats and a large spotlight focuses on the stage.

The woman's voice, when she speaks, is surprisingly deep and melodic. 'Hello everyone. For those who don't know me, I'm Karis Price and I run the Lighthouse Refuge Support Group.'

I glance at Jenny, take in her smile and the glistening at the corner of her eyes. This was our baby. Mine, Jenny and Stuart. We started this together, a place of love and respect where people can talk about their experiences of violence. Where they can hear other's stories and know that they are not alone, that you can be found, even if you've been lost for a long time.

'This charity began as a simple support group some fifteen years ago, and has so far helped over five thousand, women, children and men to talk about what they have been through and to listen to other's stories. Most of these stories are horrific. Some scars will never heal, but we hope that the Lighthouse Refuge Support Group will continue to benefit those people who need us most, for many years to come.'

I feel a lump in my throat, and Daniel, forever the protector, puts his hand over mine on the table and holds it tight.

'I cannot tell you how happy, and grateful I am to see the three people who started this group, here tonight for our celebration,' Karis smiles and gestures to our table, and to my horror, the spotlight moves to us. We give embarrassed smiles and wave to the audience.

'To that end, I would like to ask Jenny Greyson, Stuart Greyson and Charlotte Forster to join me on the stage.'

Oh my God, this was not expected. No! No! No! My friends push their chairs back and stand with elegance and dignity. Stuart takes Jenny's hand and brings it to his lips.

They look at me and I shake my head, to indicate that I don't want to go.

'Come, Lottie. This was your dream too. To help others,' Jen leans down, studies my face intently, before reaching down to take my hand. Before I know what is happening, I am being half-dragged across to the stage with my old friends, trying not to trip over my dress and I can feel my cheeks burning. The applause is almost deafening. Chair legs scrape across the vast wooden floor as people rise to their feet and offer a standing ovation.

Emotion is a funny thing, you feel happy and overwhelmed and offer the biggest smiles, but it is daunting. I remember why we started the group, the pain, the anguish that seeps through every pore, the shame and anger. Emotions that cause you to slump and want to become invisible one day and stand tall the next. To fight on and show yourself that you are more than a victim. You are a warrior. You will fight.

When we reach the stage, I stop and look over my shoulder to Daniel. He looks genuinely pleased that we three are being recognised for our part in starting this group. There is the slightest nod, to let me know that I can do this. I am not like Jenny. I haven't had to take over a huge group like the Gloverman Corporation. Or address twenty people in a room, to develop projects, monitor expenditure and make million-pound decisions. But I'm pretty sure that I can do this. I take a deep breath and take Stuart's outstretched hand and allow him to help me up the five steps to the stage. Karis waits for people to resume their seats before speaking into the microphone.

'Ladies and gentlemen, I give you Jenny Greyson, one of our Trustees, the CEO of the Gloverman Corporation and her husband, Stuart, the founders of the fabulous Lighthouse Charity.' Karis opens her arms to gesture to Jenny and Stuart, before stepping to the back of the stage.

Wiping tears with the back of my hand, I clap for Jenny, watching as she steps to the microphone.

'Good evening,' Jenny begins. Her confidence has grown significantly in the last fifteen years.

'I am so pleased to be here with my husband, and close friend, Charlotte Forster, to share this moment with you tonight.' She gestures to Stuart and me to come closer, and we do, protecting her as we always do. 'It was through our own experiences that Lottie and I, with the help of Stuart began this support group fifteen years ago. This was our first step to recovery, talking about what we had been through and listening to others. It really helped because for many of us, we realised for the first time, that we were not alone.'

'I look around the room and see some familiar faces, particularly from those early days. Amongst this sea of faces I know that many of you will have had similar experiences to those that Lottie and I had, or worse.'

'It would be great if you could raise your hands if you have been helped by the Lighthouse Refuge Support Group through one way or another.' Jenny pauses, and I stand still, holding my breath. Gosh, this is intense. I feel open and raw, standing here on this makeshift stage, with so many people surrounding us, most of whom I don't know. But they sit here and listen intently to Jenny, because she is confident, charismatic and because she is strong. I gently bite my bottom lip.

The Invisible Ones

Looking into the darkness of the audience, where the shadows of people sit at tables, or stand at the back of the room, near the food, I stand rigid and wait, to see if anyone will be brave enough to respond.

The silence stretches into the room, consuming everything, and then, I feel a huge lump in my throat as hands begin to rise within the room. Not just one hand, but many, many hands, rising and telling us their story. Telling us that they understand.

And, then one by one, people, mostly women but some men, shuffle out of their chairs and begin to stand. A sea of people standing and nodding. Some people even begin to smile. The clap, when it begins is singular and turns into a symphony of beautiful claps and cheers.

Wow, I am overwhelmed by this charge of emotion and celebration within the room. I really wasn't expecting anything like this to happen. I look at Daniel, who is also standing, he lifts a hand to his lips and blows me a kiss. It is too much. I put a hand to my mouth and stifle a sob.

Jenny pulls away from the microphone, there are rivers of tears rolling down her cheeks and I am so proud of her, so bloody proud. I pull her into my arms and whisper, 'we did that, we helped those people.'

Quietly pulling away, Jenny returns to the microphone and says in a husky voice, 'Thank you for your honesty, and thank you for taking those first steps to work through your experiences. It is a long road, and it isn't easy, but despite everything we can come out the other side. Even if our demons try to haunt our dreams. We fight back. We don't let them win.'

Slowly the applause stops and seats are retaken, to enable us to move forward with the event.

Karis steps out of the shadows and gently moves us back a few places.

'One of our major success stories is Francesca, who came to us at fourteen, following a very harrowing experience. She is here tonight and wants to say thank you to you.'

Out of the shadows of the wings of the stage, a young woman emerges. She is beautiful, graceful and almost glides across the floor. Black hair with a slight wave falls to her shoulders, and as though she has stepped out of a forties silent film with Fred Astaire. She moves closer to us, the long-sleeved, pale blue silk gown she is wearing, swaying as she walks.

I am mesmerised.

Francesca stops and looks behind us. In turn, I turn to see Stuart and Daniel have left their seats at our table and are now each holding a huge bunch of flowers. Stuart steps forward, confidently takes the steps to the stage offers the flowers to Francesca. Daniel follows closely behind, moving onto the stage. Francesca smiles steps closer to take the flowers from Stuart. She turns to Jenny and offers them to her, her movements calm and graceful.

'Thank you so much, Jenny.' Her voice is deeper than expected. 'For all that you've done and continue to do.'

Francesca acknowledges Daniel and takes the flowers from him, before turning my way and handing them to me. It is a very touching gesture. 'Thank you, Lottie.' She touches my hand briefly and our eyes make contact as my arm is filled with beautiful flowers.

Standing before the microphone, Francesca clears her throat, before speaking. Her voice is thick with emotion.

'Four years ago, I was a typical happy go lucky young teenager. I messed around with my friends, enjoyed art, dancing, and English, until that fateful night I went out drinking with friends. Then everything changed and I wasn't the same person anymore. I had scars, both inside and out.

My world became so dark, I thought the light would never come back. And, then my mum found the Lighthouse Refuge Support Group, and I began to crawl out of the darkness.'

Her words touch me, and I quickly push away a stray tear.

'Thank you, Jenny and Stuart Greyson. Thank you, Lottie Forster. Like many others, you saved my life.'

This has been a night of touching moments and tributes. A night that I will remember for a very long time.

The applause echoes in our ears as Stuart and Daniel lead us from the stage, we lay our flowers on the table and enjoy the rest of the evening. A raffle follows the delicious three course meal, and I can't help but think how much Jenny and Stuart deserve to win the main prize of a weekend for four in a lodge on one of the UK Centerparcs sites. He looks happy and chilled, more so than usual.

I am so pleased to be invited to this wonderful celebration. Over the years it is easy to forget the small, but significant parts you play in life's rich and complicated tapestry.

There is a band playing, and people are dancing. The band is good, two men are playing guitars, one on the drums and a female lead singer.

'Want to dance?' Daniel raises his voice to make himself heard above the music from the band. They are playing one of my favourite songs, 'Eternal Flame,' by The Bangles. Jenny and Stuart are already on the dance floor,

He pushes his chair back and stands, holding his hand out to me. Without hesitating I allow him to pull me to my feet.

'Did I tell you how good you look in this dress?' he whispers as he pulls me close. Guilt hits me like a sledgehammer when I remember that the one and only outing of this dress was on my honeymoon.

I put a hand to his chest, look into his pale hazel eyes, and murmur 'thanks' without losing contact, I don't want to tell him the truth because I don't want to ruin the moment. I am torn, because I think I deserve to be happy, and I know Simon would not want me to be alone for the rest of my life. Pushing the thoughts to the back of my mind, I give myself permission to focus on the here and now, to seize the day.

As though he can read my conflicting thoughts, Daniel brings a hand to cup my cheek gently 'It's just a dance, Lottie,' and those words give me the courage to focus on enjoying the moment.

I stroke his cheek. We both know that this isn't just a dance. We both know that there is something happening here, something that we don't want to admit to, yet.

'Come,' he takes my hand and leads me through the throng of people onto the dance floor. We find a space and just as we are about to dance, the song finishes, and we both stand smiling at each other like school kids.

'We really do have rubbish timing,' I joke, reaching up to brush my fingers through his hair. And then the tempo changes as the woman's sultry voice begins to sing 'Can't Help Falling in Love' an old Elvis Presley classic.

As if in slow motion, Daniel steps closer and dips his head. Closing my eyes briefly, I feel pressure on my hips as warm hands settle on me, sending a heat to my chest. My arms raise, of their own volition and find their way around Daniel's neck, relishing the feel of his warm skin against my fingers.

We sway slowly, both silent, simply enjoying each other.

I hug him close and bury my head in his shoulder.

'God, you feel so good,' he says, his voice rough with emotion as he moves his hands steadily up my back in a caressing motion.

A feeling of utter peace, settles within me, drawing me into a place where words are not needed. I close my eyes and let the world disappear.

There is only Daniel and I, and this magical moment. Nothing else exists.

Above the music, my heart thuds with excitement alongside Daniel's steady heartbeat. Moments later, a motion behind us and someone tapping my arm, startles me out of this blissful moment. It's Francesca, she has her coat draped over one arm.

'Sorry to interrupt, but I have to go,' she says as the song finishes. I withdraw from Daniel's arms and hold out my arms to hug her. 'I just wanted to thank you again. If it wasn't for the support group, I wouldn't be here.' I wait for her brief nod to acknowledge that it's OK to make physical contact, it was one of the things I remembered after my ordeal, the repulsion and need to step away from human touch.

The nod comes, and her slender body leans in to receive my hug.

'You have done so well, Francesca,' I say. 'You will get there in the end.' I reassure her. 'It takes a while, but you'll get there. Just don't be too hard on yourself.'

She smiles and to my surprise, drops a kiss to my cheek.

For some reason, watching Francesca walk, stirs a sadness within me. I'm not sure why, maybe it's the sorrow that I see in her eyes. Or maybe, she reminds me too much of the person I used to be. Before the rape, before Simon left me.

Daniel suddenly pulls me close. 'You did that, offered her a chance to get help,' he says, proudly. 'You, and your friends.' He cups the back of my head, gently with one hand and lowers his face to take my lips in the tenderest of kisses.

I begin to utter his name, but the kiss takes over, dulling my senses and pushing all my worries to one side. Opening my mouth, I allow his tongue to tenderly explore my own, as intoxicating as the whiskey he'd been drinking. It is everything I thought it would be, until he pulls away, and I'm left wanting more. This man knows how to kiss.

As we stand looking at each other, we can't help but smile. Maybe this time, life will be kind, and offer us a future that sees us together, happy with my son.

Another shoulder tap and we both look around, it's Stuart and Jenny. Their faces no longer look chilled, their smiles have gone. Something is wrong.

'Sorry, but we need to go,' Jenny's voice is full of concern. 'There's a problem at the house.'

Immediately I think of Harley, Ben and Edie and my heart skips a beat. 'The children?'

'Are fine,' Jenny reassures me, placing a hand on my arm, 'no one is hurt.'

I slowly let out the breath I had been holding in.

'The security gate alarm went off and triggered the local police to pay the guys a visit,' Stuart says, collecting his jacket and Jenny's wrap. 'We'll wait for you in the entrance hall.'

I want to thank Karis for a lovely night and look around the room, to find her standing by the stage, putting a couple of raffle prizes into a box. Moving carefully through the fray of dancers we make our way to her. I am usually quite a shy and private person, but with Daniel by my side I feel my confidence growing, as we reach Karis. I shouldn't have worried, for when she sees us, she offers a warm smile.

'Thank you for the invite and for allowing us to attend tonight's celebrations, but we need to head back to the house,' I tell her, lightly touching her arm. In another world we could have been good friends.

Karis pulls me into a hug. 'Having you here with Jenny and Stuart has been the icing on the cake tonight, Lottie. It has meant a lot, not just to me, but to everyone here.'

Tears blur my eyes. I am not used to taking credit for the Lighthouse Charity foundation, but this is one day that I am happy to be part of the group.

'You are so welcome,' I say, with genuine warmth. 'It has been an absolute pleasure to be here.'

Daniel waits patiently for me and Karis to pull apart before taking Karis' hand to say goodbye and we quickly make our way to the entrance of the hotel, where a taxi, similar to a London black cab is waiting at the entrance, ready to take us back to the Sutton Courtenay house. Thankfully, it is so big that all four of us can sit in the back.

As we sit facing each other, a young girl appears beside the window of the taxi and begins to knock vigorously. 'Stop!' She shouts, 'I have something for you.'

She looks about eighteen years old and is dressed in a long zipped up to the neck, black padded jacket, and large gold bangle earrings. Her hair is severely scraped back on her head, making her features look harsh, almost boyish.

Daniel winds down the window. 'What do you mean?' he asks. 'Do we know you?'

She shakes her head, 'No, but someone just gave me this, handed me a tenner and said to give it to the woman with the red hair, getting into this taxi. 'Charlotte?'

Bloody hell. I suddenly feel cold, and goosebumps pop up along my arms.

Daniel and Stuart open the door to the vehicle and step back out into the cool, night air, each flanking a side of the young woman. 'Describe the person who paid you to deliver the box,' Stuart says, in a clipped voice. His eyebrows are drawn together as he glances my way.

'Baseball cap, dressed in black. A man, he was sitting in a dark green car, over there,' she points to the vacant space of the car park, where she says the person parked. 'That's my car there, the red Volkswagon Beetle. I'm about to start my night shift. I work on the night room service cover.'

I step out of the taxi and watch in slow motion as Daniel takes the familiar looking box from the girl. My stomach plummets when I catch sight of the white label, with my name printed on the top. 'Charlotte.'

'Don't open it,' I whisper.

Daniel and Stuart shield me, and I feel the warmth of Jenny's hand as they carefully remove the lid of the box. My eyes flit between the two men, I catch sight of a blue handwritten note with my name on it.

'Holy mother of God!' The scrawny brown body of a wild rabbit is scrunched under the note. Again, no eyes. Just blood. Why would someone do this?

'Charlotte,' Daniel reads the note, and turns the card. 'You look lovely tonight. Enjoy your gift. x'

Nausea begins in my stomach, I put my hand over my mouth. But I know it's coming so I pull away from the group and find the nearest spot to empty my stomach.

Vomiting the contents of my stomach, by the entrance of the country house hotel is not the ending I was hoping for this evening. My tummy feels like it's rolling, and the acrid taste of retching lingers in my mouth and throat.

A warm hand rubs my back and Daniel's concerned voice soothes my mind and my poor, aching stomach.

'We'll find this psycho, Lottie. I promise you that.'

Part Twenty-Three: Harley

It's 10.30pm and I'm sitting in the kitchen of the holiday house with a hot chocolate.

Thank goodness the alarm has stopped.

I feel cold.

The old wooden table is smooth against my cold fingers, so I use the hot mug of drinking chocolate to warm my hands. Ben is sitting next to me, playing on his phone. He didn't come to the pool because he wanted to watch TV in his room. He came running downstairs when the alarm went off, found Jack and Steph and joined us in the kitchen.

Jem and Noah sit together, and a softly snoring Edie, is wrapped in a pale blue blanket, in Noah's arms. Julie and Brian are doing a routine check of the building. I'm pretty sure that we're not in any danger, or it would have happened by now. As I stare at the biscuits, my phone begins to ring. Recognising the song, one of Mum's favourites. 'Handbags and Gladrags' by Rod Stewart. Of course, it is. She's checking in.

'Are you OK?' she asks quickly. I can hear the worry in her voice.

'I'm fine, we're in the kitchen. Brian and Julie are checking the rest of the house.'

Mum sighs, 'Are the police still there?'

'No, they left about fifteen minutes ago,' I answer.

'OK, we're on our way back,' Mum says. 'Should be about twenty minutes.'

177

'See you soon,' I disconnect the phone and put it on the table. I think about her voice and how panicked she sounded on the line. It feels good to have someone worry about me.

The room is quiet, even the kettle seems to be silent as it boils quietly in the background.

***

I think of the fun we were having in the pool house a few hours ago. Tiled mostly white, with plants dotted at each corner. The pool is blue mixed mosaics with a walk-in section for the children. At the far end of the pool house is the bubbling jacuzzi, and two white doors. One for the steam room and one for the sauna. I can't even begin to think how much this must cost. Dotted around each side of the rectangular pool are wooden loungers with cushions.

Another door leads to its very own self-contained kitchen, which houses a big American fridge, filled to the top with fizzy and alcoholic drinks.

How the other half live.

Back to the fun in the pool. I'd been weaving in and out of Edie's splashing body, as she floated in fluorescent orange armbands. Her constant giggling was infectious. Noah and Jem hover near to me, messing about in the water. Her navy swimsuit with its white polka dots, swishing through the water. They hold hands a lot. Come to think of it, there weren't many times when they weren't laughing or touching each other. Mum says it's because they are 'making up for lost time.' Whatever that means.

A dull thud echoed through the room, followed by the sudden high-pitched sound of an alarm.

Then, all hell broke loose.

'Jesus, what's that?' Noah shouted above the noise, swimming to the side and climbing out of the pool.

'Not sure. Go and check the security room,' Jem shouted back. A trickle of unease makes its way along my arms, and I watch Noah as he grabs a towel from a recliner, pulls on his trainers and shoots out of the room, with the towel around his shoulders.

The noise is continuous, and Jem quickly scoops Edie in her arms and beckons me out of the pool with them. She grabs towels from the recliners, throws one to me and wraps Edie in the other.

Edie starts to cry, as she watches her daddy leave us in such a hurry. Quickly, I hold the towel around my shoulders, to stop it falling. 'It's all right, Edie,' I pat her head. 'Everything is fine. They're just testing the alarms.'

Jem kisses Edie's head, murmuring, 'It's fine darling. Like Harley says, they're just testing the alarms.'

Julie and Brian appear in the doorway, their faces flushed, as if they've been running. They scan the area. 'Is everyone all right?' they ask. The dog barks at the sound of the siren, her tail is wagging madly. She knows something is wrong. Brian bends down to pat her head.

Jem and I both nod our heads vigorously, to let them know we're fine.

'What's happening?' I ask, stopping beside one of the reclining chairs and rubbing warmth into my chilled arms and back.

'Not sure,' Brian replies, his brows are wrinkled in worry.

'Noah has gone to the security room, please see if he's all right,' Jem's worried voice, sounds higher than it usually is. Julie finds a dry towel from the storage unit and carefully puts it around Jem's almost dry shoulders.

'There you go, keep warm.' Julie offers before she and Brian disappear in search of Noah and the security room. We know the house has a security room, because Jen showed us. We weren't allowed to go in, but it is used twenty-four hours a day.

The shrill of the alarm is beginning to make my head hurt. What the hell is going on? Is someone in the house?

'Harley, with me.' Jem says, still holding Edie tightly in her arms. I nod, knowing that this isn't the time to say, that she's not my mother and therefore, cannot tell me what to do. She just wants to keep us safe.

We make our way through the hallways and doors, to the large kitchen at the back of the house. It feels surreal as we almost speed walk there, Edie holding tight as she sits on Jem's hips. Each of us are shivering and wearing wet towels around our shoulders. When we reach the kitchen, we find that the housekeeper, I can't remember her name, is already there leaning against the sink.

'Something has triggered the alarm.' The older woman announces, as though it's nothing to worry about. Her short, silver-grey hair is spiked on one side and she wears a red kimono dressing gown, which seems out of place somehow in the bright yellow kitchen with white wooden kitchen units, and more in keeping with a rich jewel coloured bedroom.

Noah rushes in, fully dressed in jeans and a blue jumper. He's out of breath, as he brings in a carrier bag and unceremoniously drops the contents onto the kitchen table. It's our clothes and stuff from the pool. Something heavy clunks, and I smile my thanks to Noah for remembering to pick up my phone. He puts a hand on my shoulder, squeezes gently in reply.

Jem lifts a hand to cup Noah's cheek, and he leans sideways and briefly kisses it. 'Hey babe,' he whispers. 'You OK?'

'Good,' Jem smiles and for a moment, I think they're going to kiss again, and I am all sorts of mortified. But then Noah looks around the room, 'Grab your things and get dressed, Jack, Steph and Ben are on their way.' He orders.

'Oh my,' The housekeeper says, moving toward the fridge and putting a hand through her grey hair, 'It's all happening tonight.' She looks at me, Jem and Edie, 'poor things, we'll have you warmed through soon enough. There's a pantry through there,' she points to the door near to a white glassed display unit, 'if you need to change. There are blankets in a store chest in there too. Now who's for a hot drink?'

I'm really warming to this woman. The way she walks into a room, and takes charge, immediately makes you think that everything is going to be alright. It feels good, reassuring.

'What happened?' I ask, grabbing my clothes and stuff and heading to the pantry. 'With the alarm.' A few minutes later, I've pulled on my clothes and return to my seat at the table.

Noah holds his arms out to Jem to take Edie from her and gives me a quick glance. 'Not sure, but it looks like the security gate on the drive was compromised.'

Jem stands up, pushing her chair to one side and gently lays Edie into her dad's arms. 'What do you mean, the front gate was compromised?'

'Not sure exactly, let's wait until everyone gets back and we'll see what happened.'

Steph and Jack push open the kitchen door, Jack has his arm around Steph's shoulders and Ben walks behind them, holding his phone. He looks at the table and walks to me, pulling the chair beside me out, and slumping into it.

'Hey, strange night,' he says, leaning forward and resting his arms on the table. His blue iPhone gripped tightly in one hand.

'You can say that again' I reply.

'It'll be alright.' Jack sighs to everyone, rubbing Steph's back gently. 'It looks like someone deliberately ran into the gate, causing the gate alarm to kick off.'

We hear someone coming toward the house. The sound of a car engine and footsteps walking across the gravel, getting nearer, makes me panic. 'Who's that?' I ask, suddenly feeling frightened that something bad is about to happen. I think Jem notices, because she puts a reassuring arm around my shoulder to comfort me.

Brian leaves the room quickly. 'I'll go and see who it is.' Julie holds onto the dog's collar to stop it following Brian.

'Come through,' I hear Brian's deep voice as he leads police officers into the room.

'Evening,' a tall, serious looking police officer with a red face and dark brown eyes look around the room, checking out faces. Next to him, is a small blonde-haired officer with a kind face.

'Hello, I'm PC Sybil Voyce, and this is,' the smaller officer explains, before pointing to her colleague, ''PC Ian Drewitt. We're responding to an alarm that was triggered earlier this evening. Can you tell us what happened?'

'DCI Brian Carter,' Brian states, 'this is my wife DS Julie Carter.' He gently touches Julie's back. 'This is DI Steph Rutland and her husband Jack. These are our friends, Jem and Noah and their children.' he points to Steph and Jack, who are standing by the fridge, who smile in return.

'Can I just ask something, before we go any further?' Brian says, looking at the officers. He moves to the sink, picks up a glass from the draining board and fills it with cold water.

'Yes, of course,' PC Voyce replies, looking at Brian with a serious face.

Emptying the glass of water and, Brian looks at the PC, 'Am I missing something here?'

'In what sense?' She replies, and I can see a small movement in her eye, like a tick. My mum has them when she becomes tired.

'In the sense that this house has a security room, there are cameras everywhere and even the gates are linked to the local police.' Brian explains, refilling his glass with water. Wow, I didn't know that. It's like we're in the Tower of London, guarding the Queen's jewels. I think back to Mum's nightmare and wonder if this is linked to the horror she was dreaming about.

Brian, Jack, Stewart and Noah are the best men I know. They are strong, but caring and aren't afraid to put their arm around you if they think you need a hug. Mum always says how lucky we are to have these people as part of our family.

Talking of strong characters, I don't know what to make of Daniel though. I think I like him, but I've only just met him. A woman's voice breaks into my thoughts, bringing me back to reality.

'I can help you with that,' the housekeeper steps forward, pulling the dressing gown tight against her body. 'This house belongs to a famous actress and former partner, who is a well-known film director. They don't live here very often and rent it out through an exclusive holiday let company.'

The police officers nod, to confirm this.

Wow! The first famous actress I can think of is that woman in The Greatest Showman. Mum has made me watch the film loads of times, and I think of the bearded lady, with the big voice.

'Is it that woman from the Greatest Showman?' I ask, excitedly. 'The woman with the beard?'

The housekeeper smiles and slowly shakes her head, 'No, dear. It's not her. I can't say who it is, but the owner is much more well-known than Keala Settle.'

Brian turns to Jack, 'We thought something similar. A politician even.'

'Or a secret agent,' Ben suddenly lifts his head from his phone, 'like James Bond.'

Jack ruffles Ben's head. He's his stepdad, but you wouldn't know, because he treats him so nice, as if he's his real dad. Steph raises her eyebrow. 'I wouldn't be surprised if Jenny knows her and that's how she knew the house was up for rent.'

'So,' PC Drewitt clears his throat and stands upright, 'do you want to talk us through what happened tonight?'

I zone out then, as the adults discuss the alarm going off. I pick up my phone and google William Shatner in space. It brings up the Blue Origin rocket ship, that was developed by Billionaire Jeff Bezos. Making sure my phone is on silent, I watch the You Tube take-off for what seems like the trillionth time. It never ceases to excite me. One day, I hope that will be me.

 A boy can dream, can't he?

When I look up, the kitchen is quiet, and I realise that there's just me and Ben.

'They've gone to the security room to check out the cameras. Noah and Jem have taken Edie up to bed. The others should be back soon.' Ben answers without looking up from his phone. 'Mum says to go to bed if you're tired.'

A few minutes later, we hear low voices as the housekeeper, Julie Brian, Steph and Jack filter back into the room, with the two police officers following behind.

'The car looks like a Peugeot, someone wearing a baseball cap, not a very clear picture. Possibly a man. We've got a partial number plate, so that's a start.' PC Voyce says. 'We'll get a team out in the morning to check for paint splatters etc on the gates.'

Steph looks at Jack as if she wants to say something, and he shakes his head to stop her. There is something going on, I can feel it. The conversation with the police officers confirms that everything is secure and that they will follow up tomorrow with the partial number plate of the car.

Finally, they leave us in peace.

***

I look at my watch again. 10.33pm. I can't remember the last time I stayed up this late, I mean there are times in my room, that I stay awake reading, looking at my phone and daydreaming about what it would be like to go into space.

Then I remember Steph and Jack's wedding last year, and it was such good fun. There was a party in the evening at a hotel and everyone was drinking and dancing. Noah and Jem were dancing slowly, with Edie asleep in their room, using the hotel's childminding service. Before she went, Edie was running around the dance floor chasing me. She is sweet really, but I'm a bit worried that she really does want to marry me, she follows me everywhere!

By 10.45pm I'd had enough, and I stand up to go to bed. I'm sure Mum will be home soon, she'll come in to say goodnight before going to bed. She always does.

'I'm heading upstairs,' I say, grabbing my phone from the table and rubbing my tired eyes. Ben follows me, pushing his phone in his pocket. 'I'm coming too, can't keep my eyes open.' He heads over to the sink where his mum is washing up, and plants a kiss on her cheek.

'Goodnight sweetheart,' Steph, hugs him tightly. 'Love you,' she says quietly, before releasing her hold. Jack is drying coffee cups, and stops to pat Ben on the shoulder:

'Goodnight son,' he says quietly. 'See you in the morning.'

We climb the stairs slowly, and Ben mutters, 'What a night!'

'You can say that again,' I reply, 'and something tells me that this is just the beginning.'

Part Twenty-Four: Lottie

I can't breathe.

It's dark and humid. I can't get air into my lungs. I feel like I'm suffocating.

The twigs and stones tear at my feet as I fight my way through wooded shrubbery, my only light is the bright full moon in the night sky.

'Mum!' my son's voice calls. But from where, I can't see.

'I'm coming, Harley,' I grind out the words quickly.

The thought of my son, out here all alone, spurs me on. Stumbling through the semi-darkness, I try to call out, but there is no breath left in me. All I can feel is the panicking burn of my organs trying to push through the lack of oxygen.

All is lost.

***

A warmth surrounds me, like a cocoon. And I think I must be in heaven. There is no pain, or worry, just the knowledge that wherever I am, holds no fear. The nightmares feel so real, and I dread going to sleep, because I know that my worst fears will take hold and ruin any chance of getting some rest.

The bed dips and a warm hand strokes my hair softly.

When I open my eyes, my bedside lamp is on, and I am in Daniel's arms. Oh my goodness, I am embarrassed that he heard me from his room, next door. I try to shuffle away, but his arms hold me tighter.

'Shh…' he whispers in his soft Scottish brogue, through the semi-darkness of my bedroom. 'It's OK, love. I'm here.'

The endearment feels good, and I wonder if he realises what he has said.

'You had a nightmare.' There is concern in his voice. I don't want to worry him. He already knows about the demons that live within me. From our earlier counselling sessions, after I had opened up to Jenny, it had been Daniel who had listened and helped me to sort through my emotions and understanding of what had happened at my cousin's party when I was fifteen years old.

It was Daniel who never looked at me in disgust. Never showed any pity, just an understanding of what I had been through. Like he had with Jenny. He helped us to put the pieces of ourselves back together.

And the surprising thing was that I never told Simon about that fateful day when I was fifteen. I'm not sure why, but I think it was because I didn't want to taint what I had with him. I wanted our love to be pure and innocent, a new beginning.

Stupidly I believed that my earlier life, including the assault and rape, was better left in the past, because once revealed, it cannot be ignored. It must be processed. I didn't want Simon to pity me or see me as a victim.

For a while it worked.

'I'm sorry for waking you,' I apologise, my cheeks warm with embarrassment. He smiles softly, and shuffles his body along the bed, so that he is sitting next to me. His long legs lift and casually rest on the top of my duvet, as he turns to face me, he raises a thumb to softly brush against my cheek.

'Nothing to be sorry for,' he answers. 'How are you feeling now?'

'Better,' I say, putting my hand against his chest. I can feel the hard muscle and chest hair underneath the material of his T-shirt.

We sit next to each other in silence for a short while, before I ask, quietly, 'what time is it?'

'3am.' He looks at me, with drawn brows and worry in his eyes.

'Do you have these nightmares often?' His eyes hold mine, and he pulls me to him gently, protectively.

'Yes, of late,' I admit, enjoying the warm rise and fall of his chest. 'They started about a month ago and I'm not sure why. They feel like an omen, as though they're telling me that something bad is about to happen. I can't explain it.'

'What, like a premonition?' he asks, his warm breath whispering across my face.

'Yeah,' I admit, knowing that of all people, he should be the one I confess my feelings to.

'Fuck,' he curses under his breath.

'What? What is it?' I ask, worried that I have done something wrong.

'I am such a fucking idiot,' he shakes his head, and pulls away from me. Pushing off the bed, he stands before me, staring at my face. He looks so appealing in his dark T-shirt and sleep shorts, but there is frustration and worry etched on his handsome face.

'Daniel?' I don't understand.

'It's never the right time, I just want it to be the right time.' He mutters, raking his hands through his hair and beginning to pace the floor.

And, then I see him. Really see him. He is a man conflicted. Tormented. How did I not see it before?

'Daniel,' I say, into the darkened room, staring at his dusky silhouette. 'Life will always get in the way.'

'I know,' he says, 'but I want to do the right thing by you. You are vulnerable, and I want to help you.'

My voice is husky, pleading for him to understand. 'You can help me, Daniel. Life will always get in the way, but that doesn't mean that we can't give us a try. Instead of always fighting it and waiting for the right time.'

'Lottie,' his eyes hold mine. I can see the indecision, the fight that goes on within him. He wants to be honourable, to do the right thing. But how can it be right to deny yourself the chance of having something that could potentially turn out to be spectacular.

Momentarily, I think of Simon and our life together, short as it was. The memories will always be precious and can never be taken away, but I'm still here and living and I need to remember that. Both Daniel and I need to remember that.

'I need you Daniel, I need you to stop running away and to give us a chance.' My voice is soft, imploring, as I try to reach him.

'You mean…' he answers hopefully, leaning forward. He brushes a stray curl from my eyes.

'Yes,' I put his hand over mine, 'I mean, this is our time.'

***

Seven hours later, the house is full of activity. The chef is here in the large, modern grey and white kitchen, finishing the last breakfast orders, Ben and Harley have eaten and are changing for the pool, in their rooms. Steph and Jack are playing chopsticks on the grand piano in the sitting room. Their laughter bouncing through the walls of the house.

Daniel, Stuart, Julie, Brian and I sit around the kitchen table as Mrs Monk fusses, making sure everyone has something to drink and eat. Lola, the dog sits quietly in her bed.

Jenny enters the room with her laptop. She's talking to someone.

Without speaking she puts the machine down on the kitchen table. She is Facetiming Jules and Sasha, who are currently living on the Greek island of Corfu.

'How are you?' she asks, pointing the screen our way.

Sasha, Jules and Zoe's happy faces, looking our way. All dressed in varying shades of white.

'We're good.' Jules answers, with a smile. He looks younger now. Now he's put his demons to bed. They do look good. They are all relaxed and tanned and that's good to see, after their hellish year, last year.

Stuart gives Zoe a wave. 'How is Peppa Pig, Zoe?' he asks softly.

Zoe jumps up and down, 'She's good.' She runs off camera, to find Peppa.

Stuart takes a sip from his mug of tea, before speaking to our friends in Corfu. 'Jenny and I have sent you something in the post. It should be with you soon.'

'A present!' Zoe claps, running into the room and stands in front of the laptop, next to her parents in her pink and white sundress riding up a little as she moves. Clutched tightly in her hands is her Peppa Pig.

'It's nothing big,' Jenny smiles, 'we hope you like it.' Her eyes flit across the wooden dining table to her husband, Stuart and for a moment they hold each other's gazes, as though they are the only two people in the world.

Jem joins us in the kitchen. Little Edie follows carrying a little pink handbag in the shape of a cat face. She looks adorable in a navy all in one jumpsuit, and a fluffy pink cardigan that's a bit on the large side for her. Noah follows closely behind his family, looking at his phone.

'Jack, Steph,' Jenny calls through the doorway to the couple. 'We have Jules, Sasha, and Zoe here, on Facetime on the laptop. Do you want to come to say hello?'

Steph and Jack appear at the doorway, holding hands. They join us at the table and wave to our friends in Corfu.

'Well,' Sasha says and falters for a moment. She speaks quietly to Jules. 'Shall we tell them together?' He nods.

Jules and Sasha look at us, their eyes bright and hopeful.

'We got married last weekend!' They say in unison, with voices full of joy.

The room is silent, and we look at each other. Jenny raises her eyebrows and I smile, reach out and pat her hand. I'm really happy for them. And, then the room erupts into a huge excited raucous noise, as everyone begins to cheer and shout congratulations.

Steph walks closer to the screen and makes a heart shape with her hands. 'We are so very happy for you both!' There are tears of joy in her eyes, and I absently wipe the corner of my eye with a finger.

A hand settles on my thigh, warm and strong. Daniel. 'That is wonderful news. Congratulations to you both!' I smile, a little choked up. It is good to have good news to take our minds off the dead animal presents, disappearance of bad guys and the usual havoc that happens within our lives.

Stuart puts his hand on his chest. 'Fantastic! You both deserve this. Did Zoe get to be a princess?' There are tears in his eyes.

Zoe jumps up and down, 'I did, I did. And I got to wear a crown and look really pretty.'

'Well done, darling!' Jenny laughs, 'I bet you looked absolutely stunning!' Zoe's smile beams across the whole of her face. Clearly, this has been a dream come true for the five-year-old.

Julie wipes a tear and offers her congratulations.

'Congratulations to you all, 'Jack says to the laptop. 'I can definitely recommend marriage! It's good to see you moving forward. You both deserve to be happy.'

Jules puts a hand to his heart and nods to Jack. 'Thank you for that, Jack. I appreciate it.' He pauses to look at Sasha and stroke her tanned cheek. 'And, to you and Stuart and Jenny for giving me a chance to start again. To you all really. I was in a dark place back then, and you saw something in me, something that forced me back into the real world and made me want to live again.'

A few people wipe their eyes. Jules and Sasha have been through so much. Their road to happiness, like many of us, hasn't been easy. They came together, both on different pathways, having suffered so much one way or another at the hand of abusers. The only difference was that Jules had taken revenge, but realised too late that this didn't take away the pain of losing his sister.

Thanks to Stuart and Jack, Jules went to live in the village of Haworth, Yorkshire, to rebuild his life. It was there he met Sasha, and her daughter, Zoe.

'Such great news. Very best wishes to you both.' Julie speaks to the newly married couple, before glancing across to her husband, Brian. He looks bemused, as he leans down to stroke a contented Lola. For a newly fostered dog, she appears very chilled and enjoys Brian's attentions. He raises an eyebrow to his wife, Julie. Wondering if anything is wrong.

'While we're talking about good news,' Julie pushes out of her chair and takes a step towards her husband. She takes his hand, gently pulling him out of the chair. I hold my breath, I'm so excited!

'Bri, honey,' she leans into Brian, touches his chest and looks up into his face. 'I'm pregnant.'

I've never seen Brian look so shocked before. His usual calm and chilled character, is replaced with that of wonder and confusion, as he shakes his head, in disbelief.

The room is silent, even the chef turns away from his pans on the stove.

'You're…?' Brian mutters, his voice is husky as the reality of Julie's news sinks in.

Over the webcam, we hear cheers, whoops and claps.

'Yep, pregnant. About twelve weeks.' Julie's petite frame stares at her husband. And, then the smile that we've been hoping for, transforms Brian's features. His face lights up and he picks Julie bodily up from the waist and swings her around in joy. The smile is wide and reveals his white teeth, what a beautiful smile.

Brian kisses Julie, soundly on the mouth, whilst we, as a group relax and enjoy the moment.

'Oh my God, I can't believe it!' he says to her. 'That is brilliant news!'

Brian looks around the room at our happy faces, 'Do you hear? I'm going to be a dad!'

We did, and I look across at my beloved friend, see the happy tears in her eyes and wonder how life could be so cruel as to not allow such a good woman, who would have made the best mother, to have children. Life sucks sometimes. I pat her hand and smile. She nudges me back, playfully. Jenny will lick her wounds in private, that's what she and Stuart always do.

Stuart rises from his seat and reaches out to pat Brian on the back, offering his congratulations. 'Well done, mate. We're really pleased for you both.' Making a bee line for Jenny, he drapes his fingers gently along the skin of her neck and leans down. 'I love you,' he whispers, before casually walking to the kitchen counter where the chic black kettle sits, checks the water gauge and flicks it on to boil.

Part Twenty-Five: Cameron

Shit! Shit! Shit! Where the bloody hell did she manage to find the time to pick up a man? He was all over her on the way to the car. That bitch just keeps falling on her feet, holidaying with her rich friends and now she even has a bit on the side.

Who the hell is he? I've been watching her on and off for months now and her life is mundane, to say the least. Her routine is predictable. She leaves her house each weekday at 8.45am and walks to a house three doors away, where she enters the house and stays in there until 6pm. Her son comes to the house after school. What she does in the house, I have no idea. She could be selling her body for all I know.

I pace the striped carpeted floor of my hotel room at the Premier Inn, Didcot South and try hard to remember if the man looked familiar. No, I've never seen him before. Clearly, she knows him well, judging by the way he helped her into the taxi, touched her back.

It worries me. There are feelings there, and that makes me angry. She doesn't deserve to be happy. I need her to be alone. Isolated. It's going to be payback time soon and I've got a front seat when she finally realises what she's about to lose.

Walking the few steps to the bed, I lower my body and stare at the blue rectangular biscuit tin that sits on the dark wooden desk, next to an empty wine bottle. Inside the tin, lies a pigeon motionless and decaying with the faint odour of death emanating from it. There is something raw and serene about the end of a life, the way it's so final and makes you realise that all things come to an end. It's the circle of life, isn't it?

A memory from long ago comes into my mind. We had a cat when I was a child, when my dad was still with us, and Mum had been happy. Before he left us. We had lived in Didcot on the Ladygrove estate near the lakes, with Samson, our lovely white long-haired cat. He was very calm and gentle, and he used to make Mum cross because he was constantly hungry.

One day, when he was seven years old, Samson ran into an oncoming car on a nearby busy road, and his injuries were so severe that we had to put him to sleep. I was devastated and cried for weeks.

I stood over him, crying as he was put to sleep. Hoped that he wasn't in any pain and that the end would be quick. That's when I first became fascinated with death, particularly animals who were at death's door. But there was a fascination, when I looked into the eyes of creatures that no longer lived. To me, a ten-year-old boy curious about death and what it means in the grand scheme of things, I found it fascinating.

When Samson was put out of his misery, we wrapped him in a soft knitted blanket and carefully took his still warm body home. Dad and I walked with him to the back of the garden, where a border of soil was being used to bring colour to the area.

Dad laid Samson on a nearby garden table and popped into the garage to find the heavy metal silver spade to begin digging Samson's final resting place. I walked into the kitchen, opened the cutlery drawer and took out a knife. Then I found a small storage container. Grasping my things, I took them to the garden and put them down next to Samson.

He looked peaceful, despite the dark red blood splattered across his white fur. Glancing quickly at Dad, I saw that he was engrossed in digging a hole for Samson, so I grabbed the utensils, one at a time. First, I used the spoon to loosen an eye from the socket. It was tougher than I thought, I had to really gouge into the crevices to loosen them. Finally, I disconnected the tissue with my knife and put Samson's first eye into the open storage container.

'Hey!' Dad stopped digging, and was staring at me, 'what the hell are you doing?'

'Just taking his eyes out, because he looks lost,' I said.

'Well don't!' he raised his voice, just as I plopped the second one out and placed it next to the first globe.

'Leave him alone,' Dad threw the spade to one side and grabbed my arm.

'Too late,' I said, looking at the eyes in the storage container, 'he won't get sad when he wakes up and finds that he can't see anything.'

'You bloody daft boy. He won't wake up. He's not with us anymore.' he said.

My father shook his head and punched me lightly on the shoulder.

'What am I going to do with you?' he asked, walking back to the muddy earth he'd been working on.

Dad didn't look at me the same way after that. He was unsure of me, of my behaviour, I could tell by the way he kept his distance.

Samson was my first mutilation. My first trial. It was easy to find wild animals to torture, or who were already dead. Poor things didn't know what had hit them.

**

The look of horror on Charlotte's face was priceless when she opened the box. There was the rabbit 'staring' up at her from its cardboard resting place, with gouged out eyes. I got a thrill when she turned away and threw up in the garden bushes.

Poor little Charlotte, always playing the victim.

Do you need an excuse to hurt someone? Because I am way past that with Charlotte. And, if her son gets hurt in the process, that's just collateral damage. Don't get me wrong, she may be my younger cousin, but I cannot let her get away with what happened to us when we three boys were kidnapped, tied up and attacked.

She has to pay, one way or another for the pain she has caused. If she hadn't told anyone, those masked people would never have known about what went on the night of the party.

The ache in my right leg is nagging and I absently rub it before, forcing myself off the bed to a standing position. Moving to the orange carrier bag that sits beside the desk, I reach in and pull out the first bottle that comes to hand. Vodka. Shit. My head is going to hurt tomorrow.

Unscrewing the metal cap, I take a deep, long gulp, and let the memories flood back.

***

'Shit! Have they gone?' Vincent says quietly. 'I can't open my eyes.'

'Fuck, I think they've broken my leg,' I moan, rubbing something sticky from my face. At this point I'm not sure if it's blood, sweat or tears. There is a silence and I'm trying to listen for any movement nearby. The only sound is that of Eric, who is sobbing uncontrollably by my side.

'Let's get out of here.' Vincent tries tugging his ropes. 'I think I can undo these ropes.' He twists, and turns, scraping the chair along the floor.

'Eric, man. It's going to be alright.' I say, trying to calm him down. 'Vincent is going to help us get out.' Vincent's chair topples over and gives a crack when it hits the concrete floor, he starts on Eric.

'We should never have done what we did to your cousin,' Eric's words are half sobbed, and it is clear that he has feelings of regret.

'We can't turn the clock back,' I mutter. 'What's done is done.'

Eric stands and both work with cold fingers to untangle my ropes and to help me to my feet. We need to call for help, but I'll be damned if I'll call the police. Not to this awful place.

'Has anyone got a phone?' I ask.

'No,' they both reply.

'Let's just get out of here and find someone to help,' with every movement of my legs I feel excruciating pain. But the worst is the right one, it has no strength and feels broken, so I have to lean heavily on the boys. Pushing through the door of plastic strips into a large area, there is a strip of light that hopefully leads to the exit. As we move closer, we realise that it's a door. Thank God, because I'm afraid I'm going to pass out at any point now.

'Do you know who they were?' Eric asks, his arm shakes slightly as he holds me up.

'No,' I wince. 'Can we stop a minute? I need to get my breath.'

They both come to a standstill as we reach the exit door. Inhaling deeply, I try to calm the nerves that make me feel jittery. I need to calm down. Who the hell were those people? There was at least one woman, but I swear the others were men. They were connected to Charlotte, somehow. But how, I don't know.

'Fuck,' I say loudly, partly out of frustration and anger. We have been kidnapped by people who knew about us and what we did.

Which means that they know about the Three Amigos, and what they did.

'Do you ever think about her?' Eric asks me, without thinking.

'Who, Lottie?' Vincent asks loudly, with a hint of frustration, uttering the words that have remained unspoken since that fateful night. We had brushed it all under the carpet, until all that was left was a carpet fractured in so many places, it was held together by a single thread. Why would he ask me that now? I mean, what would be the point? What's done is done, you can't change the past.

'Charlotte, you moron,' I correct him. 'And the answer is no. Now let's get out of here and find some help.'

'Well, I do,' Eric pulls me hard, across the disused empty car park. 'All the fucking time.'

'Me too,' Vincent says, and something unsaid passes between him and Eric. A memory that keeps them bonded.

Of course, saying I didn't think of Charlotte, was a lie. I thought of her a lot, all the time in fact. I was out of it that night at my twenty first birthday party. Like my two friends, I had been drinking for most of the day, and taking any drugs that were on offer. The one thing I wished I had done though, was taken photos, or a video.

Would I change what had happened? What we did to Charlotte? Absolutely not.

Even when we told our parents that we had been targeted by a group of thugs who had followed us down an alleyway and attacked us. Even when the GP, immediately sent me for an x-ray and referral to the highly praised Nuffield Orthopaedic Centre, in Oxford, commonly known as the NOC by staff and local residents.

Even when my right kneecap had to be pinned back in place and I needed a new knee joint. The pain and rehabilitation, that went on for months and still left me with aches, pains and weakness.

Even with all that.

It was worth it.

Because I got to fuck my young cousin, and it started feeding my fetish for drugging young innocent girls and raping them. I know that Eric and Vincent aren't that keen and didn't want to repeat what happened at the party, but I just threatened to tell their families what they had done, and they soon fell into line.

Because once you've got away with something, it breeds a feeling of invincibility. Of acting beyond the law.

And, for a few years, before we moved to Charmouth, I was able to feed my obsession. Especially, after Charlotte moved away and I knew that I would have to find another release.

***

The question now is, as I take a deep gulp from the vodka bottle, what do I do about Charlotte?

Do I want her again? Love, passion, revenge. That's what it amounts to. She was my pretty, quirky younger cousin, so in a way, I've always loved her. Passion, well it's hard to remember that night due to the drink and drugs. But even if the boys didn't feel it, there was something there, between me and Charlotte. Whether I'm imagining it or not, maybe I need to have her one more time to work her out of my system.

Revenge. Yes, that's a funny one. She shouldn't have told anyone. That made it personal. The things we did to her were nothing compared to what those three people did to us. At least she was drugged and didn't know what was happening. Anyway, who the fuck cares? She doesn't deserve to carry on with her happy life. Living in her nice little house, with her son, by the beach, and holidaying with rich friends, whilst being groped by mysterious men in the evening.

Revenge comes in many forms. My eyes flit to the biscuit tin on the dressing table. That's my first plan of action, to ready the deceased bird, which I'd lured to my car this morning at the hotel, just after breakfast. Using the uneaten croissant flakes as bait to entice the bird closer, across the car park, to the open door of my car. Waiting patiently, until the poor bird had tottered closely enough for me to scoop it into my coat and throw the whole thing unceremoniously into the backseat of my car, where it started squawking in panic, and flapping its wings, trying to escape. I was tired and it had been a hot day, but I was looking forward to killing it.

Unfortunately, by the time I pulled into the driveway of my home, the damn thing had died of heat exhaustion and shock.

My phone starts to ring, the caller ID says it's Gino Camprinelli. Shit.

Well, he can go fuck himself. I let the call go to voicemail.

Part Twenty-Six: DCI Brian Carter

There is nothing that can prepare you for the news that you are to become a DAD. It's like all your worries and beliefs change and emerge tenfold with different scenarios that race through your mind. There is also a feeling of achievement, filled with the need to protect what is mine. Achievement, that we're becoming a family, and committing to building a life together.

I can't wait to make special memories with my wife and child, and plan to do everything within my power to make sure that we all have a long, safe and happy life, together.

Day three of our family gathering and we've spent most of the day at Millets Farm Centre, Frilford, which is approximately twenty-minute drive from the Sutton Courtenay house. It was great fun. I hadn't been there since I was a child of nine, and it's grown much bigger since then.

Edie loved the playground and visiting the animals at Millets. There were alpacas, rabbits, goats, pigs and ponies. Ben and Harley were interested in the falconry and crazy golf. Jenny had booked a private room, called Lakeview Suite, above the main restaurant for us to eat a delicious selection of buffet food. The room was comfortable with its wooden floors, crisp white tablecloths, and natural brick walls. It offered plenty of space for the nine adults and children within our group.

We returned to the Manor around 3pm and the group branched off to rest in various parts of the house. Edie needed an afternoon nap after her busy morning adventure, meanwhile Harley, Ben, Steph and Jack were going to have a quick dip in the pool. Julie and I opted to chill out in our room for a few hours, before going down for drinks at 6.30pm, in readiness for dinner at 7pm.

The sound of Julie vomiting in the next room, pulls me from my thoughts and I quickly push off the bed with its white cotton duvet and rush to the en suite to help her. She is kneeling on the floor, and her head is drooping into the open toilet basin.

'What can I do to help, sweetheart?' I ask, perching on side of the bathtub. I rub her back gently, through the white linen blouse that she wears over blue skinny jeans. She has short dark hair, the same style as when I met her many years ago and carries herself with a grace and elegance that reminds me of a young Audrey Hepburn.

Sometimes, I wonder what she sees in me, I mean, I'm twelve years her senior at fifty, with floppy brown hair, heavily sprinkled with grey. But I know she sees something, because when she kisses me, she tells me that I'm her 'Johnny Cash' without the singing voice.

'Not a lot, hopefully the sickness will wear off soon.' She looks up at me and tries to smile.

Without thinking, I reach out and caress her cheek with my fingers.

She's the most selfless person I know, always thinking of others and putting them first. Her years of service to the force could have left her bitter and resigned, like many seasoned serving officers, but not Julie. She still believes in innocence, that people can be inherently good. And that is one of the things that I love about her. She never gives up.

But I know from experience, that that isn't the case. I'm the opposite. If there is a particularly hard case, like that of Jenny Greyson who was kidnapped and raped by her sadistic uncle,

Felix Gloverman, her legal guardian at the time. I just couldn't get my head around how he could do that to his own niece. When he later kidnapped and murdered, Rose Dean, Jenny's housekeeper, who was also like a mother to her, I was so angry and focused that I would have done literally anything to make him pay for the misery he had caused.

Having Julie by my side, brings a lightness to my life and reminds me to leave work at work when I can. We are both similar in that way, we live for our jobs and want to make a difference. My wife is everything. From the day we chose to be together, and make a go of things, the changes in me were significant. She makes me a better person, a happier person and that, in turn makes me a better detective.

'It will, honey,' I try to reassure her. 'It will stop soon, and then we can focus on enjoying the baby and getting the nursery ready.' I kiss the back of her neck, softly. Already, things are feeling different between us, more intense, and for some reason, knowing that she is carrying my child makes me really horny.

Lola saunters into the room, softly padding across the heated tiled floor, waiting for a bit of fuss, so I absently stroke her head. She's like a different dog from the one I collected yesterday. Her confidence is developing well, even in this short time, and there's a playfulness that shines in her eyes, whenever I scatter dog treats and ask her to find them.

The dog walks to a small white towel, which is draped over the side of the bath near where I sit. Watching her closely, she uses her paws to pull it to the floor. As the heavy material reaches the floor, Lola picks it up with her teeth and drags it across the floor to Julie. To my amazement, Lola drops the towel next to Julie, and sits quietly, with her tail wagging.

I stroke her head and along her spine. 'Clever girl,' I smile, and hope sincerely that no one else steps forward to claim the dog, because for all intents and purposes Lola seems to want to keep us too.

Julie shuffles her body so that she can rest her head on my thigh, and in a loving gesture she reaches to stroke Lola's head. The dog seems appreciative, she seems to understand that a lot rides on the next few days. After all it's been merely hours since Lola came to live with us. I just hope that Julie and the dog continue to get on well. Once she got over her annoyance with me about bringing a dog home from work, she only had to look into Lola's eyes, and she was won over.

'You feel OK to come and sit in the bedroom?' I ask, rising from bathtub, holding out my hand.

She takes it and slowly pulls herself to her feet, where I hold her carefully.

'I hope the sickness settles soon,' she smiles weakly, stroking my cheek. She leads us into the small hallway and through to the bedroom. When we sit on the light grey velvet Chesterfield sofa facing the window, she wipes her mouth absently with a hand, and looks out of the window. It's sunny and the landscaped gardens at the back of the house are stunning. Large rose bushes and palms lead along a stepping stone pathway to the grey brick pool house.

I feel a jolt on the seat, and Lola jumps up and fits herself snugly next to Julie on the cushions. Julie strokes her absently, and I can't help but feel happy that a bond is already forming between them. Lola's tail wags with contentment.

'Do you think it's because of what we did, that these murders are happening?' My wife asks, her eyes anywhere but on me.

'No, I don't,' I tell her firmly. 'Those young men were bad boys, who turned into evil men. They preyed on single females. That's on them.'

'I know you're right, Bri.' She finally turns to me. 'But what we did to those young men, was wrong. It left scars, particularly to that idiot, Cameron. His leg was busted completely.'

'Those fuckers are lucky to be alive after what they did to Lottie,' I lift my arm and drape it around my wife's shoulders.

'I know,' she pats my hand. 'I've been thinking about that day a lot recently. It's been playing on my mind.'

'Oh sweetheart,' I cup her cheek. 'You should have said something.'

She leans in to kiss me, and a stray tear trickles down her cheek. 'Oh baby,' I say, wiping the tear with my thumb, 'please don't cry. They don't deserve it.'

Cushioning her face with both of my hands, I rest my forehead against hers, 'Look at me, Julie,' I tell her firmly, and wait until her eyes catch mine. There is nowhere to hide.

'I would do the same thing, a thousand times over, if it meant protecting Lottie and any other vulnerable person who they decided to drug and rape. They knew exactly what they were doing.'

'But Bri,' she protests. I can hear that she still has doubts.

'No, honey.' I say. 'What if we have a daughter? What if she was drugged by animals like these young men, and then found herself dumped in a dirty storeroom. What would you do to them then?'

She finally gets it. Looking at me, her voice steadier. 'I would kill them. Every single one of them.'

Her answer should have shocked me, but it didn't.

I smile at her. 'That's my girl,' I whisper, kissing her hard on the lips. 'Now lie down on that massive bed,' my eyes motion across the room, 'and get some rest. I'll go in search of a pot of tea and some biscuits.'

Lola follows Julie, watching carefully as though guarding her, as my wife settles down on the bed and with a sigh, rests her head on the pillow. Once she is settled Lola looks at me and I smile and nod. Our new dog jumps onto the bed and snuggles in Julie's arms, within seconds they are both asleep.

Despite the turmoil of the visit here with Jenny, Stuart and friends it feels peaceful. As though it's allowing us to enjoy each precious moment.

Suddenly, my family seems to be getting bigger.

***

A few hours later, Julie is looking much more like herself after a short nap, and her cheeks have some colour in them. During her nap, I called Shep to see if the analysis is back on the suspected severed finger of Vincent Camprinelli, I also need to chase the data from his phone.

I had taken a walk in the garden, to make the call. The sun is going down and taking the summer heat with it. Following the eight-foot-high stone garden wall, I discovered an open white stone archway at the bottom of the garden and, to my surprise, found that this led to an oval-shaped wildflower garden. A gravel pathway jutted around the flower garden, making it accessible and inviting. Several stone benches provided seating.

Lowering myself onto the cold, hard surface of a bench, I take my phone out of my trouser pocket and call my DS.

'Hi Boss, I was just about to call you.' she sounds breathless, like she's been running.

'Any joy on the Vincent Camprinelli stuff?' I get straight to the point, as I want to get back to Julie and the dog. Absently, I brush a stray hair from my trousers.

'Yes,' I can hear papers being ruffled. 'The finger definitely belongs to Vincent Camprinelli, and Maggie says that if he's young and healthy, he may still be alive.'

Shit. I can picture the scene, with the younger Camprinelli begging for mercy! That must have hurt.

'The doc says that there are a ton of gadgets on the market that take off digits such as fingers. These gadgets are small and efficient and safer than carrying a knife. Sid, Maggie's forensic scientist, is going to try to match them against the wound tonight.'

Holy fuck why doesn't this surprise me. 'Bloody hell,' I mutter, running my fingers through my hair.

'It's pretty gory, that's what it is,' Shep answers. 'I mean, it's the sort of thing gangsters use.'

'And the phone?' I ask, feeling the sudden need to use the bathroom. I stand up and begin to walk slowly back through the stone arch to the house.

'Yes, I've made a start on that, now we've got the warrant to check his phone records and history. Recent calls include a four-minute call yesterday morning to Cameron Frost, several texts to someone called Angel, who may be the girlfriend, but nothing since 9.30am. Frost was the last person to speak to him.'

'Good work, when you've done a bit more digging around, send me a printout of the phone numbers and who they belong to. Well done, Shep.'

'Thanks, Boss. I'll get onto that asap.'

'One more thing, Shep. I'm bringing a parcel in first thing tomorrow. I'm going to pull Josie off the Shafer case and I want her looking into this. I want Sid and Maggie to see what they can get from it.'

I end the call and rush into the house to find the nearest toilet. But my mind is still on babies, morning sickness and the Camprinellis.

***

We are downstairs in the drawing room catching up on the day's events. Julie looks stunning in an off the shoulder white silk blouse that drapes softly over black velvet trousers and her usual black ankle boots. She has minimal makeup, just a touch of mascara and a hint of lipstick. To me, she is breathtaking.

I hand her a sparkling elderflower drink, while she's talking to Jem and Steph, and make my way to Noah, who sits chatting to Jack on a dark green comfy chair by the large bay window.

Noah raises his wine glass to me, 'How's Julie holding up?'

'Not so great,' I reply. 'The sickness comes and goes. It's driving her mad.'

They smile, in unison, as if they both agree and know something important that I don't.

'Ginger biscuits might help,' Noah suggests, 'they helped Jem when she was struggling.'

'Oh, that's a good one,' I park that to the back of my mind. I'll pick some up tomorrow.

'Don't worry,' Jack says, 'I'm sure she'll start to feel better soon.'

Jenny and Stuart enter the room, they scan the area as though looking for someone. Their gaze fixes on us and they walk over. They are a very elegant couple. She is tall and slender, and dressed in cream trousers and a dusky pink long-sleeved blouse.

I've known them for several years now, and they've become firm friends.

As they grow nearer to our group, Harley jumps up from the arm of green sofa and touches Jenny's arm, to attract her attention. She stops and bends down to him, giving him her full attention as she carefully puts her arm around the boy. As Harley begins to talk, they both suddenly burst out laughing.

Taking his wife's hand, Stuart leads her forward to our group, and as they reach us, he asks her if she would like something to drink. In a caring gesture he reaches out and tucks a stray strand of her hair behind her ear. It's very touching to watch, and I absently wonder if Julie and I will be like this in the years to come. I very much hope so.

She smiles. 'Surprise me,' she winks playfully at him, 'anything but vodka.' Stuart smiles and goes in search of the drinks table, which is situated by the oversized stone fireplace. The housekeeper, Mrs Monk, is busy topping up glasses and taking orders. Lola is asleep in her bed, dreaming of whatever dogs dream of.

Jenny turns to me, 'I had no idea this family break would produce such great news. Firstly, about Sasha and Jules getting married and now about you and Julie. We are truly blessed.' She is beaming with pride as always. She must feel pleased that she actually organised this break.

The distant chime of the doorbell alerts us that we have visitors, and for some reason I immediately feel that something is wrong. Mrs Monk, wearing a matching pale green knitted cardigan and skirt, scurries from the room to attend the door.

'Who's that?' Jenny asks, looking toward the doorway.

'I'm not sure,' I mutter, hearing movements and raised voices in the entrance hall. 'But I think we are about to find out.'

The feeling of foreboding continues, when I recognise the voice.

Gino Camprinelli.

Swooping into the room, like a bird of prey and wearing his trademark black suit and white shirt, all six foot six of testosterone and grey hair, is the last man I expected to seemy tea tonight. Flanked on either side of him, wearing almost identical black suits, stand his hench men.

A rather grand entrance for a person who doesn't like to bring attention to himself. His eyes look around the room and stop when he sees me. A flustered Agnes Monk follows closely behind them, her face is flushed, and she rubs her hands down her green skirt in agitation.

'Ah, DCI Carter. I was hoping to find you here.' Gino Camprinelli's voice booms throughout the now silent room. Gino is smiling broadly as though we are long lost pals who have just been reunited. But to me, the smile doesn't reach his eyes. 'We need to talk.'

'Camprinelli!' I answer, stepping up close to him so that we are shoulder to shoulder. 'With what do we owe this pleasure?'

This is Gino pushing back. He's here to make a statement, to tell me that he wants answers, and he wants them now. What the fuck he expects me to do at this precise moment in time, I don't know.

Steph nods to Jack, her eyes moving to their son, Ben, before she walks to my side. Julie has the same idea, as the only serving police officers here they pull rank and stand either side of me. It's going to be a Mexican standoff, if I can't calm the situation. Immediately, my first thoughts are, how the fuck did they get through the security. My second thought is, how the hell do I stop this situation escalating into full out war?

Stuart steps forward, gesturing to the doorway. 'Shall we take this discussion to the study? More privacy.'

The group follow him into the opulent hallway with its rich claret carpet and white walls adorned with expensive looking canvases. A few turns later and Stuart takes the gold handle of a dark wooden door, presses it down and pushes the door open.

I nod to Camprinelli, 'Perhaps you can leave the muscle outside?' I stare at the two goons, who look like they've just stepped out of a scene from a Men in Black movie.

'Stay there,' he orders to the men, and at this moment he looks every bit like the small-time gangster he is.

Stuart steps into the room and flicks on the light switch. 'I'll leave you to it.'

I offer Stuart my thanks, and watch him return to the family, before reaching out for my wife, and resting a hand in the small of her back. 'Are you OK?'

Julie turns to look at me, offering a reassuring smile to let me know she's fine. In the office, Steph scans the room and immediately assesses the walnut oak desk and matching padded chairs. She indicates for Gino Camprinelli to help himself to a chair, before closing the door.

Camprinelli shakes his head, 'I'll stand, if that's alright?' He walks to a walnut cabinet near the door and folds his arms.

I walk slowly to the desk and drop into the seat behind it. Quickly, I note that there are several pens and several blank sheets of A4 copier paper. Resting my arms away from the paper, I study Gino

Camprinelli, standing with his arms folded, as if by looking down on me, he has the upper ground.

He knows nothing.

Gino has been blessed with good looks, but his skin is now peppered with wrinkles, much like mine reflecting the signs of age and experiences that we've been through.

His grey hair is scraped back into a ponytail, almost like an aging popstar, I had the sudden urge to grab a pair of scissors and cut the bloody thing off. Whereas mine, is kept short and tidy for work.

Not for the first time, I chastise myself for tethering myself to this man, who shares some of my darkest secrets. For fuck's sake Brian, what were you thinking? How did you let that happen? You should know better.

'You shouldn't have come here, Gino,' I tell him, focusing on his face. Steel blue eyes stare back at me, but they're trying to hide something, the ever so slight tick that forms at the top of his right cheekbone, gives it away.

'I wanted to see you,' he says, unapologetically. 'I wanted to hear what news you have on Vincent.'

Steph perches on the edge of the desk. 'A phone call would have sufficed, Mr Camprinelli. You didn't need to disable the gate alarm, or whatever you did to breach the security.'

'True, DI Rutland,' he looks Steph up and down, in a dismissive way. I store this little snippet of information deep into my mind. He's not a great fan of women.

'Where are we with the phone and the finger?' Julie asks me, in her no-nonsense way, pushing her fingers along the sill of the window, as she stares into the garden.

'Ah, the lovely, Mrs C,' Camprinelli turns to look at my wife, 'I've been watching your career with keen interest, DS Carter. Will you be aiming to outrank your husband in the future?' he smiles in a provocative way, and I clasp my hands together firmly, to stop myself from punching the fucker. Julie ignores him, she knows he's trying to get a rise out of me.

'Stop being a dick,' I tell him.

Gino smiles, he's about to reply when Steph jumps into the conversation.

'That's enough! Let's get to business,' she says, looking at both of us. 'We can play games all night, but I would personally like to return to my friends and family.'

I reach along the top of the desk and take a piece of paper and a pen to make notes. 'Firstly,' I explain, looking around the room, 'the finger was severed cleanly and with little violence, and it matches the shape and clean severing of Eric's finger.'

'Secondly,' I write notes to chase up the coroner and Shep. 'We have been over to Vincent's place, collected a variety of DNA samples and they match the DNA from the finger.'

'Number three, we have a warrant to go through Vincent's phone, laptop and any tablets. We're in the process of tracking the last seventy-two hours before he disappeared. We're looking for bank withdrawals, people he's been in contact with, anything out of the ordinary.'

'OK,' Gino's face shows some relief. 'But you've still got no idea who took Vincent and where he is?'

'No,' I say. 'I assume you've had no ransom demand?'

Gino shakes his head, 'No, not a thing. That's why I think it's someone he knows. Someone close to home.'

Steph looks up, 'Was he in any trouble? I mean with anyone specific?'

I look up, something crosses Gino's face, but he shakes his head. 'He's a Camprinelli,' he mutters, 'he's always in trouble.'

That's a cop out, if ever I've heard one!

'Gino! Spit it out.' I say, I'm sick of his bullshit lying.

'It's nothing,' Gino pulls his jacket closer.

'It might be something to us,' Steph says.

Gino's shoulders shrug, as though defeated, 'Cameron said he'd been selling a few steroids at one of my gyms.'

'Ah,' Steph replies, 'Who is his supplier? And, did he owe anyone money?'

He runs his hands through his hair. 'For fuck's sake, I don't know! I've been trying to find out, but everyone is playing silly fucking beggars.'

'Well, keep trying,' I tell him, 'And let me know if you come up with anything solid.'

Gino nods in response, and I'm relieved that we all seem to be singing from the same page now. I can't have him running around threatening to cut off limbs, it'll cause a riot.

Julie leans against the windowsill, folding her arms. 'What about girlfriends, or partners. Does he have anyone special?'

The room is silent for a moment.

'I don't know, I'm not his bloody keeper!' Gino grinds out, and then he begins to mutter. 'No, don't think so, but Cameron mentioned that Eric had been seeing someone for a couple of months. Since Cameron moved to Charmouth, Eric and Vincent have only kept in touch via text or phone. Although, for some reason Vincent arranged to meet Cameron two days ago.'

I scribble some notes. 'Leave that with me. My DS spoke to Frost's mum, he left the house three days ago and hasn't been back since.'

Gino takes his phone from his jacket pocket, opens it, locates Cameron's phone number and reads it out to me.

'Let's call it a night. I need to eat.' I finish writing Cameron's number, fold the paperwork with my notes and stuff it into the back pocket of my chinos.

Gino paces the room, before slowly following the others when they move toward the door. As the last of the group leave the room, I look at the man trailing at the back, and say, 'Gino, can I have a quick word.'

The man stops still, and I wait until the door is shut before getting up from my chair. I move to the front of the desk and rest against it.

'Did you know that your nephew and his friends who were known as The Three Amigos, had an interesting hobby of drugging and raping young girls?'

'What?' Gino looks at me, and I see his eyes widen. He has no idea. 'What the fuck are you talking about!' His voice is hard.

'You heard what I said,' I tell him. 'I'm sorry to be the one to tell you, but your nephew and his so-called friends are rapists.'

He moves slightly, leaning bodily against the wall, nearest to the closed door. 'He's a fucking imbecile, is what he is.'

'That too,' I admit, feeling sorry for the man who is trying to trust a tired, old copper. 'The thing is, Gino.' I take a deep breath, push my hands deep into my trouser pockets. 'The thing is... I think, we think, that this is related.'

'Related, in what way? You mean it's someone they've hurt? A woman?' he raises an eyebrow.

I look at him, 'or a husband, father, brother... Who knows?'

'Fucking hell.' He says in a low voice and pushes off the wall. 'Regardless, of what he is and what he has done, Brian,' he walks slowly to me, 'he is my only nephew and I need you to find him.'

I pat his shoulder. Not sure why, but I feel that sometimes this man can take on the world and be misunderstood. Don't get me wrong. He's not a good guy by any means, but he sorted Felix out and that's positive in my book. Deep down, he has his demons just like everyone else.

Gino Camprinelli, keeper of secrets, avenger and general thorn in the backside, is asking for help.

I shake my head at the irony, that this is yet another one of those times, when the black and white merge into grey.

Part Twenty-Seven: Daniel

Looking around the drawing room of this beautiful manor house, I wonder what secrets it holds within the old brick walls that surround us. Tales of pain and sorrow, of heartache, cruelty and love, where mystery seeps through every rock, nook and cranny.

My imagination begins to run wild. Of secret trysts and hidden doors. I can just imagine pulling the woman of my choice, by the hand and disappearing through a hidden door.

Oh, for fuck's sake Daniel. Get a grip.

Across the room, Lottie sits in deep discussion with Jenny. Tonight, she wears a summery yellow dress that reaches her ankles. God, I love this woman, with the wild Nicole Kidman red hair, and skin so soft and pale that my fingers itched to touch it, stroke it, and do all sorts of wayward things to it.

Momentarily, I am transported to the first time I met Charlotte Peckham, which unsurprisingly, was also her first counselling session with me. All those years ago.

***

My notes are carefully laid out with my observation notebook and a pen on my wooden desk. I am so lucky to be able to rent this workspace for my consultant practice, I fell in love with the brownstone building, on the outskirts of Oxford, almost immediately. Having visited several other premises, from

Kidlington to Wantage, I knew that this building would be perfect for me.

All seems right with the world, and I feel I am where I should be. There is something very satisfying about being financially independent. I am my own boss, I own my own house, and pay my own bills. Everything that I have is here for me to enjoy. Oh Jesus! I sound like I'm part of some supergroup.

Looking at my watch, I realise that it's time for my next patient. Scrolling down my list, I note that the next person is Jenny Greyson's friend, Charlotte Peckham. It's only recently come to light that Charlotte was assaulted and raped by three young men five years ago, Jenny asked me if I could help Charlotte work through her ordeal and process what had happened to her.

Pushing out of my seat, I walk across my consultation room, open the door and step into the hallway. I am faced with a young woman, with unruly long curly red hair, staring at me, with big grey eyes that look unsure and panicked. Her body is hidden under a long dark pink skirt, with flat boots and a grey, thick cardigan.

'Charlotte Peckham?' I ask, my voice suddenly husky, as those grey stormy eyes stare back at me.

Jenny and Charlotte have set up a support group for people who have been through trauma and abuse, to talk about their experiences and offer peer on peer support. I am wavering the session cost, as a favour to her. Jenny is one of the strongest women I know, apart from my mother, Angela.

'Lottie,' she corrects, straight away and I'm surprised how strong her voice sounds. Steady, strong.

'Come this way, Lottie,' I smile. 'I promised Jenny I would look after you.'

The young woman smiles, sending a warm feeling that seeps through my body. The heated frisson makes its way down my neck and across my shoulders, before finally reaching my stomach. Every single thought leaves my mind so that the only thing I can hear are the alarm bells of my thudding heart.

The receptionist, Gill, pushes her glasses higher onto her nose. She is in her twenties, with very short black hair, several piercings in both ears and a pretty oval-shaped face. It is a joy to work with Gill because she has a lovely manner when answering the phone and is particularly kind and helpful with the patients who attend the clinic.

'Dr Scott,' she says, peering over her desk. 'I have a message for you.'

Immediately, the hairs stand up on my arm. Mrs Doreen Anders is one of my longest standing patients, I've been seeing her for three years.

Gill hands me a pink post-it note. 'Here you go,' she smiles.

'Thanks,' I say, taking the slip of paper from her and glancing at it quickly. It was another note inviting me to her twentieth wedding anniversary party. I have explained several times that it is not appropriate for me to attend, but she doesn't listen.

I glance at Lottie, who pushes herself into a standing position beside me, her face tilts so that she is looking at me and judging by the crease on her forehead and the grim line of her lips, she looks worried. Hazel eyes blatantly stare at the note.

'So sorry,' I tell her, gesturing her into my office. 'It's from one of my patient's. This way, please.'

***

The drawing room is busy. I scan the room looking for Lottie, but she's nowhere to be seen. Earlier, she was sitting on the sofa chatting to Jenny, but now Jenny is studying the paintings on the walls, with Noah. Where the hell is she?

Harley is missing too, and that makes me feel better. Perhaps they've both gone to the pool house?

'Have you seen Lottie or Harley?' I ask Jack, who is chatting to Ben on the sofa.

'I think they went with Stuart to the security office. They were looking at the cameras to see how Gino managed to open the electronic gate.'

Making my way quickly to the security room, nerves begin to get the better of me as I wonder how I must look, like a silly lamb following his flock. Or a sheep to the slaughter? I wipe sweaty palms, across my navy chinos and head to the main hall to find the security office.

Through the open doorway I spy Gino Camprinelli's two hench men, looking very out of place in their dark suits, not unlike villains in a Bond film, as they stand in the entrance and talk quietly to each other. As one moves, I get a quick flash of what looks like the handle of a gun. Shit.

Who the hell are these people? Gangsters? One wrong move and God knows what will happen. There is movement in one of the rooms nearby, a door opens and Steph and Julie step into the hallway. I nod as I walk in the opposite direction to the security room. Peeking inside the open doorway, I find Stuart standing with his arms crossed, his eyes searching across each of the four screens. He turns to me.

'Hey,' he says, looking back at the screens.

'Hey,' I murmur back. 'Found anything?'

'Yeah,' he points a finger to the screen, and stops the footage with another finger. 'Look at this. The driver gets out of the car, takes a card and swipes it twice across the key code. It's magnetised somehow to allow access through the gate.'

'Fuck.' I say quietly.

Stuart turns to me and sticks his hands in his trouser pockets. 'I'm getting really fed up with this whole situation. Firstly, we have these attacks, and secondly there are the grisly gifts that Lottie keeps getting. I'm pretty sure it's all connected. And if I'm right, Cameron Frost will be next.'

'I agree. It's all too close to home.' I shake my head absently, 'still can't get my head around you guys kidnapping and torturing three young men.'

'It just made sense at the time,' Stuart sits in a nearby chair, and brushes fingers through his hair. With slumped shoulders, he breaks the silence, 'after what they had done to Lottie, and possibly others, it was important to give them a clear message.'

'After we did it though,' Stuart's voice is husky, emotional. 'We struggled, because we knew we had well and truly crossed the line.'

'And Jenny?'

'Yeah,' Stuart closes his eyes, and a hard smile forms on his face as he recalls what happened. 'She was livid when I told her what we'd done!'

I laugh out loud. Typical Jenny. Taking a second chair, I move it slightly, until it's next to Stuart's and sit.

'I wish I'd been there,' I say in a low voice. My friend's eyebrows shoot up in surprise.

'What?' I ask, 'You think it doesn't play on my mind, what they did to her? You think I don't imagine beating the shit out of her cousin for drugging her? For raping her? I had to listen to her reliving that nightmare for months. It nearly killed me.'

Stuart looks down at the floor as he processes my words. To my surprise, he raises his face, reaches out a hand to pat my upper arm and says solemnly, 'I'm sorry man, I didn't know.'

'How could you know?' I ask, patting his hand, 'she was my patient, I was her doctor and that was the end of it.'

'And now?' He asks.

'Now, we're trying to put ourselves first. Slowly, and carefully, for Harley's sake.'

'You're a good man, Daniel, and I know you'll soon win Harley over. He's a great kid.'

I wish I felt as confident as Stuart. But I am patient and I'm willing to let Lottie and her son lead the pace, so there's hope for me yet. 'I hope so,' I reply.

'How's Lottie doing?' he suddenly asks.

'Not great,' I answer, 'she's trying not to panic about the dead animal gifts, but something is wrong, and she feels threatened.' I don't mention the nightmares, for the moment, they are private. 'I'm going to try and chat properly to her tomorrow, if she'll let me.'

'Good luck,' he laughs, 'I've known Lottie and Jenny since our university days. They're both strong women and very good at pushing things to one side.'

This is something that I have anticipated. That Lottie didn't want me to help, and if that's the case, then I will stand by her wishes.

'I can only try,' I muse, meeting his eyes. From the first moment I met this man in the hospital, during a visit to see Jenny, I liked him. He was confident and at ease with himself. He was obviously worried about Jenny, but he seemed uncomplicated, no bullshit or airs and graces. You know what I mean, just a real nice guy.

'I'm off to find the woman in question,' I say, pushing out of my chair and stretching my long legs. 'Do you know where she went?'

'I think, she and Harley went outside,' Stuart answers, his eyes focus on the monitors as Gino Camprinelli and his cronies get into their black car and pull off down the driveway. He doesn't move and is transfixed on their movements until they make their way through the seven-foot toughened metal security gate, and it closes securely behind them.

Moving suddenly, he looks my way and exhales slowly. 'Thank fuck for that,' he says cheerfully, before following me out of the door.

I laugh and shake my head. He never ceases to surprise me.

'Catch up with you soon.' I say, as I walk off.

There are moments, I reflect as I wander the corridors in search of the elusive Lottie, that you look back in your life and all you remember are the bad things. If I told you about the distress, pain and suffering that some of my patients had been and still go through. The fragile life stories, the beatings, the assaults, the fragility of the mind, trauma in all its awful shades that means you struggle for the rest of your life.

Stuart was right, Lottie and Jenny are the strong ones. They have suffered horrifically at the hands of people who should have known better, who should have respected them. Instead, they were let down. And being part of the process of recuperation means that I must be strong for her, but right now I would gladly hunt down every single one of those bastards and tear them apart.

My knuckles are twitching.

'Are you looking for my Mum?' a familiar voice asks suddenly, as I make my way down the corridor that leads to the pool house. It's Harley.

'Yes,' I answer, looking at Harley, and noting that he's changed from smart clothes to jeans and a brown, long-sleeved top. He has a folded blue towel under his arm. Taking his phone from his jeans pocket, he starts to text. 'I'm just seeing if Ben wants to go for a swim. Mum,' he looks up at me. 'She went for a walk in the garden.' He nods to his left. 'That way.'

'Thanks,' I answer.

Ben's phone bleeps and he reaches into his jeans pocket, looks at the message and replies quickly. That must be Ben replying to his text. I turn to make my way to the gardens, when there is another bleep. Harley looks down and scowls. I notice he doesn't reply. Simply pops his phone back into his jeans pocket.

'Everything OK?' I ask, casually pushing my hands deep into my pockets.

'Yeah,' he answers, looking up at me. He seems unsure of me, so I give him some space. He doesn't know me, he's more likely to tell Ben or Stuart if something is worrying him, than me. So, I tell myself that if it's important, he'll tell someone.

'You sure?' I ask, one more time studying his face. I know I shouldn't do that, but it's what I do. I'm a creature of habit, watching, listening, noticing.

He tries to play me, 'Yeah, it's nothing.' He looks at the floor.

'OK,' I say, letting him take the lead. 'Just putting it out there, but if there is anything worrying you, I'm happy to listen.'

'Thanks,' he says sullenly, before his shoulders slump and he turns in the direction of the pool area, then adds in a low voice, 'I don't need anything from anyone, so leave me alone.'

I nod, leaving him to stalk off. I'm sure I've done that a thousand times to my mum when I was younger, so I give him some space. Harley is going to take some time to win over, but that's alright. I like a challenge.

The darkness of the gardens is offset against an array of twinkling lights that loop around the seven-foot-high stone wall and hedges. Shadows fall around solar garden lanterns, and the sweet smell of roses permeate the warm, early evening air. I hear her before I see her.

She's sobbing.

I stop dead, and inhale deeply, taking in the scent of the roses. My heart contracts at the sound. As a child, the sound of someone crying always sent me into a pit of panic or impending doom. Thankfully, my parents noticed and were effective in arranging a course of counselling to help me understand that showing your emotions was a good thing, and that crying was an important process used in coping with sadness, disappointment, frustration and plain anger.

I step closer to the sobbing figure. 'Sorry to interrupt,' I say quietly, stopping when our arms are almost touching.

Taking a tissue from my pocket, I hold it out to her. She takes it and begins to blow her nose. 'Thanks,' she mutters, her voice is low and shaky.

'You want me to leave you in peace?' I ask, praying that she'll say no. I don't want to leave her here like this.

'No,' she utters looking at me. I see the sparkle of tears sitting there, waiting to drop onto her cheeks. 'God, no.' she turns to me, grasping my shirt, her head tucking deep into my chest. 'Hold me,' she urges, her words rumbling against my shirt as I envelop her within the warmth of my body.

'It's OK, I've got you,' I tell her soothingly, I have no idea why she's upset, or what has happened, that can wait for later. The here and now, is what we're striving for. For moments like this, which will define us and help us to take what we want from each other without regrets, without guilt.

'I've got you,' I say, stroking her glorious red hair, remembering our first meeting, when to touch her was all that I wanted. Well, I haven't burst into flames yet. That's got to be good, hasn't it? I rest my chin softly on the top of her head.

'Better?' I ask, my voice husky.

'Mmmm...' she murmurs. 'Yes,' her voice lingers.

'Good,' I give her a moment to settle, before asking. 'What happened? What upset you?'

'I think I'm going mad, Daniel,' she answers with such a deep sadness in her voice. I see the outline of a small border wall, the height just right for sitting on, and lead her to it by the hand.

'Why do you say that?' I look at her. All soulful eyes and curls, this isn't like Lottie at all.

'I ... I can't get the pictures of those dead animals out of my mind. Who would do that? And now Steph...' Her voice trails off.

'I don't know,' I shake my head, 'who knows why people do what they do.'

Thankfully, it isn't a pattern of behaviour I've come across before. 'Did you bring the rat with you?' I ask, trying to steer the subject onto more solid ground. It would be helpful to have both, so that Brian can send them both to the lab.

'Yes, it's in the boot of my car,' she answers. 'Jem said we needed to show Stuart and the others. She was right, wasn't she?'

I nod silently, her eyes glisten with unshed tears. We can just about see each other in the darkening evening. 'But we will find out who is doing this.'

'You can't say that Daniel,' she shakes her head. 'You can't just walk back into my life and make everything better. Life doesn't work like that.'

Facing her, I gently take her shoulders, they're chilly from the cold night air. The yellow maxi summer dress she is wears is thin, and I shrug out of my dark blue velvet jacket and gently drop it around her shoulders. 'Listen to me, I am only going to say this once.' Strangely, I had no idea what I was about to say. 'Lottie, I have been in love with you since the first time you came to my office.'

'What?' Her body stiffens, as if in shock, 'You can't be. You let me go.'

I can't believe that we're going to do this, right here, right now, and I can feel my frustration beginning to boil. 'It's true, I am. From the moment you looked at me, there was something about you. But I knew then that I couldn't do anything about it. I was your doctor for fuck's sake, how could I ask you out?'

Lottie looks across the garden at the shadows settling over the garden. 'I know we said that it was time for us, but I had no idea that you felt so strongly about me.'

'I didn't either, until I said it. I surprised myself!' I half laugh and hear a giggle form in her throat. This is good.

'I can't promise love, Daniel' she says sadly. 'After Simon, I'm not sure what I'm capable of giving. But I do know that I want to try.'

'That's enough for me.' I put my arm around her shoulder, and we sit in silence for a few minutes. Her earlier words come back to me, and I break the silence.

'You said earlier, Steph wants... what does she want?' I ask.

'She wants to take the dead animals into Cowley Station,' she answers.

'Well, that's not necessarily a bad thing, is it?' It will save us, having the grisly things here.

'I suppose not.' She mutters, before turning to me. She reaches up to touch my face. 'Now, Dr Scott, I know just the right tonic to cheer a woman up.'

'And what might that be?' I ask, tilting my head down, until our lips touch softly.

Part Twenty-Eight: Cameron

Dear All,

I want to tell you a story. It's about how a young man who enjoyed life with his college friends, drinking and playing around with girls. He also had a promising football career planned. But this all went to pot when he and his friends were kidnapped by some very strange and violent people, who ruined all chances of said football career.

The young man, still physically mobile - of sorts, and able to drive, decides to plot his revenge on those who have wronged him. From finding and torturing small animals, to gifting them to an unsuspecting cousin who deserves each gory gift.

This is the story, of a young man who grew into a bitter man, who just wants to get his own back. So, without further ado, I present, Mr Cameron Frost.

Act one:

Put more pressure on cousin Charlotte. She doesn't deserve to be happy, not while I am left in this perpetual hell. Send texts and gory photos.

Act two:

Once she is beginning to crack, find the people who kidnapped me, Eric and Vincent.

Act three:

The grand finale. What will bring her to her knees? I've got a sneaky theory, I know what.

Who will bring her to her knees? Me.

A pungent smell fills the hotel bedroom and I realise that I must get rid of the dead pigeon, before the maggots start eating him from the inside out. I pick up my phone from the desk and pose the camera app over the bird's body, to get the best gory photo I can.

When I'm satisfied that I have several good photos, I choose one and send it to Charlotte.

'Good afternoon, Charlotte' I begin typing a message to accompany the photo.

'Hope you have enjoyed receiving my special gifts. Here's a preview of your next gift. I thought of you during its death and mutilation.'

I can't help but smile, when I think of the look of horror on her face, when she sees the photo and reads the attached words.

I put on permanent capital letters to highlight my next words.

'I AM COMING FOR YOU AND YOURS.'

I press send. Act one complete.

Walking to the brown tub chair, I slump into it, and allow my aching right leg to rest in a straight position, sticking out across the carpet. I glance at the tin with the bird in it on the desk. My phone beeps, catching me by surprise, there is a reply.

'Who the hell is this and why are you doing this to me?' the angry text reads, and I can't help but feel a sense of achievement. This is what I want, to play around with her. Mess with her head.

Thank fuck!

Feeling brighter, I search for the cardboard and black marker pen before following the pattern of the previous gifts. Oh God this is epic, I wish I could see her face. The phone buzzes with the ringtone, blaring Billy Ocean's 'When the Going Gets Tough.' It's Mum calling.

If I answer, she will be pressuring me with questions. If I don't, she'll keep ringing.

I answer.

'Mum?' I say, 'What's up?'

'What do you mean, what's up?' she is angry with me. 'Where the hell are you? People have been looking for you?'

'I've just taken a few days break, that's all. What people?' I answer, trying not to reach her level of animosity.

'You would know, if you were here, you arrogant son of a bitch.' She answers with an acidic tone to her voice.

'Thanks for the motherly love, but it's a little too late.' I say sarcastically. 'What people?' I demand, harshly.

'Vincent's Uncle Gino. And the police rang wanting to speak to you.'

Shit.

'The police? What did they want?' I push, not sure if she would be spiteful enough to keep the truth from me. 'Fucking tell me what they said,' I shout, losing my patience with her.

The line is quiet for a moment.

Mum coughs, that deep raspy cough of a heavy smoker, before speaking again, 'A DS Sheppington, from Thames Valley Police rang, she just wanted to talk to you.' Again, there is silence, and I wonder if she has walked away, but then I hear heavy breathing, and her words are sad, when she asks. 'What have you done, Cameron?'

She's really getting on my nerves, and I grind out harshly and much too quickly, 'Nothing, Mum, I've done nothing.' Shit. That's the thing with mums, they know you better than you know yourself.

'I wish I could believe you, but I don't. You're not to bring problems to my door, do you hear? You and those bloody stupid friends of yours, Eric and Vincent. Always up to no good. I am no fool, Cameron, I see and hear things.

My head suddenly starts buzzing and her voice becomes distant.

Fuck.

All I can do is disconnect the phone.

Fuck.

Jesus, I need a drink.

Part Twenty-Nine: Vincent

I knew she looked familiar, but it took me a while to realise who she was. She has definitely changed since I last met her. We found her in a pub, and Cameron took a liking to her. We were getting pretty wasted with some other girls, Eric and I, but Cameron was the dominant, methodical one. When he decided to move in on a girl, I had to drink to drown out the demons, because I knew what would come next.

I knew she would be drugged and raped. But in my mind, I convinced myself that they wouldn't remember because they were so out of it. I shut my eyes to the thought that they may have flashbacks. I didn't want to know.

Eric and I were the followers, the little ants that followed the queen ant. We enjoyed the notoriety that we got at the high schools. The Three Amigos, that's what they used to call us.

That's no excuse for my behaviour. With Gino Camprinelli as my uncle, and head of the family, like the local mafioso, it would have been a surprise if I hadn't turned out bad. I quite enjoyed school, particularly literature and my grades were good. Unfortunately, it just wasn't meant to be. My uncle made sure he chose which direction my pathway took. He and mum would butt heads, they were both strong-willed, but my uncle had the weight of his men behind him.

One time, when I was fifteen, we were eating dinner of meatballs and gravy, with spaghetti in our bright yellow farmhouse style kitchen, which Mama had been working on for hours, when the front door of our house in Harwell, near Didcot, opened.

Of course, in walked Uncle Gino, stepping quickly through the small hallway and open door, into the large kitchen, wearing his trademark black suit, white shirt and grey tie. To me, a fifteen-year-old boy, he looked tall and commanding. And a bit fearsome, if I'm honest. His previously short dark hair had been left to grow, making him look a little unruly. Almost like he didn't care.

Two of his men hovered by the front door, unsure if they should follow him or not.

'Stay outside,' he said, without a glance. As if they were pets, rather than humans.

He drew up a chair, the legs scraping across the floor as he did so and placed himself next to me at the wooden kitchen table. I looked at Mama, and she looked at me. Dad had drunk himself to an early grave two years before and there was just me, my mum and my older sister, Isabella, who was now married and living in Reading with her husband, Justin, and their children, Mia and Luca.

'Rosalina,' Gino speaks to my mother, while reaching over to take a chunk of homemade bread from the centre of the table. I am mesmerised by him. Silently, he reaches into my white bowl and coats the bread in the gravy sauce. Dropping it into his mouth, I watch with interest as he closes his eyes in appreciation. I don't say anything. If I stay quiet, he may forget I'm there.

No such luck.

'It's time,' Gino says, dunking his second chunk of bread into my bowl.

Her eyes flit to me again, 'No, Gino. It's too soon.'

There is something going on, a hidden argument between them. A war of words.

'I said no, Gino,' she says, stubbornly, wiping her mouth with the blue linen tea towel sitting on her lap, and placing it, scrunched up, by her bowl of food. She looks as though she's lost her appetite.

'Mama?' I query. I have a right to know what they're talking about, especially if it's something to do with me.

'Shh… Vincenzo,' she says sharply. She never calls me Vincenzo.

'It's all arranged, he starts work at the Wallingford gym on Saturday.' Gino scrapes back his chair and stands, daring my mum to challenge him.

'Get out of my house!' mum uses both hands to push herself back from the table, all five foot nothing of her. She stands and stares at her brother.

Please don't hurt her… I say silently in my head. Please don't hurt Mama.

'Go!' She screams, with tears framing her big brown eyes and gesturing wildly at the door. 'Get out brother. I will never forgive you for this!'

Gino shrugs his shoulders, '8.30am at the gym, bring lunch and a drink.'

He left as quickly as he had entered. Leaving a feeling of impending doom and gloom in the room.

Why do I feel like the devil is about to take my soul?

Regardless of the things I saw when working at my uncle's gym, in Didcot, it wasn't as bad as my mum had led me to believe. Plus, he gave me twenty pounds a week, and all I had to do was to sit on reception and let people through the door.

'If he asks you to do anything illegal, you tell me, Vincenzo,' she kept saying. But I learned to keep my mouth shut, and Uncle Gino appreciated that. From the shady people who came to reception, wanting me to book an appointment with Gino, who had an office in each of his three gyms.

Exactly fifteen days after starting work at Gino's gym a man everyone called 'Big Steve' suddenly, came out of the changing rooms, leaned his arms on the counter where I worked and began making conversation.

'Hey man, how are doing?' he asks, with chubby fingers that snake their way through his thick beard.

'Good,' I answer, 'you?'

'Good,' he moved forward across the counter and said in a low voice, 'if anyone needs a bit of help, you know?' He winked.

I must have raised my eyebrows, not sure what he was getting at. 'You know man, stuff... as in steroids. I can get them some.'

Holy fuck, this wasn't what I signed up for! And then I think of my mum's comments and realise that this is the seedier side of working for my uncle. That night I went home and googled steroids and that's how I became interested in who was using them. In the back of my mind, there would be an opportunity to use this information, for personal gain.

***

My thoughts turn to Cameron again, the unlikely friend from school and sixth form, the head of our small group. I never knew why I didn't walk away. I was probably too weak to stand up to him and if I'm being honest here, I was shallow and enjoyed the perks of being associated with Cameron.

A cramp starts in my calf, the pain bringing me back to the present. I try to rub it, but I'm tied like a pig on the black sofa. My missing finger hand is aching like hell, I really need some painkillers. Where the hell is Ferret? She's been gone for ages and I'm bursting for a pee. My eyes flit to the wall clock, it's 3pm.

If only there was something here that would cut through this bloody rope. Looking around the room, my eyes skirt various objects, looking for anything that might be of use. The flat is on the ground floor, it is dismal, not very bright. It looks unloved.

And then I spy something on the floor by the dining table. It is the black handled penknife that Ferret was cutting herself with.

It lies there, solitary on the dull brown carpet. Making up my mind to reach it, I heave myself from the sofa, closing my eyes to brace for impact on the thin carpeted floor.

I land with several body parts hitting the floor at the same time. Notably, my face took the main force of the fall and a pain exploded around my nose, together with a cracking sound. I bite my lip hard, to stop me howling. Bloody hell, have I broken my nose? There's a wetness trickling down my face. Fuck.

Giving myself a harsh talking to, I roll in the direction of the dining table. The weight of my body and the fact that all my limbs are tied with rope, makes every inch feel like a mile. At this point I'm not sure which is hurting most. The injury where the finger was, the broken nose or the need to pee.

Needing to take some of the pressure off myself, I force my body to relax. Blocking out the pain, I close my eyes, take a deep breath and slowly count to ten. Thankfully, my shoulder blades begin to relax, making all the difference to my aching hands, arms and body. Unfortunately, the downside, was that I landed on my back and any weak attempts to block out the pain vanish, as my right shoulder suddenly goes into spasm, causing me to groan aloud.

And then a warm wet feeling seeps through my jeans as my bladder loses its battle to hold fire. Holy fuck, how did it come to this. Pissing myself on a stranger's floor, tied like an animal waiting for slaughter?

Inch by inch I move closer to the dining table, praying that Ferret won't return home until I've managed to free myself, After, what seems like forever, I have the penknife within reach, and am filled with hope, but I've still got a long way to go to break through the ropes. And, of course, this is hindered by my tied hands and the fact that I'm lying on the floor.

The smell of urine reaches my nostrils, but I know I need to keep going if I want to get out of here. Carefully, I lean forward with my tied hands and reach for the handle of the knife. No luck, I'm too far away, so I shuffle my body to bring my hands in line with the knife. A few moments later, I am relieved to be grasping the cold, hard handle of the penknife.

I place the open blade next to the rope and begin slow sawing movements to loosen the rope. Hurting myself is something I'm prepared to do, to get free from this place and from the temperamental mind of Ferret. 'Fuck you,' I say becoming braver with the knife, tensioning the rope against the blade and moving it backwards and forwards.

Part of the rope suddenly loosens, and I use the adrenaline coursing through me to slither my injured right hand under the rough material, until it is free.

Letting the knife fall to the floor, I use my hands to untie the rope at my feet. The fingers move slower than I want, especially on my right hand, but eventually my feet and hands are free. With a sore shoulder, a bloody nose and wet jeans, I use a nearby chair to help me into a standing position.

I reach down to retrieve the penknife, and on impulse decide to close the blade up and tuck it into the back of my jeans. Picking up speed, as much as I can, with a tired, bruised body, I rush out of the room, in search of the front door.

When I touch my nose gingerly with fingers from my left hand, I can feel swelling, but I don't care, as I walk down the hallway that leads to a dark blue door. I just want to get out of here. Assuming that this is the front door, I move forward, praying that Ferret hasn't locked it. With a bit of luck, she hasn't bothered, because she believes that I couldn't escape if I was tied up.

To my relief, the catch on the door opens straight away. It pulls easily and I throw myself through the open doorway. The brightness from the sunshine stings my eyes, briefly and I absently wipe the dripping blood from my nose with sleeve of my grimy blue jumper. I must look a sight, but at this point I really don't care, I just need to escape.

There is a busy road to my left, so I head for that. I wave my good hand and scream for help.

'Help!' I throw myself into the road. 'Help!'

A silver estate swerves to avoid me and clips my right leg. Bugger, that hurts.

I go down like a sack of potatoes, fast and hard.

Crashing to the ground.

And, then my world goes dark.

Part Thirty: DCI Brian Carter

The Wave Leisure Centre is a red bricked building, it has a green roof, and it is situated in the old part of Didcot town. It features a walk in twenty-five metre pool and a gym. A hive of activity, especially when the primary schools bring children in for their termly swim lessons.

My phone buzzes, it's a text. 'It's Jez at the lab. He says they found a partial print on the cardboard nailed to Eric's body.' I tell Shep, who sits in the driver's seat of her blue Ford Fiesta.

'Door to door in the area, have seen no one, and the owner of the field says that bookings are done online, that the three to four o'clock time slot was booked online using Eric Weston's credit card.'

As we enter the building, the manager appears to be waiting for us. He is tall, with a beard, and wears a dark blue polo shirt and black trousers, 'DCI Carter, and DS Shepperton?' he asks, his hand outstretched.

'Yes, Paul Wagner?' I enquire. 'Manager?'

'That's, me,' he smiles. He looks much more at ease when he smiles. He uses his lanyard to take us through to the pool and gym area, 'What can I do for you?'

We follow the man. He seems helpful enough.

'We need to talk to you about a member of your staff, Eric Weston?' I explain.

'Eric, oh no. What's he done?' The manager looks surprised.

245

Shep clears her throat. 'Erm... he's done nothing, Paul. Is it ok to call you that?'

'Do you have an office, where we might talk privately?' I ask.

The manager nods silently and gestures to a door behind the reception counter. 'This way,' he says.

When we are alone in his office, it's time to tell him why we're here.

'Eric is dead, Paul.' I watch his reaction carefully, looking for any unusual or telltale signs. The tick of an eye or cheek, not making eye contact, rubbing a chin. They are all signs that something is wrong. The manager's reaction appears genuine.

The manager rocks back in his chair, his shoulders slumping. 'No!' he says, 'that's not possible,' his eyes are wide with shock. If he knows something, he's got a damned good poker face.

'We need to ask a few questions about Eric. Get a picture of his life, who he hung out with. Did he have a girlfriend? That sort of thing.'

'Ciara knows him quite well, they dated at one point...' Paul faces the floor, I can see he's still in shock. He looks up, to correct himself, 'knew him.'

'Is she working today?' I ask, to spur him on.

'Yes,' Paul says, reaching for his walkie talkie, and pressing the button to talk, 'Ciara to the Manager's office please.'

He explains that we will need to give them time to cover Ciara's position, if she is on poolside. Five minutes later, the door opens and a beautiful young brunette with a slim figure enters the room.

Paul stands up, gesturing for her to sit in the chair facing the desk. Worried eyes flutter from myself to Shep.

'Ciara, we have some bad news,' the Manager tells his employee. 'I'm sorry to say, that Eric, our Eric has died.'

'I'm sorry,' she smiles, 'for a minute, I thought you said that Eric was dead.' was dead.'

'He is, I'm afraid,' Shep says softly from the nearby window.

Ciara looks across the desk, staring at her boss with wide eyes. 'No!' She sobs, 'not Eric.'

From my stance near the door, I watch the girl's response, and in line with her boss's she seems genuine.

'We understand that you dated Eric for a while.' I say, slipping my hands into my trouser pockets.

'Yes, from January to July last year,' Ciara mutters, in between sobs. She takes a tissue from her pocket, dabs her eyes and blows her nose. 'I broke it off, he wanted to get serious, but I'm only twenty and didn't want to be tied down.'

'How did he take it?' Shep asks.

'OK, after a while,' Ciara answers, staring at the dishevelled tissue. 'Working together was a bit awkward at first, but we got there.'

'Anyone else on Eric's radar, new friends, or girlfriends?' Shep asks.

'Can't think of anyone, at the moment.' The manager answers, looking at Ciara.

'Well, there was that girl. You know, the one he started talking to at the pool. Don't know her name, but she came to the pool, always wore a long-sleeved swimsuit.'

My eyes flick to Shep.

'Tell me more.' I say, taking my hands from my trouser pockets. 'What information do you have on her, is she a member?' And like a dog with a bone, I take my small notebook and a pen from my jacket and start making notes.

My phone rings and I take it from my trouser pocket. 'Excuse me, I need to take this.' I tell the group, leaving the room.

It's Steph. 'Brian?' She asks.

'Yeah,' I answer, worried that something is wrong at the house. 'Is everything OK with Julie and the guys?' I can feel the hairs stand up on my arms.

'Yes, Julie is fine. She's with Jenny at the house.' Steph reassures me.

'Good,' I sigh with relief. 'So, update me on what you've been doing.' I tell her, staring at a poster on the wall.

'Lottie's boxes are being analysed as we speak. Initial investigations have found a partial index print on the lid of the second box. Nothing came up, and it doesn't match the prints found from Vincent or Eric fingers.'

'Bugger!' I mutter 'Get in touch with the Dorset police and ask them to go to Frost's house, in Charmouth, and find anything with his DNA on it. Let's see if we can get a match, or least a partial match.'

'Will do,' she answers. 'Lastly, my team has been looking out for Frost's car registration. It's just flagged up at a Marks and Spencer fuel station, at Milton Gate Interchange.'

Anger and panic sets in, 'Shit. I had hoped he would leave her alone. We need to step up security. I think he's coming for Lottie.'

'Yeah, I agree,' Steph replies. It feels good to be working with someone so caring and efficient. 'I'm still at Cowley station, but I'll call Jenny to update her before I leave.'

'I'll get back to the house as soon as I can.' I tell her.'

Bloody hell, talk about ghosts coming back to haunt you.

Part Thirty-One: Ferret

As soon as I open the front door of the flat, I know something is wrong. The air feels colder, and there's an emptiness that fills the hall. Walking cautiously through the open doorway into the lounge-diner, the first things I see are the jagged and cut rope with specks of blood splattered from the sofa to the chair. The sofa is empty, the only evidence that someone has been lying on it, are the imprints that Vincent's body made.

Shit. Shit. Shit. This is all I need. Stupid, stupid woman. I hit my forehead repeatedly with the palm of my hand, until it begins to hurt. Bloody stupid woman, you can't get anything right! You should have been more careful.

Vincent. It is only a matter of time now, before he tells the police. I'm going to need to work fast and get my things together before they arrive here and start tearing the place apart.

Bloody man, I should have killed him when I had the chance. Now everything is going to unravel.

And that's why I hate my life. I absently rub my arms through the thin padded jacket I'm wearing. I can't find Cameron fucking Frost, and now one of his mates has escaped.

Collecting a large rucksack from my bedroom, I throw clothes, underwear, my laptop and chargers into the sack, before rushing into the bathroom to grab medication. The wheelchair is next, and is pushed into the hall, as I rush backwards and forwards in a panic to grab everything that I think I will need. In the bedroom, and quickly pull my single duvet off the bed and throw it onto the wheelchair.

Back in the lounge, I scan the room and my eyes settle on the taser on the table. I'm about to leave the flat when I see the wooden handle from the cheese wire and silver cigar cutter on the table, next to the book, I am currently reading, a novella by someone called AJ Warren, called The Lamp-post Shakers.

I carefully popped the cheese wire and cigar cutter from the table and put them into the pocket of my jacket.

Taking one last look at the place that has been more a prison than a home.

No happy memories. Just living from day to day, trying to find a reason to keep going.

I leave swiftly, moving the wheelchair, duvet and rucksack through the open front door.

I grab a coat to keep me warm and shut the door firmly behind me.

Time to move on.

Part Thirty-Two: Cameron

The sound of the automatic doors whooshing constantly, remind me how busy this Marks and Spencer petrol station, food hall is. It's at a place called Milton Gate, just off the A34 and is classed as one of the service offerings for those in need of a break,

Thoughts turn to Eric and Vincent. The way we were and the fun we had when we were young. Vincent's disappearance is still playing on my mind.

Moving around the shop floor, I grab a large packet of sausage rolls, and a packet of marker pens before heading to the alcohol section. I put two large bottles of vodka, the cheapest bottle of whiskey and two bottles of red wine into my basket.

Swiping my card, I pay for a carrier bag and make my way to the exit, with its whooshing doors.

And, then something very surreal happens. I see a small white van pull into the petrol station on the shop forecourt. I watch carefully nearby, as a young man gets out of the vehicle, unlocks the petrol cap and begins to fill up his vehicle. When the van is filled, he makes sure the cap is secured back into place, before pocketing the keys into his cargo trousers.

He is about to walk into the shop to pay for the fuel when his phone rings. As he reaches into his pocket to take out the phone, the keys fallout and crash quietly to the floor. Unaware, the man continues into the shop.

My heart almost misses a bit, any moment now – the man will turn and notice he has dropped his keys. 'Turn,' I whisper. 'Bloody turn.'

This is an opportunity too good to miss.

Slowly, I walk and pick up the keys. I look around, not a soul is watching. My heart is beating so fast, I'm sure everyone can hear it. Taking a deep breath, instead of handing the keys back, I pocket them and walk to the white van. Casually, with my bottles of alcohol clinking softly in the bag, and as though the van belongs to me, I open the door, put the bag on the passenger seat, adjust my seat and put the key into the ignition.

In the rearview mirror, I see the owner of the van run out of shop shouting and pointing my way as I take the hamburger roundabout at Milton Gate and head towards Milton Business Park.

At the last minute, I decide to go directly over the roundabout and head to Milton village as there will be fewer CCTV cameras about. I keep going through the village until I come across a large village green, surrounded by a village pub and follow a narrow driveway to pull up into a deserted car park. I fumble around in the shopping bag until I find the marker pens and pull the packet out.

When I have the black one in hand, I open the driver's door and walk around until I am standing in front of the boot and staring at the registration number. There is a letter C which is lucky. Massaging my leg, I force myself to stoop and change the letter C into an O. I move to the front of the van and do the same.

There, that should make it slightly harder to pick up on any CCTV cameras. Now, all I need are a few more things and I'm ready to rock and roll.

This is the moment I've been waiting for. This is where I finally get my own back.

Act Three. Bringing Charlotte Peckham to her knees.

Part Thirty-Three: Harley

I am walking along the pavement, to post a birthday card to one of mum's friends. We have just had a buffet lunch at the house and Daniel joked that there were more police officers staying in the house, than in the whole of the Thames Valley Police area. It feels good to be with our friends, and my feelings about Daniel are improving all the time. In a good way. From the moment he asked if I was OK following the text message, my view of Daniel was changing.

Steph and Brian had nipped out, on police business, Jenny said. Mum keeps telling everyone how proud she is of me. She told Stuart that she was always able to rely on me, and that I was looking more like my dad each day. I'm not usually sentimental, but when it comes to my mum, I can't help it. She's the best.

There is a walled post box about a hundred yards from the house, set into an old stone wall and it should have taken me no more than ten minutes to post the letter and get back to the house. As the letter was dropped into the post box a small white van pulled up on the pavement next to me, and a man got out. He has a bit of a limp as he walks around the side of the van to me on the pavement, and introduces himself in a deep voice, 'You're Harley, right?'

He is tall, with black hair, and a baseball cap pulled down low. He seems harmless enough, dressed in a sports jacket. He also wears a white T-shirt and jeans. There is something odd about the way he walks, it's stilted, like he's in pain.

'I'm your first cousin, once removed. But you can call me Uncle Cameron. We texted each other.' He says in a deep voice.

Ah, so this is 'Texting Cameron,' the man pestering me and my mother. If he's the one who has been sending dead presents to my mum, then he's in big trouble. I may be young, but I'm not stupid. She's my mum and I will protect her with everything I have.

Staring at the stranger, I shove my hands deep into my pockets of my jeans. 'What are you doing here?'

'Thought you'd like to put a face to the name,' he says, offering a smile.

The smile doesn't reach his eyes.

'Do you fancy a ride in my van?' He suddenly asks.

'No, thanks. I'm not allowed to go off with strangers.' I tell him.

He crosses his arms and legs in a casual manner, trying to appear chilled. 'I'm not exactly a stranger, I'm your uncle.'

'The answer is still no.'

I need to keep walking, along the pretty tree-lined pavement. I'm only minutes from the house.

'I've got some interesting stuff on space in my van. Have you ever held a real piece of moon rock? It's the best feeling in the world.'

I would love to see a piece of rock that has come from the moon.

Cameron opens the door of the van, 'Come and look.'

And then I do the one thing that Mum always tells me not to, I move closer and peer in.

The push is hard. It knocks the wind out of me, and I catch my head on the floor of the van as I fall inside. Before I know what is happening, he has shut and locked the doors. I hear movement as he gets into the van, turns on the engine and begins to drive.

My first thought is that Mum is going to kill me!

Part Thirty-Four: Lottie

I keep looking at my watch, from my wooden lounger in the pool house. Daniel and myself are the only people in here, and apart from the splashing of his impressive front crawl, and the constant ticking of the large black wrought iron wall clock, which I find myself glancing at, every five minutes or so.

Harley went to post a birthday card for me, but he's been gone for fifteen minutes.

Where the hell is he?

I'm wearing my red and black swimsuit under my cotton beach dress, but in my state of worry, I have no intention to getting into the pool at this moment in time.

Daniel pops his head out of the pool with a splash and rests his arms on the side, facing me.

'Come in,' he smiles, his voice is deep, and his eyes are glistening with drops of water.

As tempted as I am, there is a nagging feeling at the back of my mind, I can't shake off.

Forcing a smile, 'A bit later.'

Daniel makes to move, but then stops. 'Is something the matter?'

'No,' I snap, and then apologise, 'Sorry, I'm being silly.'

'About what?' He asks.

I'm about to answer when the pool house door bursts open and Jenny rushes into the room. Her face is unusually serious and there's an air of concern about her.

'What is it?' I ask, sitting up.

Jenny stands over me, wearing jeans and a purple blouse. 'I've just had a call from Steph. Cameron Frost has been picked up on CCTV at Milton Gate.'

A sense of unease begins to prickle along my shoulders. Of all the things she was going to say, that wasn't it. Cameron Frost. My brain freezes, and all I can think of, is repeating in my already worried and anxious head, that man's name.

'No!' I say, louder than I intend to. Both Jenny and Daniel look at me, concern clearly showing on their faces.

There is a silence.

Daniel leaps out of the water, with the speed and stealth of a tiger. Ordinarily, I would take advantage of anything that Daniel does, and appreciate the joy that he brings out in me, but not this time. This moment belongs to my son. Quickly, I take my phone from my dress pocket and call Harley. The dialling tone continues until it goes to automated voicemail.

'Harley, it's Mum. Call me as soon as you get this message, please.' I try to keep the panic out of my voice, in the hope that any moment now, my ten-year-old son will come walking through the door, dressed in swim shorts and ready to jump into the waiting water.

'Harley went to post a letter fifteen minutes ago and hasn't come back,' I explain, my voice thick with emotion.

'Maybe he got sidetracked, or is talking to someone?' Jenny suggests, patting my arm reassuringly.

'You stay here, I'll go look for him.' Daniel takes over. 'Keep calling him.'

'One hundred yards to the right, there should be an old post box built into a stone wall.' I tell him.

Daniel nods solemnly, listening to my instructions. Daniel throws on jeans, a turquoise jumper and brown trainers and is out of the door before I can thank him.

Pushing myself from the lounger and into a standing position, I'm overwhelmed when Jenny takes me softly in her arms, whispering into my neck. 'We'll find him, he'll be OK.'

I remember when Harley was born, Simon and Jenny were with me at the hospital. I had wanted a home birth but was advised to have Harley at the John Radcliffe Hospital, commonly known locally as the JR, which is situated in the Headington area of Oxford. I was sent to the top-level midwifery unit, called The Spires.

At the time, Simon and I were living in a three bedroomed detached property in Hinksey Hill, on the outskirts of Oxford.

This was the one and only time that I had left Shore House in Lyme Regis.

A time for new beginnings, for thinking of myself and what I wanted in life.

The memory of me howling in pain down the corridors of The John Radcliffe, wondering why, after three hours of intense pain, that there was no progress. Jenny and Simon looking at me with panic, not knowing what to do to help. Asking the midwives, why the labour was not making much progress, I remember shouting with desperation to any staff member who would listen, 'Just give me something to make my baby come.'

Eventually, I had to be moved to the lower JR floors for medical intervention.

Finally, half sedated, a drip attached to my hand and exhausted, I delivered our son, Harley, five hours later. A beautiful, wrinkly little thing, with the mellowed cry of a kitten. Simon couldn't stop touching him, he took him for a walk around the room, explaining who everybody was. Saying how much he was loved.

It was a magical time full of love, hope and promise of a life yet to be lived. Jenny had held him in her arms, with tears falling softly down her face. In that moment, I felt Jenny and Stuart's anguish at not being able to have a child or children of their own.

So, here I am enjoying a break away with my son, but instead of chilling by the pool, and enjoying good conversation with my beloved friends, I'm pacing the tiled floor, and about to have a panic attack, because my ten-year-old son has not returned to the house.

Bloody hell.

Stuart's familiar face pops around the door. 'Found him yet?' He asks, his eyebrows drawn together.

'No,' I say, 'Daniel has gone to look for him.'

'Brian is on his way,' Jenny says, 'let's go to the kitchen and I'll get Mrs Monk to make a pot of tea.'

We walk from the pool house to the main manor and find Mrs Monk sternly telling chef, who is chopping vegetables at lightning speed, not to mess up her clean floor. The housekeeper looks flustered.

'Hello, Mrs Monk. Is everything all right?' Jenny asks.

'Sorry, Mrs Greyson, just a family emergency. Nothing for you to worry about.' Mrs Monk brushes her hands down her pink flowery long-sleeved dress. She doesn't look her usual calm self.

'Oh dear. Anything I can help with?' Jenny asks, always the one to offer a hand where she can.

'No, my dear, but that's very kind of you.' Mrs Monk smiles. 'My daughter is coming to stay with me at the cottage for a little while. She struggles sometimes and just needs her mum.'

The kitchen door opens, and I clutch my chest. This must be Harley. Daniel brought him home. I'm disappointed that it's only Brian.

He comes in wearing his usual navy chinos, and white shirt. This time he's carrying a box.

My heart stops.

'Another present left for you, Lottie.' Brian states, in a flat voice. 'Don't bother looking at it. It's not a pretty sight.' He goes to place it on the kitchen counter.

'Not on there!' Mrs Monk cries. 'We'll all get salmonella,' she exclaims. 'Here,' she gestures to the utility room, and places a tea towel on the counter.

'Thanks, Mrs M,' Brian says, leaving the box there.

'Where's Julie?' he asks.

'She's fine, just upstairs resting. Jack and Steph are picking up provisions for tonight's dinner as it's Monsieur Durand's night off.' Jenny says.

'Brian,' I walk up to him and put my hand on his arm. 'Harley is missing.'

The sound of footsteps fills the room, and I find myself rushing across the kitchen, bumping my hip into the table as I do so, in my haste to answer it. Daniel is out of breath.

'I'm so sorry, Lottie,' he says, with real worry in his face. He has the dishevelled look of a mad professor. 'There's no trace of him.'

When the panic comes, it hits hard. And the world goes dark.

Part Thirty-Five: Harley

'Can you see the shape of that cloud?' My mum's soft voice whispers as we sit next to each other on the sandy beach at Lyme Bay. 'What do you think it is?'

The warm sun is shining directly into my eyes, almost blinding me. Raising my right arm, I put it over my eyes to shield them for a moment. Mum's words echo in my mind. Clouds, I'm looking at clouds. Slowly I remove my arm from my face and search for the cloud and its shape. I study it, processing its shape.

'A boat?' I say hopefully.

'No,' Mum is wearing red sunglasses to go with her red, curly hair. I love her hair. It's always so soft.

'A car?' I hope this game isn't going to go on for too long, the sun is making me sleepy.

'Shall, I tell you?' She asks, and I turn to face her so that we are almost eye to eye.'

'It's a face,' She laughs, pointing to the cloud. 'There's his eyes, nose, hair.' She sounds excited and it's infectious.

'Oh yeah,' I see it now, more clearly. See what she's trying to show me. 'It's Dad.' I can't help but well up with tears.

'I miss him,' I say, resting my head against her shoulder.

Mum takes me in her arms and holds me tightly.

'I miss him too,' her voice is husky. 'I wish we had had more time with him.'

'Me too.' I sigh.

'It was never enough,' Mum says sadly. 'But we have us now, and we are the A Team.'

I smile. Mum always knows when to say the right thing.

***

My teeth are chattering, and my head is sore.

There is a cold wind coming from somewhere.

I rub my shoulders with cold hands to find some warmth.

The ride in the van has been bumpy and I had to keep bracing myself for any motion that could make my head feel worse. Feeling around for my phone in my jeans pocket, I find the pocket empty and realise that I must have left it at the house. Trying to keep calm, I take deep breaths. Think, Harley, think. What would Dad do?

What seems like an age later, the van stops and I huddle into the farthest corner, the one behind the driver seat. Covering my head with the hood from my dark green sweatshirt, I lower my face to the floor and wrap my arms around my knees, trying to make myself as small as possible.

I am terrified and I can't stop the questions that keep floating around in my head. How could I have been so stupid? What is the man going to do with me? And why didn't I bring my phone? I'm supposed to take it everywhere. Mum will kill me. I am such an idiot.

I scrunch my eyes shut, hoping that he will disappear. But instead, the doors are yanked open, and I am met with the sneering face of my 'Uncle' against the brilliant sunshine, as he bends down awkwardly and says harshly, 'Get out, kid.'

'No,' I shout back from my crouched position.

'I said, get the fuck out! You little shit.' He raises his voice. I look up in panic, hoping he won't hit me.

He bends down and picks up something that looks like a hockey stick.

'Don't make me come in and get you!' He bangs the stick against the van, making me jump.

I know I'm supposed to be the man of the house, but I can't help the tears that fill my eyes and the sobs, when I start to cry.

'Stop snivelling, you little weasel. You're just like your mum.' He says, harshly, and I shuffle further into the back of the van. What does he mean, I'm just like my mum? Of course, I am. Well, I hope I am. Please don't let him hit me, I silently beg.

Suddenly, he leans forward, and a large hand reaches in, grabs my shoulder with a vice-like grip, and hauls me out of the van. Outside, I slowly take in my surroundings, looking at the two rundown buildings in brown stone. One has a worn sign on it, which reads 'The Blue Flag. Perhaps it's an old pub.

'Get off me!' I scream at him, but he doesn't flinch, just hauls me over cobbled ground and points me toward a door at the back of the pub. He smells horrible. 'No,' I shout, and manage to kick him in the shin.

He smells foul, as though he hasn't showered for a while and his breath is sour and bitter, reminding me the stench of the food recycling bin at home.

I feel Cameron's leg give way briefly and he swears, 'you little fucker.'

His fingers push hard into my neck, and the pain causes me to howl out loud. 'Argh…' I can hear the sound coming from my mouth, and stars float across my eyes, like I'm not in my body properly. My fingers pull frantically, trying to prise his from my skin.

My foot catches on something hard, causing me to misstep, causing my legs to buckle and it forces the 'Uncle' to release my neck. Flopping like a rag doll onto the hard uneven pebbled floor, all I can think about is, that I'm going to die. There is pain everywhere and I am crying like a baby. Cameron swears and puts his arm under my body, hoisting me up off the floor and begins to drag me to the door. When we reach it, he yanks the door open, and pushes me inside.

The pain in my neck is bad, it feels like he's pushed a screwdriver in it. Cautiously, I touch the area, to find that the skin feels tender and bruised. For the first time in my short life, hopelessness takes over and I struggle to fight the feeling that I'm about to die.

Cameron takes my shoulders and pushes me onto a wooden chair by the boarded windows. 'Ow...' I cry, 'take it easy, that hurts.'

'Just shut your bloody mouth, will you,' Cameron shouts. 'You're giving me a headache.'

Without warning, a punch lands heavy on my cheekbone, and pain explodes in my face and head. I inhale sharply, trying to scream for help. But there is nothing. Thankfully, I fall into a black cloud of darkness.

***

I sit up, enjoying the warm sun on my back and look out to sea at Lyme Bay. Sunlight sprinkles across the waves, making them sparkle and giving them a magical feel. Movement beside me, makes me turn. It's Mum.

'You need to wake up Harley,' she says, in her halter neck navy swimsuit, gently turning my chin to face her.

'It's time for you to go back,' her voice is sad, but firm.

'But I don't want to,' I mutter, my eyes fixated on the waves.

'No choice, sweetheart.' She says calmly, 'Wake up, so that we can find you.'

'Just one more minute, Mum,' I say, holding her hand. A tear rolls down my face.

'OK, one more minute,' she squeezes my hand and looks out at sea.

Part Thirty-Six: Gino

Nessun Dormer, sung by Luciano Pavarotti, booms with deep rich tones that lend a feeling of sadness to my heart. I'm sitting in my office, in behind the giant mahogany desk that oozes sophistication. God knows how many men I have killed on this desk, or how many women I've fucked on the smooth surface. Too bloody many.

The desk was the treat to myself after my divorce from Catalina. That woman never worked a single day in her whole life. And she was expensive to keep, especially in a five bedroomed detached villa overlooking the Thames in Pangbourne, Oxfordshire. Eventually, I got rid of her, and her four Shih Tzus and bought her an apartment in Cambridge. With no children in tow, it was very straightforward. Of course, I kept the Pangbourne property and invested in a new build office block on the Milton Business Park, on the outskirts of Didcot.

Back to my desk. It was crafted in Verona, Italy, by a couple of young brothers who were making a name for themselves. The Santinello brothers with their skilled hands made this desk with such exquisite skill, the symbolic statement of a damaged marriage.

Closing my eyes, I try to remember what it was like to be young again, with no responsibilities and just myself to think of. Now, so many people rely on me and the businesses that I run.

Such a long time ago. Where did those years go? I scrape my hands through my grey hair, sad that I'm ageing quicker than I want to. Too quickly.

My sister, Rosalina, called me this morning. She blames me for what happened. She thinks it's my fault that Vincent was taken. If only he hadn't started working for me, all those years ago, she keeps saying. If only, if only. If only she would bloody shut up!

Life's a bitch, isn't it?

Once my father took me to the Thames in Abingdon, when I was ten years old, to teach me to swim. We took a hired rowing boat out to the middle of the river, and he ordered me to stand up. As I looked out at the dark water and green riverbanks, I was suddenly catapulted fully clothed into the cold dark depths of the river. Water engulfed me and I thrashed my arms in panic, until I wondered if I would ever reach the surface and breath air into my lungs again.

After what seemed like an age, I could see the surface and kicked hard, still wearing my black trainers until I broke through the surface of the water. Cold, panicking and spluttering, I saw my father.

'Help me!' I begged. I didn't want to go under the water again. 'Help me, Papa. I'm going to drown.'

My father tutted, with folded arms. He looked annoyed that I was asking for help. The man was a monster, and I should have reached out, grabbed his leg and pulled him in with me.

'Keep moving, Gino. You'll soon get the hang of it,' he said, his face completely devoid of expression. He didn't care one iota, whether I lived or died. My own father couldn't be bothered to give me any quality time with him, who thought the best way to learn to swim was by pushing his non-swimming son, into the water and telling him to get on with it.

Well, obviously I managed to swim of sorts, following the boat to shore. Once or twice, I was sorely tempted to give in and grab hold of the boat. But I wouldn't give my old man the satisfaction.

'Told you you'd get the hang of it,' he had said, pushing a big hand into the water to grab the scruff of my jumper. All at once, I found myself being hauled bodily, out of the cold water.

***

That's how I learned to swim.

We all have a past, and mine is probably more colourful than most.

My Apple watch vibrates, and I stare at my phone on the desk. Rosalina again. What the hell does she want now?

I think twice before answering. I can't cope with her hysterics.

The call stops, and guilt sweeps over me. Shit. I had better call her back.

I go into my call history and call Rosalina back.

'Gino!' her voice screeches, echoing as though she's travelling. 'They've found him. Vincent.'

My heart misses a beat. I can't believe it. They've bloody found him.

'Where is he? Is he all right?' I ask, pushing back my chair and standing up. Signalling to my driver, Antonio, to get the car ready.

'He got hit by a car and has been taken to the John Radcliffe, I'm heading there now,' her voice wobbles with emotion.

'I'll see you there.'

Three hours later, and the bleeping of the machine keeping Vincent's vitals stable, is driving me mad. For fuck's sake, can it

275

be any louder? The only good thing is that it washes out the quiet sobbing of my sister. He had to have emergency surgery on his leg and the wound on his finger needed attention. We're now on the post-op ward, and Vincent has been given a room to himself, following my persuasive charm with the nurses. Which I am thankful for, as I am about to call Brian Carter and ask him to get his sorry arse over here.

'He'll be fine, you know,' I try to reassure her. 'The consultant said so. It should take about four months to recover from the knee surgery. He was lucky the driver didn't kill him.'

'Not helping, Gino.' Rosalina sniffles, pulling her brown cardigan close to her, as if to keep out the cold. Her fingers grip Vincent's hand. 'He wasn't lucky. He had half of his little finger chopped off, someone kidnapped him and then he got hit by a car. Where's the luck in that?'

'We've got him back, is all I'm saying!' my voice rises in anger. Jesus, there's no pleasing the woman, it's like walking on eggshells. Feeling the need to get away from the bleeping and from my emotional sister, I stand up, straighten my trousers and mutter, 'I need to make a call,' before leaving her alone with her son in the cold, clinical room.

Walking along the corridor, amid the hustle and bustle of hospital life, I head to the exit where I light up a cigarette and take out my phone. It's chilly this August evening, and I wish I'd worn a jacket, but in my hurry to get to the hospital, I had forgotten to bring one.

I find Brian's number and press the call button, while absently watching an ambulance pull sharply into a nearby emergency bay. Several people rush out, and I check my phone and put it on speaker, as the call continues to ring.

About to disconnect the call, I am surprised when it is answered and an out of breath voice asks sharply. 'Gino, what do you want?'

'He's been found,' I say. Vincent is the nearest I've got to a son, so I'm grateful that he's not lying dead in a ditch somewhere.

'Who? Vincent?' he asks.

'Who the bloody hell do you think I'm talking about, Brian? Charlie bloody Chaplin?' I blurt out and then take a deep breath to reign in my anger.

'Is he all right? Where is he?' Brian sounds genuinely interested.

'He's OK, got hit by a car somewhere on Great Western Park, just outside Didcot. He's at the JR.'

'Bloody hell!' Brian says harshly. 'I'll be there in about thirty minutes. Hopefully he'll be able to give us a lead on the kidnapper. Text me the floor and ward.'

'Vincent's asleep at the moment.' I tell him. 'But should come around anytime soon. I want to know who the fuck did this to him. Because I am going to fucking kill them!'

'Gino,' Brian warns, concern in his voice. 'Let me handle this. Whoever it is, is still out there. We need to stop them before they get to Cameron.'

'I'll fucking stop them all right,' I say, before disconnecting the phone.

Thirty-five minutes later the door, which stands ajar in Vincent's room, is pushed open and a dishevelled Brian Carter walks in, like a quiet but determined thinking man's Inspector Poirot. Dressed in a dark brown raincoat, black chinos and white shirt, he looks every inch the confident detective.

In another life, we may have been friends, but in this one there is too much secrecy and experience between us to allow for that to happen. That said, we have an understanding, Brian and me. I feel like we are equals, that we have both experienced the world and seen the good as well as the bad.

Pushing my chair backwards slightly, I come to a standing position in front of Brian and hold out my hand. 'Brian,' I say quietly.

He takes my hand firmly to shake it, and I feel that bond, that connection again. 'How are you holding up?' He asks me.

'Mad as hell and wondering what sort of people are they, to go after my family? They must be mental in the head to take me on!' I grit my teeth, before softening my voice, 'This is my sister, Rosalina.' My sister sits holding my nephew's hand, she looks up, tears in her eyes. 'Rosalina, this is my friend DCI Brian Carter.'

'Brian is going to help us work out what happened to Vincent.'

'Thank you,' Rosalina responds, 'Please find the person who did this to my son.'

Brian looks at me briefly, and then nods to my sister. 'I will try my best.'

Murmurings come from the bed. Vincent.

'Stay away from me!' Vincent's voice is raspy. 'Just let me go. I won't tell anyone.'

Rosalina pushes the button to alert the nurse and leans bodily over her grown-up son. She strokes his face, 'Vincent, it's Mama. You're safe now.' She cups his stubbly cheeks with its new beard growth.

Moving to the side of the bed, he looks young and vulnerable, even with the broken nose and blackened eyes. It's hard not to think of him as the fifteen-year-old spotty kid who started working for me, some fifteen or so years ago. Anger fills me, feeding a need to avenge whoever has hurt my nephew. God, I love this boy.

'Vincent,' I say steadily, and I am shocked when seconds later his eyes flutter open.

A tall, thin young man wearing a white top and navy trousers, short curly dark hair and a pair of navy crocs, enters the room. He looks younger than my nephew, as he walks to the side of the bed and looks at Vincent.

'Hi, I'm Kyle, it's good to see you awake. I'm your nurse and will be taking care of you until 8pm?' he asks solemnly.

Rosalina looks across the bed at him, 'he was having a nightmare.'

'How are you feeling Vincent? Can I get you a glass of water or a cup of tea? Then,' he looks at his watch, 'I'm going to do your observations.'

'Just water please, my throat feels really dry, and my nose is blocked.' Vincent says, his words sound dry and raspy.

Brian steps forward and take out his warrant card, addressing Kyle. 'Hi, I'm DCI Brian Carter with Thames Valley Police. I'm a friend of the family,' he glances quickly at me, and I nod. 'If Vincent is well enough, I would like to ask him a few questions.'

Kyle reaches for the jug of water, sitting on the overbed trolley at the end of the bed. He overturns a glass and begins to pour. 'If your observations are fine, I will check with the ward Sister and get permission for you to talk to him.' He says softly turning to Vincent, 'Let's see if we can sit you up a little.' He presses a button at the side of the bed and the headrest begins to rise, allowing Vincent to move into a sitting position.

'Without putting any pressure on your operated leg, I'm going to give you a hand to help you shuffle up the bed.' Kyle explains to Vincent.

We watch silently as Kyle puts his arm under my nephew's armpit. 'After three,' he says quietly, 'one, two, three...' He hoists Vincent firmly backwards, ignoring the moans and hissing that comes from his patient. He must come across this a lot in his line of work, moving patients and supporting them at their worst.

Kyle pats Vincent on the arm reassuringly, 'well done,' he smiles, arranging his patient's pillows, before handing him the glass of water and holding it carefully whilst Vincent drinks.

'Enough?' he asks Vincent, who nods and closes his eyes. He looks across the bed to Rosalina, 'Try not to worry too much. He's doing very well.' Vincent's eyes open at the sound of the nurse's voice, 'I'm going to do your observations now.'

We watch quietly, as Kyle takes a blood pressure cuff from the observation station and folds it around Vincent's arm, at the same time a small gadget is attached to the middle finger of his right hand. Finally, he takes an oblong package from the station, tears it open and puts the sterile thermometer into Vincent's ear for about thirty seconds before checking the reading and disposing of it into the appropriate bin. I look across at Brian, who is leaning against the wall, legs folded and hands in his trouser pockets. He nods, silently.

He takes the iPad slotted into the sleeve of the machine and records the observations. 'Give me a couple of minutes to speak to Sister, and I will be back to confirm that he is fit for questioning.'

'Thanks,' I say to him, liking his no nonsense approach. I've been impressed with his behaviour and quality of care to Vincent from the moment he entered the room. Of course, I am biased, because I think the JR hospital is one of the best in the country.

I make my way to the heavy wooden chair in the corner of the room and slump into it. Crossing my legs, I lean back and wait for Kyle to return.

'How are you feeling son?' Rosalina asks, sitting beside Vincent and stroking his arm.

'How do you think I feel, Mama?' The boy whines at his mum. 'Like I've been fucking kidnapped, hurt my hand and been hit by a fucking car.'

'Hey!' I say sharply to my nephew. 'Don't speak to your mother like that.' I don't care what he's been through, he has no right to talk in that manner to anyone, let alone Rosalina.

Vincent stares at me. Don't you fucking dare! I glare at him. Flesh and blood, he maybe but I won't have him disrespecting my sister.

Kyle walks through the door, with a small petite woman. Blonde curly hair is tied back as she steps in front of Kyle. Smartly dressed in navy trousers and a white polo top. 'Hello, I'm April, the Sister on this ward, I just wanted to see how you are, Vincent.'

'I'm tired,' he says, 'and sore.'

'We can check your pain meds. Out of ten what would you say you were at?' April asks.

Vincent thinks for a minute, 'about a seven.'

April picks up the iPad, 'you're due for pain relief in thirty minutes. We'll give that slightly earlier and add in extra paracetamol to go with the codeine.'

She taps away on the tablet, showing Kyle the updated dose and waits for him to nod that he understands.

'We'll leave you to it,' Sister April says, looking at myself and Brian, 'but be mindful that Vincent has recently undergone surgery and will tire easily and may not be very lucid.'

Finally, the medical staff leave and Brian steps away from the wall, closer to the bed. 'Vincent, I'm DCI Brian Carter. I'd like to ask you a few questions about where you've been and what's happened to you over the last forty-eight hours. Is that all right?'

Vincent nods.

'Going back to the beginning. What was the last thing you remember, before you were kidnapped?'

My nephew looks across at his mother, and I wonder if this is a good thing to have her here on the interview.

'Rosalina,' I begin. 'Perhaps you want to get yourself a coffee, while Vincent tells us what happened.'

My sister holds her son's hand tighter and glares at me. 'No, Gino. I want to know what happened to my son. I need to know.'

'Mama!' Vincent says quietly, tentatively touching a hand to his nose, 'please.'

Rosalina shakes her head vehemently and I know that I am not the only one with that stubborn Camprinelli streak. I just pray that the lad won't disgrace his mama, because despite everything, I don't want to see my sister hurt.

Her voice is loud and decisive, when she looks at me. 'No! I will hear no more of it. I am staying.'

'OK,' Vincent mutters, as though he can't be bothered to argue.

There is a silence, and the boy looks at Brian. His eyebrows are drawn together, something fleeting crossing his face. He seems disturbed. 'Do I know you?' he asks Brian. 'Your voice, I feel like I've heard it somewhere before.

Brian gives a wry smile, and steps forward, closer to the bed.

I look at the man standing next to me. They say there are times in life when you see what you want to, and in that moment, I have no qualms that my almost friend is telling the truth. Brian brushes his hands down his black chinos and shrugs. It is clear that he's telling the truth. 'People say that a lot.'

All the time, Rosalina, watches him like a mother cat, ready to pounce.

'You were meeting Cameron?' I bring us back onto the questions.

Vincent looks up sharply, 'I was meeting Cameron at the old disused pub where we used to meet.'

'Why? Why were you meeting?' Brian asks, sitting in the chair opposite Rosalina.

'Because I thought I was in trouble with you, and I wanted Cam's advice.'

'You are in bloody trouble!' I retort, but Brian puts his hand up to stop me. 'But we will talk about that later.'

'When you got to this place, was Cameron there?' Brian leans forward, resting his arms on his knees.'

'No.'

'So, what happened next?' Brian asks.

'Then, I heard this sizzling sound and before I knew it, my body went into painful muscle contractions. I couldn't move for about a minute but when I came to, there was someone there and we got into a fight. They knocked me out with an old kettle.'

'You were tasered?' Brian summarises.

'Oh, Mio dio!' Rosalina puts her hands to her mouth, to hide her shock.

'What happened next?' Brian asks quietly, glancing at me quickly.

'I woke up, tied with rope in a living room, with my hand sore and bandaged.'

'Fuck!' I mutter, this is like a Netflix True Crime documentary. Some mentally ill or psychotic person is triggered to take their revenge, and no one will stop them.

'Your kidnapper, what did he look like? Did you ever see his face?' Brian leans in closer.

'Her,' he says, so quietly I almost miss it.

'I'm sorry?' Brian asks, 'are you saying that the person who did this to you was a woman?'

'Yes,' he answers and his eyes flit quickly to his mother, before staring at the wall ahead.

'We used to call her Ferret.' Vincent continues staring at the wall, as though he's still there, in the flat, living in that moment, reliving his ordeal.

'You know her?' Brian asks. 'In what capacity do you know her? And who is we?'

'All of us, the Three Amigos, Eric Weston, Cameron Frost and me.'

The room suddenly goes cold, and I feel the hairs stand up on my arms. Something clicks into place, and I realise that this is no ordinary kidnapping. In fact, he's lucky to be alive.

Brian looks at me, eyebrows drawn together and lips forming in a grim line. 'I'll send someone to you later, to try and locate the place where you were kept. Also, I'll send a sketch artist to see if we can get a photofit of what this woman looks like.'

There is a short silence, in which I am trying not to upset my sister. But then, I can't help it.

'What did you three do to her?' I ask in a hard voice, pushing from the chair and standing over him at the foot of the bed. 'What the fuck did you do, Vincent?' I repeat, I am so disappointed in him, that I can't look at Brian. Can't let him see the look of shame I have for this nephew of mine.

My head feels as though it's about to explode. The pounding in my ears pushes me to my limits, and in the background, all I hear are the quiet sobs of my sis.

Part Thirty-Seven: Lottie

There are voices talking quietly. They feel far away, as though I'm in a field and they are walking at a distance toward me.

Opening an eye slowly, I decide to face the world again.

'Lottie, thank God you're awake,' Daniel looms over me, he draws his brows together and his lips form into a grim line. His usually handsome face is fraught with worry. I look around to find myself lying on an ink blue velvet chaise longue in the formal lounge. What a sight I must look? Like a fair maiden fainting at the drop of a hat, waiting for the handsome hero to come and save her.

Jenny rests her arms over the beautiful ornate and comfy chaise longue. She stares at me, as though she's seen a ghost. 'Please don't do that again, Lottie. You frightened the life out of me.' She offers a weak smile as she pats my arm. I suddenly feel cold through my thin, green cardigan, desperate for warmth and am shocked when Daniel suddenly puts his arms around me, in front of everyone and holds me tight. I close my eyes and concentrate on using Daniel's strength to warm my body.

'Any news on Harley?' I whisper.

Julie sits on the dark blue velvet sofa nearby, she leans forward. 'Nothing at the moment.'

'Where the hell is he?' I ask, looking around the room.

'We don't know,' Jack looks across at Noah and shakes his head. Jem walks into the room, holding Edie's hand. 'Aunty Lottie, sad.' She says, bouncing up to me in a purple summer dress, green socks and pink sandals. Edie lunges towards me, 'I'll give you a kiss to make you feel better.'

'Edie, be careful with Aunty Lottie,' Jem warns her three-year-old, gently patting her back.

'It's OK,' I stifle a sniffle. 'I could do with a hug from my favourite niece,' I pull Edie to me, and hold her tight for a moment, taking in the scent of her and remembering how precious these moments are.

'You are such a good hugger, Edie,' I tell the child, softly as I stroke her satiny curly hair. The innocence of young children and how they see everything in rich colour. Their lives are not marred by the dark colours of the world, well not all of them. They see you for what you are and that is such a refreshing feeling in this world of wars, strikes and poverty.

Simon always told me that it was important to remember that there is always hope, that heroes can be anyone, from the person who helps to carry your shopping bag, or who stops to rescue an injured animal, basically, someone who gives more of themselves than they need to.

And that is true. Hope is needed now more than ever.

Releasing Edie from our warm hug, I shuffle myself into a sitting position on the chaise longue and watch the little girl run to her mum where she subsequently clutches onto Jem's long flowing pink skirt, declaring 'Mummy, I give the bestest hugs!'

Jem pats her daughter's head lovingly.

A movement catches my eye, and a slim, young woman walks into the room. She wears a sweeping long-sleeved cherry-coloured dress with flat shoes. With her dark hair pulled tightly into a bun behind her and pale, delicate skin, she looks like a fragile supermodel. 'Mum, I can't find my phone, have you seen it?'

There is something very familiar about the young woman. I am sure that I have seen her somewhere before. Perhaps she is the well-known actor who owns the house?

Mrs Monk walks across the room, stuffing a tea towel into the front pocket of her apron, until she stands beside her daughter. 'No, Francesca. The last time I saw it, it was on the mantlepiece in the living room.' She looks around the room, 'Sorry everyone, this is my daughter, Francesca. The one I was talking about. She's staying with me for a few days.'

Everyone nods and murmurs hello. 'Right, let's head to the kitchen,' she says briskly, 'I think a nice pot of tea will do us all some good.' She ushers her daughter a few steps, when it dawns on me where I know this young woman from.

'Francesca?' I catch Jenny's face, glance at her expression. She's thinking the same thing, surely. 'It is you? We met the other night at the Lighthouse Celebration!' I look to Stuart and Daniel and see that they realise who our new visitor is too.

Francesca looks up from the floor, as though in a trance. 'Lottie? Jenny? Is it really you? What are you doing here?' A big smile spreads across the young woman's face.'

'We're here on holiday with the family for a few days,' I explain.

Jenny steps forward and pulls Francesca into her arms. 'Oh, my word. I can't believe you're here. What a small world we live in.'

Mrs Monk's jaw drops, and she glances at her daughter, 'Francesca? You know Jenny and Lottie?'

'We met at the Celebration evening a couple of nights ago. I told you, didn't I?' She hugs Jenny back.

'No,' Mrs Monk replies, shaking her head, 'I'm sure I would have remembered.'

Jenny releases Francesca from her hug, and immediately Francessca rubs her arms up and down her body as though she's cold. Which is strange, because it isn't cold. My inner alarm begins to ring, and when that happens, usually there is something wrong. Her whole demeanour has changed. She no longer looks relaxed, but skittish, anxious.

'Are you all right?' I ask her. But before she can answer, her red-faced mother puts her arm around her shoulder and guides her to the door.

'She's fine. Just needs a cup of tea and a biscuit,' she mutters, with panic in her voice, 'she gets low blood sugar sometimes.'

I look at Jenny, raise my eyebrows at the strangeness of the situation.

Brian enters the room, 'Where's Julie? And who is that woman with Mrs Monk?' he asks, dropping into a nearby chair. He looks serious.

'Julie is lying down with Lola in your room.' I explain, looking around the room. 'Steph and Jack were at the office, and they are now collecting something for dinner tonight. It is chef's night off.'

'As for the young woman, that is Mrs Monks' daughter,' Jem answers, looking in the basket of toys that had been put to one side of the baby piano. She tips its contents upside down onto the soft beige carpet, and Edie's eyes bulge with excitement. 'A baby dolly,' she coos, picking up a beautiful, blonde-haired doll with her clumsy little hands, and thrusting onto her shoulders. 'I'm going to give her a cuddle.'

Brian pulls himself upright and watches them. I guess he must be wondering what it feels like to be a parent. How can you not be terrified of raising a baby. To fear for them as you do, hoping that they grow up happy and healthy.

And, then Brian pushes out of the deep blue chair and walks across the room to me. He rests a knee on the beige patterned carpet and looks at me. Daniel sits beside me, offering a gentle, reassuring hand on my thigh, catches Brian's eye. Brian finally looks up at Jenny, taking in her worried face as she stands behind me, her fingers holding on to the back of the chaise.

He nods, before talking.

'I notified the station that Harley is missing, we really need to get ahead of this. There is no time to waste, so Stuart, Daniel and I, will go knock on doors near the post box, to see if anyone saw Harley or if anyone new has been hanging about in the area.'

A warm hand rests on mine, offering comfort. Daniel. My eyes smart and a tear escapes, slithering down my cheek.

All I can do is nod.

'Do you have any idea who may have taken Harley?' I ask, flatly. I really need to find my son.

'Possibly,' Brian's eye catches Daniel's again.

'Tell me.' I demand, 'Tell me, who would do this to me,' My voice rises, and I grasp tightly onto Daniel's hand.

'Cameron Frost,' he says simply, pushing himself to his feet with a small groan. 'Fingerprints have come back with Frost's on the lid of one of the boxes sent to you. We know he's in the area. I think it's linked to Harley.'

My heart stops when I hear Brian's words. Silently, I have been telling myself that it couldn't possibly be Cameron. Hasn't he already had his pound of flesh from me?

'Why?' I ask, voicing my concerns 'Why would he do this to me? I don't understand.' Without meaning to, I raise my voice and I am quite sure that my stress levels are shooting through the roof.

'Please tell me that this isn't because of what you did to him and his friends?' My heart is beating so fast, I wonder If I am going to have a heart attack. Anger flows through every pore in my body, I need someone to blame, someone to be the fall guy for my cousin's actions. It's irrational.

Brian looks at Stuart, who is playing on the floor with Edie, and Noah and the toys. The men shake their heads. 'Honestly, we don't know,' Stuart says quietly.

Stuart looks at me, we have been friends for many years. I know, hand on heart, he wouldn't harm someone unless there was no option. Or he felt justice was not being served. 'We are heartfelt sorry if it is. We wanted to punish him and stop him hurting others.'

'I know,' I say quietly, looking at my dearest friends. 'I know.'

Silent tears fall down my face. If Brian is right, my cousin has my son, and he means to do him harm, to punish me. Where the hell are you Cameron Frost? I'm going to kill you for this.

I watch in slow motion as Brian pushes his hands deep into his trouser pockets and begins to pace the carpeted floor. He suddenly looks tired, rubbing his face and pushing fingers into his eye lid sockets, making them squeak. And, making me feel guilty, that I have added to his stress. 'I need to check on Julie; and then Daniel, Stuart and I will take a walk to the post box.'

Nodding silently, I let the world carry on and fall into my own personal hell. People move around me talking, but I don't hear anything with clarity. Don't understand that they are talking to me. I just want everyone to leave me alone.

A movement beside me, brings me back to reality. Daniel and the others have gone, and Jenny is sitting beside me. I feel her arm slip around my shoulder.

'It's going to be alright, Lottie,' she says quietly. I can't answer, I just stare at Edie, with Noah and Jem playing with the toys on the floor.

I sit feeling cold and waiting for news.

Jem stands up and wanders to some curled up throws squeezed together in a basket beside the fireplace. She takes a pale blue chenille throw, unfolds it and drapes it carefully around my shoulders. 'Thanks,' I say in a low voice.

I have known Jem since she came to Shore House when she was fifteen years old. She was a quiet youngster, always doodling and sketching, with a beautiful smile and sad eyes. Despite her volatile home situation, I could tell that she had experienced kindness in her short life, which she later confirmed. Her friend, Noah, and his Gran were the people who took Jem under their wing.

And now Noah and Jem are married with a small child. Life is looking good for them.

'They've gone,' Jenny is saying. 'Brian is sending a couple of colleagues to talk to you,'

Harley, where the hell are you? I scream inwardly. I don't care what anyone is saying or doing, I just want my son back. Throwing my head into my hands, I close my eyes to shut out the world.

***

'Mum, help me.' My son's frightened words cause me to panic.

'Where are you, Harley?' I cry. 'Tell me where you are?'

'I don't know mum. But I'm scared,' He sobs.

'I know you are baby,' I choke on the words. 'But I will find you.'

Pain sears across my forehead, not a migraine. Not now. 'Hang on, Harley. I'm coming.'

Pushing myself out of the chair, I throw the blanket off me and force myself to stand upright. I don't care that I'm only wearing slippers, or that my hair looks like bird's nest. I stumble across the room, holding on to furniture and doorways as I make my way toward the front door.

Voices call out behind me. I don't care. I keep moving, and forcefully grab the front door catch and yank it open. The sun has gone down, but I can still make my way across the gravelled forecourt, past several cars.

'Harley?' I shout through tears, 'Harley, I'm coming!' I reach the end of the driveway and open the catch to the gate, and don't stop running until I'm stopped by a pair of strong arms.

It's Daniel. He pulls me close into his chest. 'Let me go, Daniel' I sob, 'I need to find my son.' Even as I say the words, a part of me is glad that he is here. For, I don't know where to go. I don't know where my boy is.

'Lottie,' He strokes my head, pulling me closer, and I wince through the pain. My head feels tender. 'Come back to the house. We have knocked on the doors, we have spoken to the neighbours, I'll update you when we get inside. The police are on their way. They want to speak to you.'

'But my son,' I say.

'We will find him, but we need to go back.' He turns me toward the house. I give in. I have no energy left.

Not long after we reach the house, the police arrive. I remember that they were very kind. Everything after that is blank.

The next time I wake up, it is daytime.

***

Bloody hell. What has happened to me? I think Daniel gave me a sedative.

I try to recall where I am and what the time is. Forcing myself to look up, my eyes rest on the opulent, tall ceiling with its beautiful glass chandelier. Sadness sweeps over me, when I realise that I am not in my own home, but I am in this luxurious manor house, our holiday home in Sutton Courtenay.

That my son is missing.

This is hell on earth.

I reach out to disconnect my charging phone, which sits on the Queen Anne set of drawers beside my double bed. Jesus! It's 8am!

Memories of last night come flooding back to me. The kind women police officers who asked questions about Cameron Frost, about Harley. Did he know anyone here? Did he know Cameron?

Harley's phone was found under his duvet in the bedroom by the woman DS, they call Shep. She said that they were going to go through it to check who he had been in contact with. Brian, Daniel and Stuart had come home, with nothing but a possible sighting of a white van, near the post box.

'That's got to be him!' Jenny had said. She had been looking at me funny, 'Lottie, are you OK?'

I didn't answer. Couldn't. Could only stare at her.

The bedroom door creaks open. My heart flutters. It's Harley, he's back. But I am mistaken, as Jenny and Steph walk slowly into the room. They sit on either side of the bed.

'Any news?' I ask quietly, as my eyes begin to burn with hot tears.

'No,' Jenny says in a soothing voice, making me feel like a child. But I don't care. Nothing matters anymore.

Steph strokes my arm, 'Come downstairs and try to eat something.'

I promise to, once I've freshened up and watch silently as they close the door behind them. There are so many things going through my mind. My eyes scan the room for my laptop, finding it charging on the dresser. Pushing my tired limbs out of the bed and upright onto the red patterned carpet. While every bone in my body seems to be screaming out in protest, I force my feet to pad tentatively across the floor.

Where is my son? Where is Harley?

Collecting the laptop, I push the heavy floral curtains open, and let the daylight fill the room, Sunlight tips from behind a white cloud, threatening to break through, and I feel an urge to throw myself back under the duvet and block out the world.

Who am I kidding? How can I block Harley out. Lowering my head, I stare at the carpet. And a gentle knock at the door reminds me that I am not alone.

The door slowly opens, and Daniel pops his head into the room.

'Can I come in?' he asks, quietly. His face is serious, I know he's worried about me, about Harley, but somehow, I can't muster the strength to reach out to him.

'Yeah,' I try to smile, but it feels too painful. I let him step into my room, before asking, 'You gave me a sedative?'

'Yeah, sorry. You were becoming very distressed.' He answers, carefully. 'I wrote a prescription and Stuart went to a late-night pharmacy to collect it.'

'Thank you,' I tell him, and this time manage a brief smile, 'It really helped.'

'Thank God!' he says, exhaling with relief as he strides across the room to me, each step, marking his intention, reducing the barrier that I've put up between us. Soft hands take my shoulders and hold me gently to him.

The scent and feel of him brings me comfort, and my hands reach for his top to keep him close.

'We'll find him Lottie,' he whispers. 'On my life, we'll find him.' His voice deepens and develops into a husky promise.

'You don't know that.' I argue through wet tears that spread like wildfire on his dark green coloured top.

He gently pushes my unruly curly hair from my eyes, 'maybe not, but I can feel it in my gut.' He fists a hand and puts it swiftly into his gut area, steadying it against the soft material of his top. As if I am a prized possession, he cups my face, raising it to his, so that our eyes meet.

'Trust me,' Daniel whispers, and suddenly I feel that I am not alone anymore. 'Let me be your strength, let me take some of the weight.' His words move me, it's almost painful, the way my heart skips a beat, as it tries not to break in half. The hot salty tears, that are never far away, trickle down my cheeks like a river that has burst its banks.

Warm thumbs reach out, catching my tears and sweeping softly to one side. It's time for me to find that inner strength, because my son needs me, and I'm no good to anyone in this state.

I look into his beautiful brown eyes and decide in this moment, that I would gladly let Daniel's strength take some of my strain. That, no matter what happens in all of this, I will be forever grateful for what this man has done for me.

Fifteen minutes later, I have showered, washed my face and brushed my teeth, dressed in jeans and a longline pink V-neck jersey top and am ready to go down to breakfast. Daniel waits patiently for me at the bottom of the stairs and gently takes my hand to lead me into the kitchen.

Clattering plates and muted conversations fill my ears as I enter the large room. In my current state, I forget completely that I am holding Daniel's hand, Jenny immediately makes a beeline for me, throwing her arms around me, forcing me to disconnect from his touch. 'Latte, hon?'

Daniel is determined. As I nod to Jenny, 'please,' for the coffee, I feel a warm hand at the small of my back and it is both reassuring and comforting. I allow Daniel to lead me to a heavy wooden chair at the kitchen table. Like something out of a Brontë novel, he pulls out the chair with a thud and scrape, I smile weakly. Noah, Jem, Stuart and Edie face me, chomping at scrambled eggs, bacon and brown toast. Daniel takes his phone from his pocket before sitting next to me.

'Are you OK?' he asks quietly. I nod slowly.

Monsieur Durand, the chef is busy cooking at the stove, shaking and stirring pans, whilst systematically checking the oven. Mrs Monk is studiously making hot drinks, using a combination of the kettle and Nespresso machines.

Francesca joins us in the kitchen. 'Mum?' Her eyes scour the room, looking for her mother. The young woman is dressed in black jeans and boots, a black top and a long flowing black cardigan, as though she is going to a funeral.

Resting her gaze on the sink, she stares at the back of her mum who is emptying coffee cups and rinsing them ready for the dishwasher. Mrs Monk turns to her daughter. 'We're out of milk. Can I borrow some from here?'

'Of course, I meant to get some yesterday and then forgot all about it.' Mrs Monk replies. Today, she wears a long flowery A-line dress.

'Why don't you join us, Francesca?' Jenny, and her kind heart asks. 'We have plenty here, and Monsieur Durand, our chef won't mind one more for breakfast. Will you Monsieur?' she looks to the chef who raises his hand, without turning away from the pans.

'Bien sûr,' he shouts across the room.

Julie, Steph, Brian and Jack enter the room together. Ben follows behind, looking at something on his phone. 'Morning everyone.' They say solemnly, finding seats and waiting as Mrs Monk begins taking drink orders.

Francesca hovers, so Jenny takes her under her wing, 'do sit down, Francesca. You look as pale as a sheet of pastry.' Jenny raises her hand to gesture the young woman to the empty seat next to me.

'Now what drink would you like?' Jenny asks.

'A plain black coffee please.' Francesca answers. Jenny moves around the kitchen with ease, diplomatically keeping out of the way of the housekeeper and chef.

Monsieur Durand brings me my plate of scrambled eggs and bacon and brown toast. 'Keep your strength up,' he says in broken English.

'Thanks,' I say awkwardly, still finding it hard to have people cooking for me.

Mrs Monk brings my latte over, placing it carefully in front of me. 'There you go, my dear.'

I smile appreciatively at her beaming face, before lifting the hot mug with both hands to my lips. The hot liquid is delicious.

'Any new developments?' Jack asks.

I shake my head. 'Nothing,' I say sadly. 'Not one phone call or message,' I take another sip.

'News?' Francesca raises an eyebrow, 'What news? Has something happened?

Steph looks up from her phone. 'It's Lottie's son, Harley. He went to post a letter yesterday afternoon and never came back.'

'Oh my God!' Francesca's face paled, 'that's awful. How old is he? You must be going out of your mind!'

'I am,' I say simply, wiping my eyes with the arm of my jumper. I'm holding on by a thread, but I don't tell her that. I need to be strong. Warm fingers find mine, resting on the kitchen table and thread their warmth and strength through. Daniel. I look at him, and to my surprise, he leans close and kisses me gently on the side of my temple.

'You're doing really well,' he says quietly. 'I'm here for you.'

Jack turns to the kettle to make himself, Ben and Steph a drink. 'He's ten, ten years old.'

'Holy shit!' Francesca says, before covering her mouth. Steph and Jack, look at Ben but he is still engrossed with something on his phone. At fourteen, he's probably heard much worse than that.

Her mum doesn't look happy with the slip up. 'Sorry,' Francesca seems mortified, and offers a heartfelt apology for her outburst, before turning to Lottie. 'That's awful. I'm so sorry you're going through this Lottie.'

'Thanks,' I take a deep breath and concentrate. 'I'm pretty sure that my cousin has taken him,' I tell her. 'He's a nasty piece of work. The only thing that gives me hope is that he won't harm him, because it's me he wants.'

Brian walks into the room, his phone next to his ear, as though he's listening to someone. 'Are we talking about Cameron?' he says walking to the cupboard, taking a glass and filling it with water.

'Cameron bloody Frost,' Stuart says, and I feel Francesca stiffen beside me.

'Cameron Frost?' Francesca repeats, her voice has a shakiness to it. She brushes a hand through her hair, and as she does so, her sleeve rises, and I notice red scars of self-harm. Poor girl. I know she must have been through a lot, and that can take its toll on your stress levels, on your physical and mental health. I say nothing.

'Do you know him?' I ask, watching her hands visibly shake as she brings the coffee mug to her lips.

She doesn't answer for a moment, but the telling signs of panic show clearly on her face, as she bites her lower lip, and her dark eyes flit from the table to the warm mug.

'No.' Francesca replies quickly, placing the coffee mug onto the table with a hard thud, and before I can say another word, Francesca pulls a black thin hair band from her wrist and scrapes back her chair.

Adding the band to her hair, she pulls it into a tight ponytail. 'I need something from my car,' she mutters, without making eye contact. I watch in silence as she picks up speed and rushes from the room.

'Don't be long, your breakfast is nearly ready?' Jenny calls, taking a plate from the cupboard and putting it on the counter for Monsieur Durand to fill.

A strange feeling in the pit of my tummy, tells me that something is wrong. I look at Mrs Monk and see a fleeting moment of panic in her eyes. She is worried for her daughter.

As expected, my appetite has completely disappeared. I can't face pushing food into my mouth, not until I know that my son is safe.

A phone bleeps, we all look at our phones, and I plead inwardly, hoping that Cameron will try to make contact. No such luck.

'It's me,' Brian says. He pulls out the phone and presses some keys. He stares at the screen.

'Holy crap!' He mutters.

'What is it?' Julie walks to him and rests a hand on his arm. Brian just shakes his head.

'Shep just sent the photofit through from the sketch artist, of the person who kidnapped and tortured Vincent Camprinelli. Who we think also killed Eric Weston. You won't believe who it looks like!'

Quickly, he shows the phone to Julie. 'No!' she says, putting her hand over her mouth.

Pushing back chairs, Stuart and Daniel stand and walk over to the phone. They look hard at the screen until recognition fills their faces, then they look at me.

'What?' I panic, 'Who the hell is it? Tell me!' It's all too much, I just want my son back, I don't care a fig who killed Eric or tried to kill Vincent.

'We know who Ferret is.' Stuart says. 'Ferret is female.' He looks at Mrs Monk and Steph throws her bag over her shoulder, ready to leave in an instant.

Something clicks into place. My mind starts to scream NO! I stare at the housekeeper.

'I'll take Edie into the lounge to play with the toys,' Jem picks up her three-year-old and hugs her close, before leaving the room. 'Ben,' she offers him a quick look, 'do you want to come too?' Ben nods a yes and follows them out of the kitchen.

Brian glances around the room. 'Julie, Steph and Jack, you're with me. Hopefully, she's still in her car. Let's go.'

Everyone nods, as though they know what is expected of them and leave the kitchen to go in search of Francesca. A sudden, sharp crash to the floor, breaks the silence. Mrs Monk stares into space, she knows that something is wrong. Monsieur Durand gently takes the tea towel from her hand and guides her to a chair at the table, giving Stuart time to pull it out and to gently encourage Mrs Monk to take a seat.

Jenny is busy at the counter, making Mrs Monk a sweetened, milky tea. I watch idly as she sets the kettle to boil, takes a mug, adds milk and sugar, stirs and takes it to the table, placing the mug carefully in front of the housekeeper.

'Here, drink this, Agnes. May I call you that?' she says kindly.

Mrs Monk nods slowly, without lifting her head. She stares at the kitchen table. 'I'm so sorry, sorry for ruining your break. Sorry for everything. You see, I didn't know.'

Jenny, Stuart and Noah exchange a look. I've seen that look before. It's the look that says, finally we are fitting the pieces together. 'What didn't you know, Agnes?' Steph asks softly.

'I didn't know who had hurt her. You see she never said. But I knew someone had.' Agnes talks as though she's reliving a dream or a nightmare, her eyes never leaving the table. 'She changed overnight. Started hurting herself, became solitary, depressed. I thought it was her age, but then she started to lock herself in her room and wear dark coloured clothes.'

'Oh my God,' I say. 'It was them, wasn't it?' The chills that run down my spine cause me to shiver. They did it again. And, I could have reported them. I could have stopped it. No. Please don't let me be the reason Francesca got hurt.

'Lottie,' Jenny looks at me sternly. 'This is not your fault. You know that, right?'

'But if I had reported what they did...' I begin.

Daniel looks at me, from the table pushing out of his seat. He begins pacing the floor. I've never seen his anger before. 'No!' he says firmly, his beautiful face overcome with anger. Eyebrows raised and eyes blackening with his frustration, 'Stop!'

A sob starts in my throat and threatens to force itself out.

'Noah,' Steph lays a gentle hand on her friend's arm, 'can you please make sure that Jem and the children are OK.' He nods and leaves the room in a hurry. I know she feels paranoid that something bad is about to happen. I feel it too.

The silence doesn't last long. Agnes' accusing voice echoes across the room. 'Who are they?' 'The ones who changed my daughter. The ones who took the life she should have had.'

I look at the pale faced, broken woman before me, the scrunched white handkerchief in her hands. 'I am sorry,' I say, 'so very sorry for what happened to Francesca.' My nose is running, and I can hardly speak, as the tears run down my cheeks.

Agnes doesn't acknowledge me, instead, puts her hands on the table, lowers her head onto them and howls as though her heart is breaking.

Footsteps disrupt the sobbing as Brian, Julie, Steph and Jack return to the house and appear at the kitchen door. He shakes his head.

'She's gone,' Brian says flatly, taking in the scene before him. He pulls up a chair beside Mrs Monk.

'Mrs Monk, I know this is hard. But I need to ask you a few things,' he speaks quietly.

Steph puts her hand on Mrs Monks shoulder.

'We need to know,' Brian presses, 'About Francesca. Why is she staying with you?'

There is no movement, so I look at Steph.

'Mrs Monk, we really need your help.' Steph says, but there is still no reply.

'Agnes,' I put my hand on top of hers. 'Please. We need to find Francesca. For her safety and for whatever she plans to do next.'

Mrs Monk slowly raises her head and swollen red eyes look at me. 'She said she needed to stay with me for a few days.' Her voice is quiet, and we all strain to hear her words.

'Did she say why?' Brian asks.

'No, she wouldn't say.' Mrs Monk shook her head sadly.

'What car does she drive?' Steph places a pen and piece of paper on the counter. 'And, if you know it, can you please put the car registration number on this paper.'

Mrs Monk looks at me, 'It's a Peugeot 2008, dark green, but I don't know the registration number.'

'Where does she live? Can you tell us her address and phone number?' Julie asks. 'Anything that will help us to find her.'

The woman looks at the paper in front of her, 'She lives on the Great Western Park estate, just on the outskirts of Didcot,' she starts to write down her daughter's address and phone number.

Julie mutters, 'Bloody hell, Vincent was held captive and knocked over on Great Western Park.' Everyone looks at her, mostly with relief that we are now getting somewhere with the case.

The pieces of the puzzle are starting to come together, and my mind tries hard to process the information. When I look at Mrs Monk's face, her eyes are dull, and her skin is pale. She looks defeated as she reaches into a pocket for a tissue. After blowing her nose, she rests her arms on the table and lowers her head onto them.

'Fuck!' Daniel mutters, and within a couple of strides he's in front of me, leans down to hold me close. 'It's OK, honey.' A small comfort, but his warmth and strength bring me solace. Reminds me that I am not alone. Through a gap above his shoulder, I see Agnes with her head still down, her shoulders bobbing up and down. From one mother to another, I can feel her pain.

But there was nothing that each one of us could do, to support each other.

The chef, who has been quietly moving pans on the stove, suddenly stops, shakes his head and leaves the room, without saying a word.

A cloud of oppression fills the room.

Part Thirty-Eight: DCI Brian Carter

The kitchen is quiet. You can cut the air with a knife. I walk over to my wife and slip my fingers in hers.

'You alright?' I ask, quietly. She looks a bit pale.

She turns to me, reaching up and curls a hand around my neck. 'I'm fine.'

I kiss her hand quickly, before leading her to a chair. 'Rest for a minute, it's going to be a long day,' I say in a low voice, pulling out a chair.

Everyone in the room is deep in their own thoughts. We are just waiting, hoping. For what, we're not sure. Good news. Any news. I called Shep to chase the registration number for the Peugeot registered to Francesca Monk. Now, I have it, she is checking CCTV to see if the car flags up at any CCTV points, alongside Cameron's.

My phone bleeps. It's a text, from Gino.

'I know who kidnapped him,' I read and my heart stops. Another text, and I stare at the words.

'When I find her, I will fucking kill her!'

Shit! There is an urgency to find Harley and Francesca, not to mention Cameron – before someone else gets hurt. My phone rings, it's Shep. Cameron's car has been found in the Waitrose Carpark in Wallingford. It's a start.

'Julie, Steph and Jack, we need to go,' I say, looking at my wife apologetically, because she looks pale, and I want her to rest. Grabbing my car keys from the table, I take a step forward.

'Let's go.' I tell them, leaving the room. Steph disappears to tell Ben that she and Jack need to go out and to stay with Jem, Noah and Edie. Julie throws her small bag over her shoulder, pushes out of her chair and follows Jack out of the door.

Time is of the essence. I need to get to Harley in time.

Part Thirty-Nine: Harley

Someone is talking.

'Can't wait until I phone her, and tell her what I've done,' a male voice says. It sounds like Cameron's. There is movement, I try to open my eyes to look but they won't open. 'Yes, this is the day I've been waiting for. This is payback for this bastard leg.'

I can't hear all of it, because it sounds vague and muddled, as though someone is ranting to themselves.

'Please don't hurt him, she'll beg,' his voice sounds higher, as though he is impersonating a woman. Who is he talking about? I wish I could see and hear clearly. Then it goes dark again.

The next time I wake up, I'm lying on something hard. There is a thick rope tied around my right wrist and it is knotted on a hook on the wall. I'm surrounded by a foul-smelling odour that forces its way up my nose and makes me want to vomit.

My jeans feel wet and cold, as if they are stuck to my skin, and I realise that the odour is coming from me. I've wet myself. Shame fills me, even at ten years old, it feels wrong to have allowed this to happen. I try not to dwell on it, I peed myself and it's the least of my worries. My face is sore, and one of my eyes feels thick, like it's swollen.

'Smile young man.' Cameron says, pointing his phone my way, he clicks it several times and taps away at the phone before walking closer. Dropping his phone into his jeans pocket, he slowly stoops before me, his legs wobble slightly, until he's kneeling in front of me.

His eyebrows draw together in a wince, and I have a quick flashback. I think there's something wrong with his legs.

Cameron brings his face close to mine, and we are almost touching. I can feel the whisper of his breath on my skin. He stares at me for the longest time, with one hand resting on his knee, and for a second, I think I see a little bit of my mum in his face, he has her nose. Small and straight. He pushes a hand through his dark hair.

'Tell me about your mum,' he asks in a low voice, he looks around, stands up and stretches one of his legs. He rubs it and winces, before walking slowly across the room.

I say nothing.

'Tell me about your mum!' he repeats, raising his voice.

Closing my eyes, I ignore him. 'Don't ignore me, you little shit!' His voice resonates around my head. You must answer him, I think, but be clever, don't give anything important away. Just stay alive.

Taking a deep breath, I open my eyes, 'What do you want to know?'

Cameron moves his hips from side to side and lifts his right leg onto a wooden pallet, forcing it to bend. When he feels happier with his knee, He smiles, as though he is pleased that I am answering his questions.

'Here's a few to start with...' he taps his chin, with a finger, thinking, 'what's her favourite food? Is she dating?'

Mmm, strange questions. Why does he want to know what she eats? Does he have a food phobia?

'Favourite food... pizza. Pepperoni.' He repeats this information back to himself. 'And dating, sometimes she dates, not much since my dad...' I stop, almost clamp my hand over my mouth. Immediately, I realise that I've said too much.

'Yes, your dad,' he says, his eyes light up and I can tell he's enjoying this. 'I was getting to him. Your mum was such a pretty teenager. Your dad was lucky to have such a beautiful young woman as his wife.'

A sudden feeling of apprehension sweeps coldly along my arms. This doesn't sound right. His words sound strange and contorted. It doesn't sound right for him to speak of my mum like this. Is he in love with her? The notion makes me feel sick and I force myself to take deep breaths.

Cameron begins to pace the hard concrete floor, it's scaring me.

'Let me go,' I say quietly. 'This isn't the right way, Cameron,' I plead quietly, as he puts a hand to his forehead and begins to mutter to himself. His pace quickens. The damaged leg can't cope, so it drags slightly to keep up.

'She doesn't deserve to be happy, after what she did. What she did, what she did.' he repeats quietly as he moves.

'What did she do, Cameron?' I ask, sitting up and crossing my legs, I wince when my sore ankle knocks against my other foot.

He continues for a few moments before abruptly stopping in front of me.

'She did this,' he points harshly at his leg. 'She caused this.'

My mind tries to make sense of what he is saying. My mum wouldn't hurt anyone, not willingly. I don't believe a word this mad man is saying, but I know enough to realise that he believes she did it.

311

'How? How, did she do that?' I query. 'My mum wouldn't hurt anyone.'

He starts to laugh. 'Of course she wouldn't, little Charlotte Peckham, always everyone's darling. Never did anything wrong.'

I think he's forgotten I'm here. His head turns to focus on a cobweb in the corner of the ceiling. Mesmerised, he stands there, as if in a trance. It is so quiet and eerie, my heart is beating so loudly, I wonder he can't hear it. But he stands there, looking at the cobweb, which can be seen through the streaks of light that have broken through the boarded windows.

Rubbing my rope-tied wrist, I look to see if I can undo the knot, frantically I force my left hand to feel the rope, trying to get my fingers in some of the tight crevices to loosen them.

Scanning the room, I wonder if the door is unlocked and wonder if there's time to escape. Thankfully, the rope begins to loosen, but I keep my movements small, because I don't want to draw any attention. Gently, I twist my wrist to see if the rope has loosened at all. Bugger, no, there's hardly any movement.

I have a vision of a film my Mum once told me about, when a young man fell between two boulders in a canyon in Utah, wherever that is and injured his arm. He survived but Mum said he had to make the ultimate choice, for survival. He had to cut his own arm off to escape.

It sounds very brave, but I'm not like him, I'm not a hero.

'Don't.' The word is so quiet, I wonder if I've misheard it.

When he looks at me, I realise that whatever window of opportunity I had, has gone, along with my energy.

I am ten years old, and I am going to die.

'She'll never forgive you for this,' I say flatly. 'Never.'

'I don't want her forgiveness,' he says, walking over to me. 'I want her dead.'

Cameron silently takes his phone from his trouser pocket. For a moment, he studies the screen before unlocking it, pressing a button and taking a photo of me. Focusing on the phone, he presses several numbers, waits a moment and uses his forefinger to make a call.

'Let's see what she's got to say,' he smiles, putting the call on speaker. The dial tone breaks through the deadly cold air of the room, he takes it off speaker. 'Charlotte?' he says. He's the only person I know who calls my mum Charlotte.

Holding the phone in his open hand, we hear my Mum's frantic voice talking at speed, accusing, demanding, begging. When she is finished, Cameron starts to talk. Confident, gloating.

'Calm down woman. It's only superficial. Well, you'll have to come and get him if you want him.'

In silence, I watch as Cameron brings the phone to me, and almost jams it into my face.

Trying hard to hold back the tears, I hear my mum's worried voice, 'Harley? Are you alright honey?' She asks, her words shaking with worry.

'I'm fine, Mum,' I try to be brave, reassure her. 'I should have been more careful,' I say sadly, before the tears fall and I find myself crying like a baby. 'I'm sorry,' I sob, rubbing my wet nose and eyes with the sleeve of my sweatshirt.

'You've got nothing to be sorry for. You just need to hold on, I'm coming to get you.' She sounds strong, determined.

I sniffle an 'OK' as Cameron pulls the device from under my chin and disconnects the call.

'See, I knew it would be easy.' He says, slipping the phone into his jacket pocket and giving me the biggest smile.

The smile fills me with dread, it doesn't reach his eyes, but dips slightly at each corner. He's like two people, the sane Cameron, and the crazy, staring, chanting Cameron seeking revenge for something that happened a long time ago.

I lower my head onto my crossed arms and don't try to stop the hot tears that make their way down my cheeks. All I did was go to post a card... how can such a simple thing lead to this? How stupid was I to get close to his van? I am so angry with myself for being stupid, and letting Cameron take me.

'Shut up, boy. And keep quiet.' Cameron moans, like a sulking child. His character seems to be changing with the wind, he has so many different faces. I yank at my rope, trying to get the tiniest bit away from him, but I'm too late, a punch comes to my ribs. Hard and fierce, making me scream in pain and sob loudly. It hurts when I take a breath, so I throw an arm over my ribs and hold it there tightly, to calm my breathing. And to protect myself.

Hot tears fill my eyes. This man is a demon, and I hate him. Hate that I am related to him, and that my mum is related to him.

He watches me intently, waiting for a reason to hit me again. And I worry that, he is past that stage of waiting, that he will find any reason to punish me to get at my mum.

We don't hear the creaking of the door behind us.

'Cameron Frost, I've been looking for you.' A deep female voice breaks through my sobs.

My abductor and I turn to see a young woman with dark hair scraped back into a ponytail, she is dressed all in black, with a black flowing cardigan wrapped around her middle. The woman stands unfazed in the open doorway.

There is a look of shock on Cameron's face. And, then his brows draw together as though there is something familiar about the woman who now stands in front of us.

Despite not being overly tall, she holds her head up high and oozes confidence.

'Step away from the boy,' she says, harshly. Slowly stepping forward in our direction, she is almost ghost-like, gliding through the semi-darkness of the pub.

'Do I know you?' Cameron asks, taking a step closer to the woman.

She stops.

He stops.

Like a Mexican standoff.

She suddenly smiles, and her face changes completely. She is beautiful when she smiles. She pushes a hand through her hair and looks at me. 'Are you alright?' she asks quietly.

I nod, wondering who my rescuer is. This woman dressed in black who might just be here to save my life. Whoever she is, I don't care, I am just so grateful that she's here.

'I said, do I fucking know you?' Cameron says in a harsh voice. I'm scared, and worried that he's going to hurt her. He's so unpredictable. Rubbing his leg, his focus stays on her face. They are almost within touching distance, and I am dreading what will happen next.

'Untie him,' she orders Cameron.

'No fucking way,' he says shaking his head, 'I need him for collateral.'

Suddenly Cameron stops talking, and his face goes deathly pale.

'I know you… it's Ferret, isn't it?' He steps away from her, off guard. 'I remember a night, a long time ago. You were drunk and really up for it. So, my mates and I sorted you out.'

'You mean, you drugged me.' She replies.

'You didn't say no.' Cameron gloats, 'You were up for it.'

'You raped me. The three of you.' The woman says in a flat tone.

My blood goes cold. He knows her.

'I found your other two cronies. One's dead and the other is not far off.' She says, rushing forward and at the same time, reaching into her cardigan pocket and taking out a small black object.

She stops a short distance away, activates the object and points it at Cameron. I watch, mesmerised, as a loud buzzing sound accompanies the electrical current, that she forces into his body. Cameron begins to shake uncontrollably as though he's been hit by lightning. He has been tasered. Something I've never seen before.

'You're the one I want, though.' She waits until Cameron stops moving on the floor and rushes over to me to help me get the rope off my wrist. It's sturdy, and she takes a penknife from her pocket and begins frantically sawing through the rope to free me.

After, what seems like an age I am finally detached from my tether.

'Get his phone and run. Phone your mum or 999 for the police,' she says urgently as she takes rope from her pocket and secures his wrists and arms.

I fumble around in his trouser pocket and find the phone.

'Now, go!' She shouts, 'run as fast as you can.'

'What are you going to do with him?' I ask her quietly.

'Nothing that he doesn't deserve,' she says flatly, focused on securing him before he comes around.

'Thank you,' I say, and she nods. No words are needed.

My feet are rooted to the spot in this semi-dark, cold building with the unconscious man, who calls himself my uncle, lying on the hard floor at my feet tied with blue rope. Whoever this man is, he's done nothing to make me feel sympathetic to him. He kidnapped me, attacked me and was willing to use me as a pawn to make my Mum pay for something that happened before I was born,

The woman suddenly turns her face to look at me, and our eyes meet. The look on her face is so sad, her eyes are lifeless. It reminds me of how Mum was when Dad died.

I run from the building, and don't stop, until the building is no longer in sight.

Part Forty: Jenny

People who know me, see me as someone to aspire to. Stuart often says that I am the strongest person he knows. I am driven, compassionate (his words, not mine) and forgiving. I like to see the good in people and I firmly believe in second chances.

Most days I am strong. But there are days, like today that seem to spiral out of control and drag me down. So many things are going around in my mind.

I just wanted a few quiet days with my family and friends.

Obviously, as the world moves, things change all the time. My friend Lottie is really struggling at the moment. What with the ghastly presents that someone keeps sending to her, the reappearance of her cousin, the death of her cousin's friend and now the kidnapping of her son, Harley.

A picture of Judy, lying in her bed at home, waiting to die, comes into my mind. That poor woman, she doesn't deserve this. Doesn't deserve to come through the other side of domestic violence at the hands of her partner and now to be struck down, her body ravaged by cancer. A sob escapes me, without warning, when I think of the twins.

I'm staring out of the window, in the drawing room.

And I just want to scream, life is unfair!

'Hey,' Stuart's voice whispers in my ears, and I close my eyes and let the warm touch of his hand on the small of my back, heal me. As it always does.

'Hey,' I reply. 'Are you OK?'

'Yeah, you?' his husky voice is soft.

'I am now.' Part of healing and processing is being kind to yourself and allowing yourself to be sad, angry or frustrated sometimes. By allowing these feelings in and validating their importance and your emotions, you're enabling these thoughts to be acknowledged, therefore accepting that they are important.

I am that person who wants to make things better, wants to fix them. Stuart often says, 'Jen, you can't fix the world, but you can help a little, one bit at a time.' And I do, when I can.

'Where are Agnes and Lottie?' I ask.

'Still in the kitchen,' he answers, stroking my neck softly. 'Shall we go and check on them?

I nod and take his hand, as we walk in silence through the hallway to the kitchen.

The kitchen door is open, but apart from low voices chatting at the far side of the large room, it is silent. Agnes and Lottie sit on opposite sides of the table, staring at each other solemnly, with their hands resting on the table, fingers clasped. I'm loathed to interrupt, but I need to be here, to support my friend. Daniel talks quietly to Noah by the large, built in glass display cabinet, each with mugs in their hand.

'Where is everyone?' I ask, no one in particular.

'Brian, Jack, Steph and Julie rushed off. Brian had a call about Cameron's car,' Noah explains. 'Can I get you both a drink? I'm making one for Jem. She's going to take Edie and Ben to the pool house in a little while. She's trying to keep them busy.'

'I'll have a latte, please.' I tell him, as I walk behind my friend and put my hand on her shoulder.

'Make that two, please.' Stuart says, 'I'll be in the lounge with Jem and the youngsters.' He touches my waist tenderly as he makes his way out of the room.

'How are you holding up?' I ask her softly.

'Not good, I should be out there looking for him,' Lottie answers.

'We need to let Steph, Brian and Julie do their job,' Daniel reminds us. 'We've done what we can. Cameron will make contact soon and we can get Harley back.'

'But what if he doesn't?' Lottie asks. 'What if he doesn't phone?' I see her pain and lean down to hug her tight.

'He will,' I say. Even though I have no idea if Cameron will call or not. I need to believe to have hope.

Noah hands me my hot drink and I smile my thanks, as he leaves the room to take Stuart's drink to him.

Lottie's phone comes to life, and the room goes quiet. Stuart stands in the doorway. Lottie, quickly looks at her phone, hoping that it is Cameron. It's not, she puts the phone on speaker mode.

'Hey Brian,' she says, loudly, 'You're on speaker.'

'Hey,' he says, 'I've just had a call from Shep, and she found recent messages on Harley's phone.'

'What messages?' Lottie asks warily.

The room is silent. 'Your cousin, Cameron, began sending text messages to Harley last week. It looks like he meant to get to you through him.'

'Bloody hell!' Stuart's voice is hard with disbelief. 'I can't believe he would stoop so low as to go for your child.' He brushes his fingers over his designer stubble beard. 'We should have stopped him when we had the chance. The man is evil.'

'What did the messages say?' Lottie pushes for answers. We wait for Brian to speak.

'Bloody hell, get off my backside, will you?' Brian suddenly shouts. 'Sorry, someone on the A34 is tailgating me, ah – that's better,' he sounds calmer. 'There were only a couple of messages. Cameron introduces himself as your cousin, he is clearly trying to befriend Harley.'

Lottie's face pales and I worry that she is going to faint, so I move to the sink to grab her a class of water.

'We're heading back to the house. Will be home in about ten minutes.' Brian states.

'Thanks, for the update, Bri,' Stuart says, as the line goes dead.

I am about to take Lottie the glass of water, when Daniel steps over to her, reaches down to take her hands and carefully pulls her to her feet. Slowly he pulls her into his arms and holds her close.

My heart is heavy, when I think of Cameron deliberately focusing on Harley, to make a point. To punish Lottie, to make her hurt and feel pain again.

I can't help but feel the frustration building within me. 'What a bastard!' I mutter under my breath and gulp down the water myself. Apart from my cruel Uncle Felix, I have never wanted to hurt someone as much as I want to hurt Cameron Frost. He deserves nothing but contempt.

Daniel tips his head and his eyes hold Lottie's, it is as though they are in a trance. That look reminds me of the way Stuart stares at me. The feeling of safety, of being connected, is the best feeling in the world.

'A few days ago, Harley was being pestered by someone on his mobile,' Daniel, pulls away and looks into her face. He tells her solemnly, 'I don't know who was pestering him, but when I asked, he said that there wasn't a problem. Bloody hell. I should have insisted.' Daniel chastises himself.

'You weren't to know, Daniel' I tell him. 'This is not your fault. The only person who is to blame, is Cameron Frost.' The truth is a sad fact of life. I learnt a long time ago, that I couldn't take the blame for someone else's actions. That they alone, had to face the consequences.

'Jenny speaks the truth,' my husband, moves to my side and gently places his hand in the small of my back.

Occasionally, when I'm low or tired, doubts creep in, and I give myself a stern talking to. Telling myself to put my big girl pants on and lay the blame at the hands of Felix Gloverman, for what he did to me, to Rose and the others.

Stuart sees my inner struggles. He can tell when the only things I need are his arms to hold me tight and his tough words to pull me back from the abyss.

'My poor boy,' Lottie sobs into Daniel's chest, dropping her head against his top and gripping it tightly.

A phone starts to buzz, and we look at the table. It's Lottie's phone.

'Quick, get that Lottie,' Stuart urges, as Brian rushes into the kitchen, dressed in brown chinos and a long-sleeved navy top. He looks windswept, and slightly breathless, as though he's been running. When he reaches the dining table, he takes Lottie's phone and hands it to her. Julie, Steph and Jack stand in the open doorway, waiting for Lottie to answer the phone.

Daniel releases her quickly, but Lottie stares at the phone, unable to move.

Finally, she reaches for the phone. 'It's a text,' she says and opens it. 'Oh god, oh my god! It's a photo of Harley.' My son has a red mark on his cheek, his face looks swollen on one side.

The phone she is holding springs to life, and swiftly she presses a button to accept the call. 'Cameron, what the hell have you done to my son?' She screams at the phone, and we all watch helplessly as Lottie's anger increases. There is nothing but her shouting. 'Cameron, I am going to kill you, do you hear me! Don't tell me to calm down. You tell me the place and I'll be there. Do not touch another hair on his head.'

Brian indicates for her to put the phone on speaker mode. She does. 'Harley, are you alright, honey?' Lottie sobs.

Harley replies, sounding much younger than his ten years, 'I'm fine, Mum,' he says a little too quickly. My heart skips a beat when the shaking of his voice echoes across the room. suddenly feel like I'm interrupting a special mother-son moment as he apologises to her, for not being more vigilant, for allowing himself to be taken by Cameron.

Harley starts to cry. Bloody hell, I can feel my blood boil at the thought of his distress.

Lottie tells him that he has nothing to be sorry for, and my eyes start to blur with hot tears. She mutters something about coming to get him, Harley sniffles before the phone goes dead.

'Nooo!' Lottie stares at the phone. 'He didn't tell me where my son is!'

Bloody hell, I rush to Lottie and hold her tight. 'He didn't tell me...' she weeps into my shoulder.

'Shh...' I try to calm her, 'maybe he'll send a text.'

'I would gladly give my life for that of my son,' she wails. Daniel, Jack, Brian and Stuart stare at her.

'It won't come to that,' Daniel says harshly. 'I won't let that happen.'

Brian reaches into the pocket of his brown chinos, takes out his phone and studies the screen. His face looks pensive, with drawn brows and the grim line of his lips. He looks agitated.

'Everything alright, Brian?' I ask, watching him walk across the room to the dining table, he pulls out a chair next to Agnes and drops himself into it. He stares at Agnes.

Brian looks my way, and I catch the tiredness in his eyes as he scratches his day-old stubble wearily across his chin. My first instinct is to rush to his side and give him the biggest hug. To tell him that everything will work out, that it will be OK. But we all know that life doesn't work out that way.

'Agnes,' he turns to the housekeeper, his voice is gentle. 'Agnes, please look at me.'

It's taken some time to process the fact that Agnes is Francesca's mother. And, as her mother, she seems to have aged considerably over the past few days. Wrinkles pepper her face, particularly around her eyes and her lips.

'Agnes,' Brian says, 'we need to talk about Francesca.'

'What about her?' The older woman looks up quickly. 'Has something happened to her?'

Brian takes her hand, 'Nothing that we know of,' he reassures her. 'But I have someone who is very angry and he's looking for your daughter.'

Agnes puts a hand to her mouth, as tears fall freely down her cheeks. God, this is awful. How can you not be moved by a mother's desperate need to protect her child. I can't help thinking that under different circumstances, Lottie and Agnes may have become friends.

'We need to find her, before he does,' Brian says. 'I'm not trying to frighten you. I'm trying to keep Francesca safe.'

Shaking her head, as though to clear her thoughts, Agnes focuses on the glass display cabinet. 'I can't think!' she says with desperation. 'I can't think.'

'Where would she go?' Daniel asks, sitting beside Agnes. 'Was there somewhere she liked to go? Somewhere that she felt safe? Or somewhere that lifted her spirits?'

Daniel's words must have unlocked a memory in Agnes' mind, because her eyes suddenly brighten, and her cheeks begin to flush. She twirls her fingers in a continuous circle, just above the table.

'What?' Lottie asks. 'You've thought of something, please tell us?' Her face is red and puffy, and she takes a silver scrunchie from her wrist and uses it to pull her hair into a ponytail.

'Please,' I beg, 'let us help you to find Francesca.'

Agnes looks at me, and I watch sadly as a stray tear makes its way slowly down her cheek.

'When we first moved here, she enjoyed our trips to Days Lock at Little Wittenham. I know she's been back there a couple of times in her car, since she left home.'

Everyone looks at Brian. It has got to be worth a shot. As things stand, we've got nothing to lose.

'I'll take Lottie, Julie and Agnes in my car.' I feel better, now we're doing something. 'I think Francesca will respond more to us and her mum. So, we'll take the lead. What do you think Brian?'

Brian pushes back his seat and stands with his hands resting on the dining table. He looks at Steph and nods. 'Stuart, Daniel, Julie and I and I will hover in the background. Steph, can you and Jack stay here with Jem and the kids.'

I suddenly realise that I have made a big assumption that Lottie would leave the house. Feeling guilty, I want to give her the option of where to stay, while we're waiting for Cameron to call again. 'Lottie, do you feel OK coming with us, or would you prefer to stay here?'

'I just want to find my son, Jen.' she smiles sadly. 'But I can't sit here a moment longer, it's driving me crazy. I'll come with you.'

With that settled, we are all ready within minutes, we are all ready to take on our respective roles to try and save Harley and Francesca.

We hope we're not too late.

Part Forty-One: DCI Brian Carter

Depressing the clutch on the Audi I bring the car into fourth gear. The traffic moving along the Abingdon Road is crawling, so I drop down to third gear again. Bloody hell. Traffic in Oxfordshire is a nightmare.

My phone rings, and I see that it's Gino. 'Better answer this,' I say, leaning forward and using my forefinger to accept the call. I hope he hasn't found her, my heart slams in my chest.

'Gino,' I tell the car, 'I'm driving, so you're on speaker.'

There is a brief crackle, before Camprinelli's voice booms through the speaker system. 'I can't find this fucking girl anywhere. She's like a fucking ghost.'

Thank God! I glance across to Stuart, check my rear-view mirror. Both men look as relieved as I do.

'I don't know where she is Gino,' I lie through my teeth, to give me some time. We just need to check out the lock.

'Anyway, I'm on my way to see you at the Sutton Courtenay house. I'll be with you in a about twenty minutes.' Gino snaps.

'She's not at the house, Gino' I tell him. 'I'm not at the house either!'

'Don't play me, Brian.' Gino responds, 'I know Jenny and Lottie know her through the Lighthouse charity. It's all I've got to go on.'

'Wait,' I say, looking across at my wife, who puts a reassuring hand on my knee. 'We think we know where she will be.'

Bloody hell. I hope I've done the right thing.

Part Forty-Two: Lottie

As my head rests, bumping slightly, against the window in the rear passenger seat of Jenny's red Volvo, I allow my mind to think about Harley and all the things he will never get to experience if his life is cut short. He will never grow up and have a girlfriend, a wife or children. I won't be able to cry happy tears as he says his vows to his new bride.

If Cameron decides to kill him.

I have failed my son, and as a mother, there is nothing worse. I just want to crawl into a corner and cry.

My phone rings.

'Hello,' I answer. The name comes up as Thames Valley Police.

'Hi, this is Detective Sergeant Jake Allen from the Thames Valley Police. Is that Charlotte Forster?' A deep voice asks.

'Yes, why?' My heart skips a beat in my chest. I sit upright, the only other sound is that of the car engine purring as we make our way to the village of Little Wittenham.

'I have someone who would like to speak to you.' The deep voice relaxes, and for a moment I stare at the grey leather head rest in front of me.

'Mum?' My boy's voice booms through the phone. The best thing I have ever heard.

'Harley?' I burst into tears. 'Is that you?' I say, through sobs, disbelief and happiness.

'Yes, it's me, Mum. I'm OK and at the John Radcliffe. They want to keep me in overnight, to check on me.'

'Oh, my darling boy!' I am so happy, I could scream. 'Are you sure you're all right? I'll be with you as soon as I can. We've all been so worried.' We speak for a few more moments, and I ask him to put the DS Allen back on the phone, so I can confirm where they are keeping him.

Oh my God, he's safe!

I see Jenny wipe a tear from her cheek. 'Thank God,' she says.

Texting Daniel the good news, we draw to a stop beside the church at Little Wittenham. There is a green Peugeot already there.

'That's Francesca's car,' Agnes says quietly as she unbuckles her front passenger belt and opens the car door.

The crunch of tyres behind us makes me look up and I see Daniel open the door before it has even stopped. He rushes over to me and pulls me into his arms. 'Thank God he's safe,' he says loudly.

We stand together and Agnes begins to lead the way, down an uneven dried mud pathway with hedges either side. Walking over a white fenced bridge, we see them, in the distance. Francesca is pushing somebody in a wheelchair towards the lock bridge. We watch in horror as she stops, takes an object from her pocket and points it at the person.

In the distances we watch as Francesca tilts the wheelchair, and the body falls onto the grass. Reaching down, she begins to drag the body onto the bridge, stopping and hauling – but determined to move him to her chosen place.

We realise that time is against us. That, whoever she had there in the wheelchair, is already not far from being her next victim.

Fleetingly, I wonder if it is Cameron, but there is no time to think further. As a group we nod to each other, reach an understanding, before making a silent decision.

We start running.

Part Forty-Three: Gino

'What do you mean, she's got Cameron?' I shout at Brian, through the car speaker phone. 'I don't fucking believe you! What a bloody nightmare. I'm parking up now.'

Bringing the car to a stop near the hedge bordering the field at Little Wittenham Church, I open the car door and step into the crisp morning air. There are three deserted cars, two Volvo's and a Peugeot, and it looks as if they've been dumped in a rush. Damn, am I too late?

I've never been to this place before, so I'm following google map area on my iPhone. The image shows a pathway, through thick shrubbery, that leads onto a bridge that sweeps over the Thames. Following this trail, I walk over dried mud to reach the bridge.

In the distance, sirens from the emergency services break through the quiet calmness of the village, and I begin to move faster. There are two pathways that lead in opposite directions. To the left of the bridge, I see Brian, and his friends Stuart, and Daniel. They have slowed down. I take that pathway. There are voices shouting.

Further along, there is another bridge, and I can just make out figures on it, like tiny ants. As my feet drag, I think of my nephew, Vincent, safe in his hospital bed. Of Rosalina, comforting her son, as only a mother can. There aren't enough hours in the day to keep everyone safe, it's bloody exhausting. But I'm a realist if nothing else, I know that if someone gets hurt, that there will be repercussions. It's human nature, we want to explore our own individuality, and we want to experience things, but there is also a need to challenge and exact revenge.

I get that too.

Finally, I reach the small group of men, and breathlessly acknowledge them. 'What's happening?' I ask, willing my heart to settle back into a normal rhythm.

Brian speaks first, 'She's got Cameron. We think he's injured.'

'Bloody hell! You need to stop her!' I shout, as I begin running to the lock. The men follow me, but instead of rushing forward, Brian puts his arms out to stop me.

'No, let her mum, Jenny, Julie and Lottie deal with it. They know her best.'

I stop, stubbornly wondering how I get myself into these scrapes. Bloody hell!

Part Forty-Four: Ferret

'Francesca, stop!' My mother's voice pierces through the warm air, as I kneel on the hard, white-painted bridge at Days Lock, Little Wittenham. Cameron's limp body is lying on the floor, but leaning into me, still bound at the wrists and ankles with cable ties. Earlier, I gave him water that I'd grounded a couple of my mother's sleeping tablets into. It's important to keep him subdued.

 The taser is still in my hand. Looking at my watch, I'm surprised to find that the hours have passed quickly, and the sun is already high and giving off an August heat that makes me want to throw off my long-sleeved cardigan. But I need the pockets.

Quickly, I drop the taser into a pocket and find the cheese wire with cork ends from the other pocket. I place it around his Cameron's throat and cross the cork handles at the back. I pull slightly, but not too hard.

My mind briefly thinks of Harley, and I hope he managed to get to a safe place. I want them to have a happy ending, to be reunited with each other. Some people deserve to be happy, to live with hope and know that their lives are worthwhile. No matter what I do, all seems lost.

I lost the hope a long time ago, and the worthwhile,

When did I change? When did I lose myself and my faith in humanity? I can't keep blaming those boys for what they did to me, but that was the beginning of the end. That was when the young Francesca began to disappear into the shadows.

There are no clouds in the sky, just a crystal blue hue that expands across the horizon, like a beautiful topaz jewel. The Thames is a buzz with wildlife, insects and sun sprinkled rays that scatter across the water. 'Please don't do this.'

I steal a peek through the slats of the bridge, and see the wild, natural grey waters of the lock. The noise from the gushing water hurts my ears, but this is where I want to be. My fingers tighten around the cork ends that pulls the wire tight into Cameron's neck. There is blood everywhere, colouring my hands and fingers, making them sticky.

I don't want to do this, but I have to. I can't stop.

It is the only way I can find peace.

Somewhere behind me, my mother sobs, heart wrenching sobs that force tears to my eyes. I am a monster. I have done terrible things. Cameron makes a strange gurgling sound and I know that if I don't do this now, I will regret it. Like that night so many years ago, the night that changed my life.

'I'm sorry, Mum,' I sob, as the sun scorches my hot tears. 'I thought I could move on, I tried. I really did. But I just can't get their bloody faces out of my head. They haunt me.'

'I know baby, I know you've been struggling. But please let me help you.' Mum cries, her voice sounds nearer.

Looking up, I see Jenny, Julie and Lottie, shadowing Mum at the entrance to the bridge.

'You brought them with you,' I can feel the anger forming in the pit of my stomach. How could she bring these two women here? I don't want them to see me like this. Broken and bruised. A killer. and my fingers begin to tighten on the wooden handles of the cheese wire.

'Please, Francesca. Don't do this.' Lottie cries, her wild hair wilting in the heat. I will never forget the look of panic on her face.

'I'm sorry, so fucking sorry.' I wipe my runny nose, as they step closer to me. Cameron stirs next to me. I haven't got much time. 'I never wanted to let you both down. But I'd become invisible you see. I couldn't find myself. I was lost.'

'I know,' Jenny's husky voice echoes in the silence. 'Let us help you.' She begs. In the distance I can hear sirens, and I know that the police are on their way. I look across the field and see a group of men standing, watching. Waiting.

Julie takes a step forward, 'Please think about this Francesca. Let's talk and see if we can figure something out.'

'Too late,' I mutter. 'Can't stop. Need to finish this.'

Lifting Cameron's head on to my lap, I wait for his eyes to flutter open, before I pull the wooden handles on the cheese wire, tighter.

'Nearly done, Cameron,' I whisper, watching a new wave of bright red blood oozes from his neck. The look of fear in his eyes as the taut wire forces its way through the skin of his neck slowly, his hands reach up to grab the wire. He tries to flail but his body is still subdued under the sedative.

His heavy arms try to grab mine, but I hold on. There is only one outcome here. That Cameron Frost will not live past this day. A plan which I have been working to for a long time. Jenny and Lottie drop to their knees beside me, their hands on my forearms, trying to pull them away from Cameron's neck.

Julie stands with her arm around my Mum. They both look on in horror as Cameron's blood seeps from his throat and through my fingers.

Suddenly, Cameron's arms go slack and very still, but my slippery grasp remains firm. Ignoring the cramp in my fingers and the pressure from the women's fingers as they pull at my arms. I feel satisfaction in the knowledge that I've done a lot of damage, but I don't let go. Not this time. He doesn't deserve to live, not after what he did.

There are some things that you simply cannot come back from, believe me, I've tried. It's just not meant to be.

'I'm sorry, but you should never have done it,' I say without emotion, to the dying man who has haunted my dreams for so many years. I can see the life dimming from his eyes. Not long now. Silently, I allow the women to pull me away. 'You should never have hurt me. And Lottie, and the others.'

Lottie wipes her face, and quietly begs, 'Please Francesca. How can we help you?'

Dropping the wire, I push the body onto the ground and try to stand. But my limbs suddenly feel very heavy, and my legs give way, Jenny catches me and helps me gently to the floor of the bridge. Next to the body of the man who raped me when I was a teenager. Cameron's eyes study me, even as the life drifts from his body, he lingers on.

'Bitch,' he whispers softly, blood trickling from his lips as his chest rises for the last time.

My mother sobs somewhere in the background with Julie, while the two women join me on the floor, quietly sobbing and holding me close. Out of the corner of my eye I see the group of men and police officers heading our way. I haven't got long.

'They had to die, because I couldn't live knowing they were still alive after what they had done.' I tell them in a flat voice.

Mum rushes to me, 'My beautiful girl.' She says pulling me to her in a tight hug, as she strokes my hair. 'My beautiful girl. You deserve to be at peace.'

'I know, but that's never going to happen. Not in this life.' I stroke Mum's face and slowly get to my feet. 'I love you, Mum. Don't forget that.'

Then, with as much strength as I can muster, I yank myself away from everyone's grip and run. Halfway across the bridge, I haul myself up onto the railing and climb over to the other side. The thrashing of the water is noisy, the current strong. But it matters little to me.

I look at Mum, her face is pale, her eyes are wide with horror. 'No...!' she screams, rushing towards me.

Sometimes in life, you need to look in the mirror and see what you are. Well, I've looked hard at my reflection and I don't like any part of it. I don't want to be a killer. I don't want to be a monster, and I certainly don't want to be a victim, or invisible.

I just want to be me.

The scream comes quickly, like a release, better than any slicing into my flesh, better than the pain I inflicted on my three attackers. The scream is the sound of a tortured animal, forcing itself from my throat, and is as relentless as a river which has burst its banks.

And, when there is no breath left, I stare up and watch the birds soar gracefully through the beautiful blue sky, their wings splayed for maximum effect.

Oh, to be free.

It feels good to empty my body and mind of every painful moment, of guilt, of panic, of fear and ultimately of anger.

Tears flow freely down my cheeks.

And then, I throw myself into the water.

Part Forty-Five: Lottie

The soft snores are like nectar to my senses.

I look at my ten-year-old baby, the dressing that protects the wound to the front of his head, the bruise to his cheekbone and surface cuts above his right eye. He lies in his bed at the hospital, the white bedding covering his young body. His face looks at peace and I am so grateful that I have him back safely. He looks much younger than ten, and so vulnerable.

I am torturing myself by thinking about what my son has suffered at the hands of my cousin, Cameron Frost. The feeling is so strong, I feel like howling.

My heart cries silently in my chest. I need to be strong for him, but as I sit on the wooden padded chair next to my son's bed in the white sterile room stroking his hand, it's getting harder every second. Despite, the fact that it's Summer, I feel cold, and can't stop shaking.

Before I can stop, a sob escapes my throat. Holding a hand over my mouth to stifle the sound. He's all I have left, since his father died. Someone comes quietly into the room, and I look up to see Daniel and note that he's holding a pink blanket.

Daniel gently places the heavy knitted blanket over my shoulders, keeping his large, warm hands there for a few minutes. Reaching out, I place my hand on top of his, giving him a quick smile to say thank you.

'He'll get through this, Lottie,' he says quietly, 'he's young and strong.'

I nod, even though I don't hold much hope. The consultant says to give him time, that Harley will need time to process what has happened, following the trauma of his kidnap, the beating he has taken at the hands of my cousin.

'I'll get us a hot drink,' Daniel says. He knows the John Radcliffe well, works here part-time. I feel Daniel swoop down and place a gentle kiss on the top of my head.

'Thanks,' I tell him, pulling the blanket around me because I can't stop shaking.

I think back to yesterday at Days Lock, with Cameron and Francesca. What a mess! Three lives lost to bitterness and revenge. Two more lives almost taken away and left with deep scars that are embedded within the soul.

I am so bloody tired. I feel like I've run a marathon. My limbs feel very heavy, making it hard to move and my eyes are puffy. The bed looks so comfy. Maybe I will just put my head down for a moment to rest.

'Mum... Mum!' I can hear a muffled voice calling me, but it's so peaceful, here in my sleep-filled haze. Just let me stay a little longer.

There is movement in the room, forcing my subconscious to stir and awaken.

'Mum!' That sound again.

I open my eyes, it's time to get back to reality. I must have been leaning on the bed, because my arms have cramped while I've been asleep. I rub them slowly.

My son's worried face stares back at me, his big brown eyes study mine. I offer a silent prayer to whoever chose to save my son.

'Hey Baby,' I say, gently pushing stray hairs from his forehead, 'you gave us a fright.'

Nurses and a doctor move silently around us, and I push my chair backwards to give them space.

The consultant, Mr Ray Jenner is tall, slender and losing his hair. He walks with an air of authority and confidence that offers a degree of reassurance to those who need it.

He touches Harley's shoulder. 'Hello young man. Good to have you back with us,' he says, 'the nurses are continuing to check your vitals.'

Harley looks directly at Mr Jenner and nods.

Mr Jenner looms over Harley. 'How many fingers am I holding up?' He asks, showing four fingers.

'Four.'

'What is your date of birth?'

'Second of February 2013.' Harley answers straight away.

I let out a deep breath and reach out to take my son's hand.

'The police want to call in and see you and your mum in a short while,' Mr Jenner, glances at me. 'They would like to ask you both some more questions. But we will hold them off until you have had something to eat and drink.'

'For now, everything is looking good. So, we'll leave you and your mum in peace for a few minutes. Well done, Harley.' With that Mr Jenner exits the room with a flourish.

Standing up, I stretch my tired limbs and reach over to gently kiss his cheek.

'Don't do that again,' I whisper, only half-joking. 'I was out of my mind with worry.'

Harley tries to smile, but tears flow down his cheeks.

'That woman saved me.' He suddenly says quietly.

'What woman?' I ask.

'The one with dark hair, the pretty one.'

'Francesca?' I ask feeling goosebumps travel along my arms.

'He called her Ferret. She was crying and screaming because he had hurt her a long time ago. She said her name was Francesca.'

Shit. Shit. Francesca.

I feel as though my whole body has turned into a block of ice. Despite everything that Francesca did to try to be a better person, her demons were too strong. She tried so hard to overcome what those three young men did to her, just like I did. Only, she couldn't do it, she was too damaged.

Those bloody men, how dare they hurt such a brilliant young girl. A girl who had her whole life ahead of her. She couldn't cope with knowing that they were all walking around free, laughing and joking as though drugging, kidnapping and raping was the norm, and that she should pretend like it never happened.

My head starts to hurt. I can't focus or see straight.

'If it wasn't for her arriving and taking on Cameron, and giving me time to find Cameron's phone, to run away and call 999. I would have been dead,' Harley says flatly.

Tears fall down my face.

I have no words.

Epilogue: Three Months Later

Daniel

'Come join us, Daniel!' I chuckle as Harley and Ben call me, taking it in turns to kick and be the goalkeeper in front of the netted goal, in the garden of Lottie's house in Lyme Regis. I sit on the decking on one of the wooden seats, slotted around the patio table, in my padded jacket, resting my arms on the cold table, my hands warmed by the hot mug of tea in front of me.

It's a glorious November, Saturday lunchtime and although the autumn leaves have darkened into jewel colours of darkened browns and reds, and cover much of the ground, the weather is cold, but milder than it should be for this time of the year.

Harley now seems to be actively involving me in things he does. He is a great lad and would make any dad proud. I am quietly hopeful that he more accepting of the growing relationship between his mother and me.

'Just a quick one,' I shout to the boys, pushing out of the chair. 'Don't want to cramp your style.' I smile, running on to the grassed lawn.

'David Beckham waits patiently as Ronaldo pushes the ball effortlessly to him,' I commentate, as Harley kicks the ball my way. I touch the ball gently with the tip of my black boot, before adding further comments.

'He studies the goalkeeper,' I look at Ben, over-exaggerating my movements, by pulling my brows together in a fake attempt to concentrate. 'Winks at the crowd,' I tilt my head and wink and smile, 'before bringing the ball home.' My right foot, aims the ball at Ben who is standing guard, crouched with arms splayed out.

'And he does it!' Harley shouts, as Ben misses the ball, and it hits the back of the net. Harley quickly walks the few steps across the lawn to me and offers a hand to high five me. I raise my hand, surprised and happy, as our hands slap together.

His action is thoughtful, and it warms my heart to feel that he accepts me.

Striding back to my seat, I call back, 'Sorry guys, but that's all you get from David B today,'

Laughter comes from behind me, and Harley remarks, 'And Beckham's number comes up, and he's substituted off, due to being too old for the game.'

I splutter into my cooling mug of tea. He's quick, I'll give him that. Cheeky little bugger.

Lottie is in the kitchen cutting cake into slices. Steph and Jack are in charge of sandwich fillings. Every now and then, Lottie bursts into giggles and feeling of contentedness envelops me. I feel that I am where I'm supposed to be and that the puzzles pieces are fitting into place.

Knowing that Lottie is happy, and that Harley seems to be recovering well from his ordeal makes me feel grateful each day. They are both strong. I walk to the bottom of the garden and stare up into the now changing sky:

'I promise to look after them both, Simon,' I say quietly to a passing cloud. 'Promise, that I will love them, protect them and do everything in my power to make them happy.'

Pulling my coat around me, I acknowledge the shifting of the cloud, that sends the sun shining into the garden. As though Simon is giving me his approval.

Checking my watch, I see that it is almost 2pm, and that Jenny and Stuart are due to arrive any moment. They have some exciting news, that they want to tell us in person. I hope they are both keeping out of mischief, which isn't easy when they are always helping others. They just can't help themselves.

To show Lottie how serious I am about giving our relationship a fighting chance, I come to stay with them both every weekend, plus anytime I can work from home. I am also exploring job opportunities in local hospitals or privately, in fact I have an interview lined up for this Monday at the Royal Devon and Exeter Hospital. It would mean winding down my private practice in Oxford, but that's a small price to pay to be with the woman I love.

Sometimes, you need to take a leap of faith.

If things continue to work out well, I will buy a property here and rent mine out. I would also consider bringing my parents here to live, but that is something that needs a lot of thought and commitment on both sides.

Francesca's funeral took place last month, her body was found a day after she jumped into the water. Agnes, her mother has taken companionate leave, and I spent some time talking to her about Francesca, her traumas and discussing reasons about why she did what she did, following her sexual assault. The self-harming was a key issue with the way Francesca coped with the day-to-day challenges in her life. I hope that the poor young woman has finally found some peace.

Cameron's mum came to take her son home to rest in peace, near their home in West Dorset. When I think of him, I remember the cruelty he inflicted on people, usually those who were vulnerable, unable to fight back. I remember the sexual assaults that could so easily had turned Lottie down the same pathway as Francesca. Not the killing, but the feeling of loss, lack of control and depression.

I remember the grotesque presents he left for Lottie, just to make her miserable. Of course, the kidnapping and treatment of Harley, will always be at the forefront of my mind. What must Cameron's mental health have been like to do that to a child?

Brian and Julie kept Lola, the dog and Julie continues to flourish as she enters her sixth month of pregnancy. She is adamant that she wants to work until the very end. You can see Brian's eyebrow lift as he listens to his wife making decisions that will affect them all in years to come. I can see fireworks heading in their direction.

Lottie and I often look at each other and shake our heads, she understands what it is like to carry a child, and how your body lets you know when it's had enough and needs to rest. But they will find that out for themselves.

The doorbell rings, and Lottie calls me to answer it. 'Sure,' I call, grabbing my cold mug, finishing the dregs of cold tea and making my way across the decking. Jenny and Stuart smile back at me laden with wine, chocolate and flowers, as I open the door.

'Hi Daniel, how are things?' Jenny says, wearing a navy woollen dress, long red cardigan, matching navy tights and knee length boots. She kisses me on the cheek, as she walks past. She has taken to Lottie and I being together, very well.

Stuart, dressed in black jeans and a black and white striped zip neck jumper, puts out his hand.

'Hey Daniel, hope Lottie hasn't been giving you grief over the new Nespresso machine?' He laughs. It's good to hear his deep, throaty laugh. Of course, Lottie was totally against me bringing my Nespresso machine to the kettle, she couldn't see the point in using it, when you can put a teaspoon of coffee into a mug and boil the kettle. We make life too complicated, she tells me, jokingly rolling her eyes and filling the kettle.

'You know damn well, she has,' I retort, 'Although, I came downstairs this morning and caught her making herself a latte.' My voice is light, 'you should have seen her face.'

When we reach the kitchen, Lottie hugs Jenny and tells the boys to come in and wash their hands, ready for lunch. Jack and Steph are putting plates on the table, and I sort the drinks so that we can sit down to eat around the large wooden table.

After we've had time to eat a sandwich and nibbles, Stuart clears his throat. Everyone stops speaking and I have a sudden worry that he or Jenny are ill. That something is wrong. We sit in silence and wait for Stuart to speak.

'We, that is Jenny and I, we want you to know that about three months ago, when we hired the house in Oxfordshire, during the summer, well we had some bad news.'

'What?' Lottie puts her hand on Jenny's, as it rests on the table. She watches Stuart carefully.

Stuart nods to Jenny and continues. 'A friend of ours, called and said that she was dying.'

Bloody hell. The hairs on my arms freeze and my first instinct is to reach for Lottie. My hand rests on her thigh. Harley and Ben, look at each other.

Jenny pats my hand, 'I'm sorry, but it was Judy who came to Shore House a couple of years ago.'

The colour leaves Lottie's face, and she puts a hand to her mouth in shock. 'No, not Judy! I remember her, and the little ones. Lovely family. She set up a flower business in Lyme?'

'Yes,' Stuart says quietly. Jenny reaches to hug her friend, and I look at Steph, Jack and the boys as they sob quietly for a few minutes. Jenny pulls away and takes a deep breath.

'Sadly,' Stuart continues, 'To cut a long story short, Judy, died last week, and Jenny and I are going through the process to be the legal guardians of her two six-year-old twin girls, Anna and Amy. It was Judy's one and only wish, written in her will.'

'Oh my God,' Steph speaks first, she moves out of her chair and stands in between Stuart and Jenny. 'That's awful. For Judy, I mean. But for you guys…' She tucks blonde hair around an ear. 'You are going to make great parents.'

I pull out of my seat and walk to Stuart, holding out my hand.

'So sad, but great to hear that you're going to be parents.' I say as he pushes out of his chair, grabs my hand and pulls me in for a quick hug. I can't help but think that this gift, despite the horrific circumstances in which the situation offers itself, is still a gift meant with love and respect. The gift of parenthood to these most selfless people.

'Thanks Mate,' Stuart replies, 'Means a lot.'

I turn to Jenny and gently pull her close. 'You are going to be such a good Mum. It must have given Judy a great deal of peace to know that her girls are going to be brought up by you.'

While Steph and Jack talk to Stuart and Jenny about their news. The sadness of Judy's pain and happiness of having the chance to bring up two beautiful girls, the flip side of two coins.

When I'm close to Lottie, I reach forward to hold her, before placing a soft kiss at her temple. She looks worryingly at Harley, but he just rolls his eyes, and I shrug my shoulders at them both and smile. Sorry, kid but you'll need to suck it up. I think we're coming to an understanding though, because he suddenly winks at me.

'What do you think?' Jenny's voice breaks through my thoughts, she is looking at Lottie, her oldest friend.

Lottie throws herself into her arms and hugs her tight. 'Oh Jenny, I'm so pleased for you,' she chokes out the words. 'You didn't bring them with you?'

'No,' Stuart clears his voice, 'they are staying with Brian and Julie for a few hours. We wanted to talk to you first, freely. The grief process will take a while, and we didn't want them to overhear us explaining to you about their mum.'

Jack raises his glass of water, 'To Jenny and Stuart. May you enjoy every moment of being a parent.'

Everyone raises their glasses, 'Here, Here.'

Isn't it strange how things seem to fall into place? I can't help but smile, as I raise my glass to my friends, who are in every sense, my family. Even during moments when you feel you've lost hope, things can work out. You just have to have a little faith and be ready to make that leap when the time comes. If Jenny hadn't invited me to the house at Sutton Courtenay and Lottie and I hadn't reconnected, life would have simmered on, uneventfully. There are lots of 'ifs' in life.

If Francesca hadn't seen Eric, Vincent and Cameron again, she would never have followed through her threat to harm them. But then she would never have been able to find Harley and send him to safety.

I could go on forever.

Life is a jigsaw, and we just need to put the pieces together.

Vincent

My finger is throbbing like a bitch. How can that be? When it isn't even there. I rub my hand against it, to cause friction and relieve the itch. A sudden picture of me being tethered like a pig whilst lying on that black sofa, in Ferret's living room comes to mind, the thought makes me shiver.

My stomach turns at the memory, and I force myself to take a deep breath. She was one psychotic lady. In addition to kidnapping and hurting me, she killed my two oldest friends. I still cannot make sense of it, or of what she hoped to achieve. Did it make her feel better? No, she jumped into the bloody water. Which brings me to why I cannot move forward. I am still angry with her.

Deep down, I know the Three Amigos played their part in shaping the person she became, and that is something that I must live with.

My leg is better, but I still have a limp. Especially, when I get tired. I can't and I won't let it get me down like my old mate Cameron. Uncle Gino drove me to Cameron's funeral near Charmouth, I must admit, I felt like an old man – hobbling in on crutches and wearing sunglasses, to hide my panda eyes. Thankfully, there were only a handful of us in attendance. But I wanted to say goodbye, because he had been a good friend to me.

The pub is situated in Summer Town, north of Oxford city centre. It is busy for a Tuesday night, and I'm thirsty, so I stand at the bar with my replenished pint of Stella. A deep, female voice calls over my shoulder to the bartender, 'Hi, can I have a large glass of house red please?'

I turn to see the most stunning woman. Black hair in sleek bob which stops effortlessly just short of her neckline. An off the shoulder grey sparkly top, reveals soft silky tanned skin, that makes me want to reach out and caress it. She pairs this with tight leather trousers. The sight of these causes my pulse to race.

The woman manoeuvres her body, until she stands next to me. 'Hi,' she smiles with cherry red lips, 'sorry to shout in your ear.' God this woman is every man's dream, like a chilled ice-cream on a gloriously hot day. No wonder the blood in my veins is beginning to pump hard, with an undercurrent of excitement.

'I'm Vincent,' I smile at the woman briefly before my concentration turns to watching the bartender pour red liquid into a large glass.

'Louisa,' she replies, looking across at me. Our eyes meet for a long moment. The bartender's voice breaks in, 'Cash or card?' Louisa raises her hand, a bank card sits snugly between her fingers, bright cherry nails match her lipstick. Casually, she taps the card reader without checking to see the price.

'How about us finding a quiet corner, so we can get to know each other?' I ask.

Taking her wine glass, she smiles and gives me a nod. I turn to make my way through the throng of people, taking my pint of lager with me, and am pleasantly surprised when warm fingers link mine. 'Lead the way,' she laughs softly just behind me.

Full of bravado and a confidence I never knew I had, I lead her to a dark corner of the room, away from the noise. Perhaps life is going to pick up after all. We place our drinks on the table, and she snuggles next to me.

'So, Vincent,' Louisa drawls in a deeper, melodic voice, transfixing me, 'tell me about yourself.' She smiles. There is a tone in her voice that feels a little off. I'm not sure what it is, and I don't care. I just want to taste the cherry lipstick.

Her hand slowly creeps up my thigh, and she leans forward to take my lips. Closing my eyes, I relax, smile – looking forward to this moment.

There is a faint click sound.

And, then something sharp suddenly pierces my thigh. Louisa cups my face hard, to keep our lips connected. The searing pain causes me to whimper, and I try to pull her hand away from my body. The object is cold and slim, a switchblade knife. I'm not sure what is happening, but the pain increases, until she pulls away from the kiss.

'This is for Francesca,' she whispers, withdrawing the knife. In a daze, I watch her click it shut and tuck it into the back of her leather trousers. Time stands still as blood pools across my jeans. Louisa doesn't flinch as she finishes her wine. Fuck! What did she do? My leg feels weak, and a coldness seeps through my body. With a racing heart, I put my hands on my bloody thigh.

Louisa stands, and without a word, she walks away.

Bloody women…

Acknowledgements

I am so pleased to finally finish this book and to tell Lottie's story. From the beginning, I knew she wanted to be heard. But the scenario of mirroring what she went through and the different paths that people take, was too interesting a plot to miss.

Thanks to Declan and the gang at Berro Lounge, here in Didcot, where I spend much of my time, sipping lattes and munching on delicious food, whilst tapping away on my laptop, in my 'Work office.'

To my fab team of pre-readers, who read the various drafts and give feedback. Denise, Rose, Wendy and Lisa. It is always great to have your comments, to make sure that my work makes sense, and flows well.

Thanks to Lisa, my editor – who I've known for many years, and who always has my back as she tracks through the words and manuscript to make sense of the often chaotic thoughts of my mind.

Thanks to my family, who humour me in my author endeavours and thankfully, jump in to help during my panicked moments. Especially, the hubby!

And finally, a huge thanks to my readers. For those who invest time and money in buying and reading my books, who give such wonderful feedback and love the characters as much as I do. Even the bad guys.

AJ Warren (Andrea) x

Read on for reviews of my previous books

What readers say about my books

The Lamp-post Shakers

'Fantastic read. Really enjoyed it!

Very well written and kept me gripped to keep reading more.

Look forward to reading the next novel!'

Donna

The Ghost Chaser

'A really good follow up book. Lovely location and great story.'

Steph

The Box

'Another excellent read, the third in the Lighthouse Series! If you want a good read, these are the books for you!'

Beryl

The Lost Soul

'Just finished The Lost Soul. Wow! What a fab book, it's definitely my favourite. I was up until 2am so that I could find out how it ended!'

Denise

Printed in Great Britain
by Amazon